Bleeding Blue

DON WESTON

Copyright

ISBN:
978-0-615-78273-7

Chris,

Thanks for your support.

Don Weston

DEDICATION

This book and all of my accomplishments in life have been possible because of my wife, Carol Weston. She has always supported me in my writing efforts and anything I have done in life.

Author's Note

Although the setting for this story takes place in Portland, Oregon, and the locations are real, I have taken the liberty to fictionalize Billie Bly's home, the warehouse scene and a scene where Billie was nearly run off the road. The locations are true enough; I just imagined a location within the real location. Also any murders or mayhem taking place at specific locations in this book are truly imagined. They never happened. Any persons depicted in this story are also fictionalized and not based on any real person.

ACKNOWLEDGMENTS

I want to thank those influences in my life that enabled me to write and get this book published. First, my father, Vernon Weston, who was taken from me early in life, but has been with me always; my critique groups which helped me sharpen my writing skills, and Dee Lopez, a writing instructor who believed in me and steered me toward writing a novel.

Chapter 1

On the morning of my death, my psychic, Edna, warned me I might stumble upon a murder. I wish she could have given me more details. It might have saved my life.

Death and mayhem are common occurrences on the streets of Portland. Police are searching for a killer who eats his victims on the Grimm television horror drama filming on a vacant lot near the waterfront and Union Railroad Station. A few blocks away, the Leverage TV cast is plotting revenge on an unscrupulous Portland businessman in a room above a Chinese bar in Old Town.

My life as a Private Investigator feels like a television drama too, except at the end of the day my problems are still with me: a missing person determined to stay missing, my recent termination as a cop from the Portland Police Bureau, and a pending lawsuit from a con who I roughed up a bit for stealing my purse.

My name's Billie Bly. I'm told I'm pretty, smart and tough--not necessarily in that order. Because I'm a blonde, some people don't take me seriously and that's when being tough comes in handy.

In my little drama, I died on a beautiful September day with summer still in the wind. I was oblivious to danger as I walked the streets, not noticing the new paintings hanging in an art gallery in the Pearl District. It also didn't occur to me to swing in Powell's Bookstore and check out the new police procedurals. I had finished my workout at the gym and changed from my sweats into a tan jumpsuit, and I should have felt renewed not depressed.

Instead, I worried about a ruling on the lawsuit filed against me by Chris The Creep, a.k.a. Chris Johnson. He's a dumb thief who tried to steal my purse twenty months ago when I was off duty and shopping for Christmas gifts, and he's also the reason the Portland Police Bureau wanted me gone. I had slammed his head in a revolving department store door for his efforts.

Internal Affairs asked me why I had to slam his head in the door so many times—five or six by my guess. *What else could I have done?* My gun was buried in my purse and if even if I'd wrestled it away from the creep, he'd likely bit a bullet. So in my eyes he got off with a warning. I mean, stealing a woman's purse is the lowest. Forget the credit cards and money. Do you know how much cash I have tied up in makeup?

I should have shot the son-of-a-bitch. Then there would have been no complaint filed, no lawsuits pending, and the piece of crud would have been off the street for good. He was out of jail a few months after sentencing in my case, but returned soon after on a breaking and entering rap in which he scared an old lady to death. I guess he got bored in prison and decided to sue me for something to do.

In a subplot of the Billie Bly series, after turning the city upside down, I had failed to find a missing husband for a client, and she was pressing for results. I was beginning to second guess my decision to become a P.I.

And that's when it happened. I was feeling sorry for myself even as the rain started drizzling again, and I spotted another drama up the street. A flash of bodies struggling half a block ahead of me. It was two grown men against a kid. One was a thin guy with greasy brown hair dressed in lime green pants and a paisley green shirt (I know the seventies are making a comeback, but somebody call the fashion police). The other perp was a wiry Asian in dirty blue jeans and a yellow print shirt. The kid struggled not to be dragged down an alley.

I looked around for other witnesses, but the rain discouraged pedestrians from venturing out for lunch. My adrenalin kicked in like two pit bulls fighting over a porterhouse steak. By the time I got to the scene and did the procedural backing against the safe side of the wall and pivoting around the corner with raised gun, they were gone. Had I imagined it? I spent so much time mind-racing lately anything was possible. I took a couple cautious steps.

The alley dead-ended abruptly with doors into the backs of a pharmacy and a warehouse on each side. I eyed a garbage dumpster too small to hide two adults and a kid and walked ten paces to the drug store door on the left side of the driveway.

I peeked through the window and spotted a pharmacist in a white coat standing behind a counter chatting with a young lady with reddish hair. The door on the opposite side of the driveway looked more like the place I'd find trouble. The solid metal gray door had no window, yet I knew it would offer no resistance. I turned the knob slowly and it responded by groaning a warning to me. At least it wasn't a revolving door.

I wondered if I was about to take the law into my hands again, causing trouble where no trouble was warranted. I took a deep breath and pushed the heavy door open with my gun dramatically stuck up in the air like they do on the television cop shows. I was thinking I was going to shoot the first thing that made a move at me because I do try to be careful, and in my book shooting first is the height of being careful.

The dark and gloomy interior offered no answers, only oblique aisles surrounded by rows of shelves stuffed with oriental rugs and drab-colored window drapes. I walked among the narrow shelves, thinking they might be a good place to stuff a body and shuddered at the thought of mummified corpses rolled in rugs and jammed into the deep vaults.

"Help me, mmmph."

I scanned some 50 feet down the aisle of darkness toward the muffled cry. It sounded like the kid, although a little throaty. I continued forward and stared open-mouthed as the kid ran across my path at an intersecting aisle about 30 feet ahead and disappeared. He wore baggy short pants that hung off him like he was proud of his butt. The kid appeared maybe older than the ten-year-old I first made him to be. Could be a gang member, I cautioned myself.

Before I recovered, the guy dressed in green darted down the same aisle. The other guy was nowhere to be seen.

I shook my head, resisting the impulse to charge after them. About the time I reached the spot I'd seen them and cautiously turned the corner, two gunshots echoed in the air. One of the bullets whistled a foot over my head the other slammed into a wooden shelf somewhere in front of me. A dull sensation crowded my brain, searching for a way out.

Someone had gotten the first shot off and it wasn't me. I inched down the hall, hugging the wood shelves, taking splinters instead of bullets. My progress seemed to take days. My face flushed and my blond bangs dripped greasy sweat into my eyes.

Ahead, double doors splayed open inviting me into the murder scene. My psychic had been right on her prediction, even if she was wrong about the supposed anonymous victim. The kid and the guy in green lay supine and motionless on the floor, a pool of blood between them. I gazed at the scene, trying to figure out how so much blood could be on the concrete floor already.

I pivoted in all directions searching for the shooter and it occurred to me, even in the dim lighting, the liquid pool between the bodies looked too red, instead of the maroon or burgundy color you'd expect of blood. And the bullets came at *me*. How could these two be dead?

I turned back to check out the scene and the kid sat up and grinned at me like something out of a surreal movie. He held a big gun in his hands. His crazed eyes radiated evil and his yellow teeth flashed a grin. I realized, too late, he was not a kid. He was a full grown man—a dwarf with childlike features.

Before I got a round off, because *every* single nerve in my body screamed *danger,* a big ball of fire erupted from the dwarf's gun barrel. I didn't hear the explosion, but I swear the bullet came at me in slow-motion. I tried to get out of its way, but my body wouldn't cooperate.

At first, I didn't feel the bullet, but I slammed onto the concrete floor anyway, fading in and out of consciousness, becoming aware of a little sting in the center of my chest. I don't remember the second bullet hitting me. Because of the first, I guess. I wondered if maybe it wasn't a bullet but the toenail of an elephant because a minute later it felt like the beast had one foot on my chest and the other on my head.

"She's dead," a voice said.

"I don't think so, but she will be in a couple minutes the way she's bleeding." I recognized the second voice as the gravelly one I mistook earlier for a child's.

"Billie Bly, the P.I. She's not so tough. I thought she was going to be hard to kill." I didn't recognize this third voice, but I was memorizing all three just in case I didn't die.

Damn! Edna should have known I was the one who was going to be murdered. I made a mental note to get a new psychic.

"You want I should put another bullet in her?" one of the voices said. "Just to make sure?"

"Nah. Don't spoil her pretty little face. At least she can have an open casket. She's dead. She just doesn't know it yet."

"This was easier than I thought," the third voice said. "The boss said she might be a difficult hit. See her laying there, peaceful as an angel? No trouble at all. Ha, ha, ha!"

I had fallen into a trap. They knew when I would be walking by the alley because I worked out at the gym every morning and came home by the same route each time. I felt safe because of the nicely dressed citizens along Tenth Avenue in the trendy Pearl District, with all its art galleries, healthy eateries, and such.

Five blocks down, in Old Town, where crack dealers work with impunity, would have been the logical spot for an ambush. But I was on my guard down there. They found a solitary one-block stretch on the fringe of the Pearl District and lured me in to a private murder.

I heard them laugh and call me an angel. I worried about my assistant, Angel, back at the office. What would happen to her if I died? Their voices softened as they departed. I tried to call out for help, but I couldn't cough enough air from my lungs to make a sound. I fought passing out and flashed back to that guy in the revolving door who got me kicked off the Portland Police Bureau. *Move over, buddy, I've got someone else to hate.*

I tried to crawl from the warehouse through the darkness. I remember seeing a blinding light, the whitest, brightest light I'd ever seen in my life. Peace and contentment embraced me. I answered the call to serenity and fell into a deep slumber.

Chapter 2

My psychic and the guy who shot me were wrong. I was still alive.

Not the *alive* where you go out boogying on the town. More the *alive* as in barely generating a pulse with a truck parked on your chest.

Still, it was better than the alternative. I learned I was still alive when I woke up from a dream where my four cop brothers chattered like playful squirrels coercing a dog into action.

"What-are-you-guys-so-excited-about?" I sat up stiffly and coughed.

"She's awake," Dag shouted. Of all my brothers, Dagwood got the worst moniker. We tell him it's cool, but I laugh when I say it, so he knows I'm lying. He has sandy brown curly hair, is solidly built and is as strong as he is tall. No one makes fun of his name to his face, except me.

"Where am I?" I asked. "The last thing I remember is that freaky little weasel pointing that huge gun at me."

"You're in the hospital, little sister," Dan said. He stared at me like you would a miracle. Dan's the oldest, and he's more like my dad than my brother since mom was busy raising a family without our cop father, who was shot in the line of duty.

"I thought I was dead."

"Not yet," Jason said. His big blue eyes met mine and a tear flowed down his chiseled face. Jason is the only Bly other than me with mom's overtly blonde hair. He has a fair-colored pencil mustache which you have to look at twice to see.

"I must be dead," I said. "My psychic predicted it and that damn runt made it come true."

I spotted a bunch of bandages as I peeked inside my gown. Half a dozen plastic snakes extended from my arms to several plastic bags feeding me saline and antibiotics and such. A machine sucked something somewhere behind me and another machine blipped and bleeped alarms.

My younger brother, with an older soul, smiled broadly. "You've been mostly sleeping for the last three days," Darrin said.

I reached for a mirror someone had left on a side table and gazed upon my face. Not dead, but not really alive. A ghostly yellowish tint shadowed my lower right cheek highlighted by the largest black eye I've ever had. I remembered the jolt when my face hit the concrete floor. My head still felt trapped in the spin cycle of a washing machine. All of my thoughts jumbled in the process. It was like trying to separate the whites from the colors in the middle of the wash cycle.

"Is this Heaven?"

"No," Dag said. "You're in the hospital."

"And you're all with me? How long have you been here?" Still trying to sort out reality and dreams.

"We've been here all three days since the surgery," Darrin said. "Telling stories, remembering how you use to thump us all the time. We've been trying to get you to wake up."

"But I *have* to be dead." My head felt like a two-by-four with a nail through it. "I saw the bright light. I think I saw God. I remember going toward it. It was the brightest, whitest light I ever saw."

"Shit," Dan said. "You crawled a hundred feet out of that warehouse with two bullets in your chest and pushed open the warehouse door to call for help. Then you crawled into the alley. The bright light was daylight. You'd been in that dark warehouse."

"What about seeing God?"

They acted puzzled for a moment.

"A tall, old guy with a scruffy white beard?" Dag asked.

"Yes, of course. That's what God looks like. Did you see him too?"

"That's the homeless person who found you." Dag grinned. "He called for help."

I didn't believe him. Part of me wished I had stayed with the white light and followed it to Heaven. Maybe God wasn't ready for me yet. I must have drifted off to sleep, because when I opened my eyes again I was surrounded by doctors in white coats and nurses in maroon scrubs.

"It's good to see you awake," one of them said.

"How can I sleep with you shining a flashlight in my eyes?"

"I'm Dr. Hoffman. Your brothers said you came out of your slumber, but when I got here you were out again. I was checking to make sure you were okay."

I peered around the ray of light into his brown eyes. He was young and serious, and I could see the early signs of worry lines on his forehead as he switched off his little flashlight.

"It's great to have you among the living again," he said. "You've been in and out and pretty groggy when you did wake up."

"How long have I been here?" My brain bounced around the room trying to follow his words and make sense of them.

"I make it three days including today," Doctor Hoffman said. "We kept you pretty doped up. A bullet nicked your left lung, collapsing it. We had to insert a chest tube in your lung to inflate it with negative pressure. After we made sure all of the blood and other fluids were removed, we covered the area where the tube was inserted with an occlusive dressing to prevent any air from reentering your lung."

"Thanks," I said, and drifted off again. When I woke up the third time, the doctors and nurses were gone and my brothers sat in chairs around my bed.

"Why aren't you guys working?" I said.

"We took leave," Dag said. "We've been here by your side all this time."

"Well, who in the hell has been arresting all the crooks out there if you guys are off the job?" I struggled to push myself upright and felt pain in my chest. "Did any of you deadbeats find out who shot me?" I thought it was sweet they worried about me so, but I wouldn't let them know it. Those goofballs just sat there and grinned.

"The investigators got a couple of leads, but they went cold," Darrin said. "They're still trying to track your would-be killers down."

"I suppose you're waiting for me to get better and go get them for you."

They grinned.

"Well, I'm not so sure I want to. I had a lot of time to think about things during my unconsciousness, and I think maybe God has other plans for me. I think maybe he's trying to tell me to slow down."

Darrin frowned "Are you okay? You aren't talking like yourself. Maybe you have some brain damage. You must have hit your head pretty hard when you fell."

"Do I sound like I've got brain damage?"

"How would we know the difference?" he said, and they all laughed. "But seriously, it's not like you to turn the other cheek. Are you sure you feel okay?"

"I think so," I said.

"Your heart stopped twice," Jason said. "You actually were dead for a while."

"Then my psychic was right."

"Psychic?" Jason said.

"Yeah. She said I'd stumble onto a murder, but she didn't say it would be mine."

"The bullets just missed your heart," Darrin said. "One punctured a lung and the other one cruised around missing any vital organs. The lung injury and loss of blood almost did you in."

Seeing God had changed me. I know Dag said he was a homeless person but to me he was God. I felt like maybe he didn't want me to do this P.I. stuff anymore. Dealing with the dregs of humanity had somehow lost its appeal. But I didn't like the idea of someone out there hunting for me, and I knew the only way I could quit this racket would be to find the person or persons responsible for wanting me dead before they found me. And I had an obligation to a couple of clients before I could retire and get a real job and maybe someday have a family.

"I'm going to stay in bed and be good for one week," I said. "Then I'm going hunting for the people who did this to me."

I gave my brothers, who now seemed to think that maybe I *was* okay, a description of the three guys who set me up and then chased them out so I could get some rest. I talked tough, but I felt like crap.

I woke up the following morning in a regular hospital room. The attendants transferred me from ICU some time during the night. They drugged me so I couldn't put up much of a fight when they jostled me around.

I was cross and bitchy and hungry. I told the day nurse I was famished, but she wanted me to wait for a doctor to say it was okay to eat solids. I told her I was going to get up, disconnect all my tubes and hustle my butt down to the cafeteria if she didn't bring me a steak or hamburger or something I could get my teeth into. Of course it was a lie. My butt wouldn't be going anywhere for a couple of days, at least. She shook her head at me and walked away.

I had practiced a vegan lifestyle for a while before my near-death experience, but after nearly dying without benefit of meat or dairy products ever crossing my lips again, I decided to make an exception. It might be a permanent exception.

Quite a few people stopped by to see me, including a bunch of the cops I used to work with. Some of them I hadn't seen for several months. A few others, not since I quit the force. I was doubly humbled because I didn't think any of these people were my friends any longer.

Lt. Steve Thomas dropped by the day after I regained consciousness. Steve is built thick and muscular. He has a square jaw, fleeting smile, brown hair and bright blue eyes. We used to be partners when I was on the force and we're still friends. Truth be known, I still have a crush on him.

He leaned over me with that stupid *I told you so* grin to show me I screwed up. Only this time there was some kind of warmth behind it. "How you feeling, kid?"

"I've been better. What little food I've had is bland and the coffee Dag snuck in tastes like they used the grounds I threw out the morning I was shot. Jeez, I hope you brought me something."

His eyebrows arched a bit and his grin widened. He pulled a paper bag into my view and I saw a familiar grease stain.

"You didn't," I said.

"As a matter of fact, I did. I got the feeling the nurses wouldn't approve, so I tucked it inside my jacket." He opened the bag.

"Mmm. A bacon maple bar, a chocolate Voodoo doll, cake doughnuts with Captain Crunch and Froot Loops on them and lemon chiffon crullers. Voodoo Doughnuts."

"Damn right. I had to stand in line for twenty-five minutes out on the sidewalk after I stopped off at Starbucks and picked you up a Cinnamon Spice Mocha."

He lifted a liter-sized container of my favorite hot drink from a Starbucks bag. "It might not be too hot by now."

"Double shot Espresso. You know me too well." I took a hit from the coffee. "I haven't eaten *real* solid food in four days."

He opened the doughnut bag and started to pick through it. I snatched it away quicker than a bear with his paw stuck in a bee hive and winced at the pain surge in my chest.

"That's mine. Go get your own."

"I'll bring you some more the day-after-tomorrow if you're good."

"You darn well better bring me some first thing tomorrow morning if you know what's good for you."

We laughed. I relented and let him have a cruller. We attempted small talk but neither of us is good at intimacy. Eventually Steve sobered up and directed his comments at a wall.

"You know, you aren't out of the woods yet," he said. "I'm worried about you."

"The Doc said I'm doing fine. I passed almost all of their tests. He said I'll be out in a week or two if I'm a good patient." Steve nodded slowly. "So I asked, 'how long if I don't follow orders, Doc? Cause I'm kind of headstrong that way.'"

"I'm not talking about your health. Someone tried to kill you, and they might try again."

"I've got open cases I have to get back to," I said. "I don't get paid for lying around."

"Dammit, someone put a professional hit out on you. These guys won't stop until you're dead. I think you should forget your cases and take a vacation until we catch these killers."

"I don't think they're pros," I said, ignoring the suggestion. "A pro would have given me a head shot to be sure. They're amateurs and that might say something about whoever hired them. Besides, you and I both know the cops will never find these guys unless they give themselves up or get picked up in a traffic stop."

"That's not fair. Half the department is hunting them now that we have your descriptions to go on. Even though you're private now, you're still a cop to most of us. And it's not safe for you until we find them. Why do you think your brothers have been by your side the last three days?"

"Double time and a half?" I sassed.

"Because they're worried the assassins might try and finish the job," Steve said. "They took turns guarding you around the clock."

"Well, they can go back to their own lives now."

"Don't be rash. The department doesn't have the manpower to stick a guard outside your door twenty-four-seven. I'll bet whoever shot you is checking and hoping you would take a turn for the worse. Now that you're back with the living, the pressure is on them to finish the job. Why don't you go visit your aunt in Tacoma?"

"I'm telling you, I can take care of myself," I said. The frown on his mug told me he wasn't buying it. I pulled a Glock 22 from under my pillow and nodded toward it.

"Where in the hell did you get that?" he said.

"Darrin gave it me for protection. When I chased them out yesterday he came back with it a few minutes later."

"So you've been armed ever since you woke up?" he asked.

"Yeah, it's unnerving because I never know when someone is going to come in and start moving me around. I don't want to blow a hole in some orderly by mistake. I'm lucky I didn't shoot anyone last night when they moved my bed from the ICU because I don't remember a thing."

"I'll bring you another one if they take it away." He was serious.

"Bring me something bigger. This has good stopping power, but I want something that says, *bang, you're no longer on this earth.*"

"I could bring a sawed-off shotgun." It was his attempt at sarcasm, but he changed the subject when he saw me nodding. "Speaking of arsenals," he said, "Angel should be by a bit later. She said she had some errands to do."

Angel is no angel. My diminutive brunette secretary stands five-foot-one in high heels, dresses like a hooker, and has too many tattoos. She also carries at least three guns on her person at all times. She gave up smoking a few years ago and walks around with a permanent space between two fingers on her left hand where a cigarette rested for 10 years. When she's nervous she takes a phantom puff.

"How's she been?" I asked.

"I only saw her for a minute this morning, but I'd say she's up to three packs a day if she still smoked."

"It must be hard on her running the business while I've been incapacitated."

"Yeah, about that." Steve stared at the wall again.

"What's wrong?" I tried to sit up.

"Ah, I got some bad news for you." He took a long time in the windup to throw me the knuckleball.

"You know that jerk Johnson who was suing you? The judge finally ruled yesterday. He's awarded Johnson one and a half million dollars."

"What?" It felt like I ripped a stitch when I lurched at the news.

"How did the city let that happen?" I said. Slowly the truly bad news slipped up on me like flesh-eating bacteria. "Don't tell me they cut a deal with Chris The Creep."

"I'm sorry, Billie. They said you were off duty when it happened, and claimed they fired you because you weren't following departmental procedure."

"The liars. I quit!"

"Rather than be terminated," he reminded me. "The city agreed to pay five hundred thousand dollars and left you owing the rest."

"But why didn't they wait for me?"

"The Creep's lawyer said the trial could be delayed indefinitely and the plaintiff needed his due process. I think he was afraid you would die before the judge ruled."

I threw my bed sheets off. "I would have if it meant that creep couldn't collect. I'll give him his due process right up his keister."

"You can't get out of bed. You're in no condition."

I hate it when Steve's right. I had no sooner gotten my weight on my feet when my legs quivered like Jell-O. My gut argued with that doughnut and coffee, and my head spun. Steve lifted my traumatized legs up onto the bed, one at a time, and eased me back onto my pillow. After a couple of deep breaths, I relaxed.

"How did Angel take it?"

"The judge froze all your assets. Angel's a nervous wreck. I think she's planning to use some of her own money."

It took a while but Steve finally calmed me down.

"I'll see you in the morning with some more doughnuts," he said.

"Forget the doughnuts." I tightened the grip on my Glock. "Could you bring Chris The Creep instead? Maybe you could get him a day pass. Tell the authorities the court wants to rule on one of his many motions. Oh, and if it's not too much trouble, maybe you could encourage that city lawyer and my former union rep to drop by since I'm not well enough to call on them."

"Oh shit." Steve kicked at the floor. "Chris Johnson got out the day before you were shot. I only heard second-hand, but I think he won an appeal on the burglary charge. I guess the D.A. doesn't want to put the city through the cost of another trial. He's out walking around now."

I screamed into my pillow. Steve left abruptly after making some awkward apologies. I *needed* to get out of this business and maybe I was getting some help. The forces all seemed to be against me. I had no money, very little health insurance and apparently no rights.

I fell asleep and had sweet dreams about shooting my gun at the firing range. Instead of targets, I sighted down the barrel at Chris The Creep, the judge who ruled against me, the city lawyer, and my former union rep. I was in heaven until my dream was hijacked by the face of the little man who put me in the hospital. Then I was in purgatory.

Chapter 3

I spent the rest of the morning being poked at by nurses and doctors and blowing into a plastic tube to make a gauge rise. It reminded me of hitting the gong with a sledge hammer at the carnival, only with a punctured lung this was much harder.

Doctor Hoffman also scheduled an EEG to make sure all my brain synapses fired correctly. The handsome doctor wanted to make sure I hadn't suffered any brain injury or concussion when my head bounced on the warehouse concrete floor. But the good doctor couldn't stay and chat so I rolled over, tired from all the activity, and dreamt the Doc and Steve arm wrestled to see who would take me out for dinner.

Angel showed up soon after my nap, dressed nice and cheery in a thin white blouse with a black lacy bra underneath. At least, I told her she looked nice. Her ensemble included a blue miniskirt, about ten years too young for her and red spiked heels. She applied her makeup liberally, her lips painted bold red, and her hair was pumped up like some model in the magazine *Seventeen*, with lots of rebellious curls. Did I mention Angel's a fashion-disaster? The girl has no taste and I think she might be color blind.

"Good morning," she said, and moved in for a careful hug. "Gee, it's great to see you awake. I've been here every day except yesterday when you woke up. I was in court trying to keep Chris The Creep from getting your money. And last night they said you were resting. Did Steve give you the bad news?"

"I'm afraid I didn't take his news very well," I said.

"That bottom feeder," she said, and took a puff of her phantom cigarette.

"How did The Creep get sprung already?" I asked.

"I don't know. I didn't even know he was out until I saw him in court yesterday." Angel brushed some unruly black bangs from her eyes.

"He killed that little old lady when he burgled her house," Angel said.

"At least he *did* call for help," I said. "That's how he got caught."

"I didn't say he was smart," Angel said. "I guess they took that into account, and I hear that lawyer of his is really good. Of course he can afford the guy because of his settlement with the city and his lawsuit against you."

"Ohhh. . . I don't have a million dollars."

"You don't have to come up with the whole amount," Angel said

"I don't?"

"No. Your liability insurance covers up to five hundred thousand dollars. That leaves only a half million for you to pay."

"Are you trying to cheer me up?"

"Well, yeah . . ."

She continued cheering me up by telling me the judge had frozen my bank accounts and appointed a trustee to go over my assets, sell my property, and pay The Creep off. She also told me my attorney had already filed an appeal so my beautiful Victorian house in the high rent district of Northwest 23rd Avenue, left to me by my favorite Uncle, was safe for the time being.

"How are we paying the bills?" I asked.

"I planned to use some of my money from my Christmas savings."

I shook my head and regretted it instantly. My temple throbbed so I settled into my pillow for refuge.

"I want you to go to my place and take down the shower curtain rod in my bathroom," I said. "Open the end closest to the showerhead. It's got one of those plastic stoppers that come off. The tube is hollow."

"Yes?"

"There should be some money rolled up inside. Hundred dollar bills. I've been putting them in there one or two at a time for years. I'll bet there's a couple thousand dollars by now. It was a forced savings plan. Once I got the little buggers in there, I couldn't reach them to get them out."

Angel grimaced.

"*What?*" I said. "I don't trust banks. Use the money for operating expenses."

"How am I supposed to get the bills out of the shower rod?" Angel asked.

"That's your problem. All I know is a coat hanger just pushes them further inside."

"I'll stop by the hardware store and get a pipe cutter," she said.

"A what?"

"It's a little gizmo like a clamp with a blade that makes circles around the pipe until it cuts through.

"Why didn't I think of that?"

"Possibly because you aren't very mechanically minded," Angel said.

She leaned over and gave me a hug. I smelled like antiseptic hospital sheets and stale coffee and she of garish and overpowering perfume, but it felt good to hug someone again.

"Well, isn't that sweet. The two buddies in a clinch. Hey, are you two lesbos? We should get together and have a threesome at my place."

I cast my eyes up to the unctuous face of the newly sprung Chris Johnson. He wore a pair of Calvin Klein blue jeans, a beige form-fitting knit shirt, and a cheesy smile.

"What the hell are you doing here and how did you get past

security?" Angel said.

"I just waited for the cop guarding your door to go to the bathroom," Chris said, matter of fact. "The way he was guzzling coffee, I knew it wouldn't be long."

Angel started after him with her purse cocked, and he backed around my bed with his hands up as a defense and laughed. "Are we going to play now? Maybe I can take your friend to court too."

I reached out and somehow managed to grab Angel's wrist and reel her in. She got a second wind and started flailing her arms and, for the life of me, I don't know how I managed to hold her back. I realized it was only my white-knuckled grip on her blouse doing the job. The rest of me was sliding off the bed. Angel realized I was heading for the floor and caught me. Angel is strong despite her small stature. She lifted me back to my bed, her face now flushed at what she had done.

"I can't take much more of this," I said. "He isn't worth it. If I can control myself, you should be able to do the same."

"I'm sorry. I'm usually pulling *you* off of people."

Chris The Creep rubbed up against me from the other side of the bed and whispered in my ear, touching it with his slimy lips.

"I've been waiting for you to wake up."

And that's when I realized maybe Angel was right and this role reversal we were doing *was* out of character for me. Even sick I didn't need to put up with this shit. I shoved the barrel of my Glock under his chin and showed him a wicked smile.

"Want to go for double or nothing, Creep?"

He stood immobile, unflinching, and I watched for the telltale beads of sweat that would show me he knew I was serious. About the time the perspiration appeared, he managed to take a slow step away from me.

"Hey Billie, you got me all wrong. I just came here to see how you were doing. All I've been hearing is about you being on death's door. So when I heard this morning that you're alive again, I said to myself, 'I got to thank that bitch for making me rich.'"

Angel picked up a vase filled with daisies and clipped him alongside the head. Neither vase nor head broke open, but the daisies and water splattered on the floor. Chris yowled and staggered back to the wall.

"Crap, call her off. Will you?"

"I'm surprised you got the balls to show up here." I slipped the Glock under my pillow.

"I was just talking to one of my detective friends and asking him about maybe bringing you by. I think he was afraid I might shoot you or something because he declined."

Chris had recovered and grinned again with one hand holding the side of his head and one eye on the pillow hiding my Glock. "I'm not afraid of you."

I know false courage when I see it. I watched Angel take a puff from her phantom cigarette while hunting for another solid object to throw. Chris noticed too and took a step toward the open door. I grabbed Angel's arm and shook my head, which made me feel lightheaded. I wanted to question The Creep about his motives and I needed him conscious.

"So, Chris, don't you think it was a little premature to kill me before you won your court case? The judge might have had to throw your petition out for lack of a defendant."

"Hey, I didn't have anything to do with it. You're my meal ticket, and I was still in jail when you were shot." His dirty brown eyes lit up, and he paused as if considering his position. "I see what you mean about me having a motive, though. I thought about you a lot in stir. Man, it really hurt when you rammed my head into that revolving door. I was in the hospital for a week and I still get migraines."

"Knock it off," I said. "You aren't playing to a jury now. I heard you were caught robbing a house within a week of being bonded out. And you were only in the hospital overnight to make sure you didn't have a concussion."

"Yeah, you're right," he said. "I was headed for a seven-to-ten stretch 'cause some old lady croaked when I was doing her joint. Then Ron Epps called and offered to be my lawyer. He remembered me from the revolving door thing and thought he could get me off and maybe get me some money from the city for your unprovoked attack."

"Unprovoked?" I said. "You stole my purse."

"Hey, that's what I do. Don't take it personal. Just like you go around finding guys cheating on their wives, I steal purses and do the occasional burglary. Shit, I put as much effort into my craft as you do. I spent years learning how to spot a mark. I do a lot of research on the places I hit. It takes planning and skill, the work I do."

Angel laughed and plopped herself in a nearby chair, crossed her legs and took another puff from the cigarette that wasn't between her fingers anymore.

"I think I saw you on that TV program," she said. "*The Dumbest Crooks Caught on Video*. Weren't you the one who got stuck in the ducting trying to crawl into a restaurant through a chimney on the roof?"

"Good one, shrimp," Chris said. "She's got a mouth on her, huh. So where was I? Oh yeah, my lawyer. So Epps gets me a deal where I have to serve one-to-three years, but because of prison crowding I catch a break. Next thing I know, I'm standing in front of a parole board and being ushered out the door. Doesn't the justice system rock?"

"I thought you got out on appeal," I said.

"What? Nah, I'm on probation. Even the system thinks I'm not that bad a guy."

I was getting tired of this jerk and decided to hurry the interview along. "Angel, could you excuse us for a second?"

"What? Leave you here with this asshole?"

"Angel! Please?"

"I need a cigarette," she said. She made a huffing noise and stomped out of the room. I asked her to close the door and she slammed it shut on the way out.

"Chris, I want you to know I don't think you're dumb," I said. "I notice how people talk, how they think, how they carry themselves. And you, my friend, are a smart bird."

"You're not BS-ing me, are you?" He smiled, not wanting to but he couldn't help himself.

"Nah. You and I are a lot alike. We notice things. We plan things. We're careful most of the time."

"Yeah, you gotta be in our business." He kicked at some imaginary dust on the floor.

"See, that's what I mean. You think things through. That's why I want to believe you didn't try to have me killed."

"Hey, I wouldn't do that to a pretty thing like you. Of course, you aren't very attractive lying in a hospital bed with messed up hair and no makeup and that huge shiner you got going, but . . ."

"You're turning my head with all your flattery." He actually acted a bit sheepish when I said it. Who knows, maybe crooks have feelings. "Like I said, I don't want to think you put a hit out on me, but there's this one thing that has me questioning my instincts."

"What?" Chris's face turned serious.

"Well, when I was lying on that cement floor, my blood pouring out of me, I was still conscious, you see."

"Yeah," he said, real intent now, like I'm going tell him the secret of life or something.

"First they were talking about how easy it was to knock me off," I said. "They thought I was dead or dying, see." He nodded. "Anyway, one of them started talking about you."

He stood there still nodding his head, and I waited to see if it ever was going to sink in when he cocked his eyes and head in one motion.

"Talking about me?" he said. "What do you mean? Why would they be talking about me?"

"That's what I'm wondering, Chris. They said I wasn't so tough and how you said it would be hard to catch me off guard."

"What? That's ridiculous. I don't even know those guys."

"What guys?" I asked.

"The guys you're talking about. I never met them before."

"How do you know? Do you know what guys I'm talking about?"

'Well, no." He thought about that for a moment and slowly a smile crept to his lips. "No, *I don't know* who you're talking about."

"That's funny," I said. "They seemed to know you. One was a tall thin white guy with greasy brown hair and a tattoo on his shoulder. The other was a short wiry Asian with black hair. The third guy was tiny. He was four-foot-six, maybe, baby faced. Shit, I thought he was ten at first glance. He looked Asian. Thin as a rail with short hair and mean, beady eyes."

I watched him for any sign of recognition but he played it cool and disinterested.

"I know a lot of guys, but I never come across anyone like what you're talking about."

"The tall guy with the tat said they'd be getting paid when you got out of stir." I frowned. "I didn't know at the time that you were that close to getting out. No one called me and I'm off the police bureau, so I don't have the inside scoop anymore. Plus, I was kind of busy trying not to die."

"You. . . You're not going to tell that story to the cops are you? That's all bullshit. You'll make me prime suspect in your shooting and violate my probation. And you know I didn't do it. Like you said, why would I kill the golden goose? You were going to make me rich."

"I don't know," I said. "I'll have to think about it. On one hand, it might take care of my financial problem. I mean, being found guilty of an attempted capital crime would probably keep you from collecting on your lawsuit. Or, I could appeal my case and probably win it now that they'll see you for the scumbag you really are."

"You can't do that," he said. "You're lying. I never hired anyone to kill you."

Beads of sweat glistened on his forehead and that's what I wanted. Unfortunately, I believed him. He was sweating not because he was guilty of the attempt on my life, but because he thought I was going to frame him. And maybe I could.

"Come here." I patted my hand softly on the mattress.

He hesitated and reluctantly stepped toward me wringing his hands. I grabbed him by the balls and squeezed hard enough to let him know who had the upper hand.

"Jeez, they're softer than I thought. Angel was telling me earlier you had brass balls."

"Ouch, let go. Shit, you're killing me. Let go."

"In a minute. I want a few things from you first."

He squirmed to get away from my grasp, but he didn't try *too* hard. He stopped short at a swing toward my jaw when I squeezed in self-defense. It must really have hurt.

"First, I want you check around and see if you can locate these three guys or find out if anyone has heard about them and where they might be."

"Shit, I'm small time. I got no connections around town."

"Shut up. Just go around and shoot off your mouth about how you're taking me to the cleaners and how someone shot and almost killed your golden goose before you could collect. That gives you a chance to say 'Gee, I wonder who could have done that?' You wanted to keep me alive until you collected your money. That's your angle."

"Ohhh! I don't know," he said. "Someone might roll me for the cash I haven't got yet."

"That's your problem. You have until I get out of the hospital to come up with some names. Got it?"

"Okay. Anything you say. Please let go." He flinched as I squeezed for emphasis.

"Don't get bossy. It makes me cross. Next, you're going to

renounce the lawsuit against me. Get to your lawyer and tell him you've changed your mind. And if you say one word to him about *why*, I'm going to go straight to the cops and tell them what I know."

"I'm not going to do any such thing," he said. "I got that money fair and square, and I'm going to keep it. Ohhh. Please let go."

"Finally, you're going to apologize to Angel for all the nasty things you said. It doesn't bother me, but Angel is very sensitive."

"You mean the Lesbo remark?" he said. "Ouch, and the threesome thing at my place? Yeeouch. Dammit, stop it. They're turning blue."

"Can they do that? Well, yes I bet that *is* possible. Yes, that would be nice, but I'm talking about when you called me a bitch."

"What? I don't get it. I didn't call her a bitch."

"No, you called *me* one and believe me I am one very tough bitch. I can say it about myself, but in Angel's eyes, no one else ever better say it to or about me. I don't know why, but it sets her off."

"Okay, you got it. Please let go."

"What about that second thing? Are you going to renounce your claim?"

"Ouch, ouch, ouch." He did a little dance. "No way. No way. You can cut 'em off, I'll still have the money to spend. I'll buy new balls."

"You won't be spending my money in prison and without balls you might be the main attraction for the guys at the big house."

"Jeez, please let go. I'll find the guys that did this to you. I promise. And I'll apologize to your friend. Two out of three, Billie."

"You have until I'm released to change your mind," I said. "Then, I go to the cops. Or maybe I take the law into my own hands. You doubt me? Check out the newspaper article where I blew away a guy last year who tried to rape me. Turns out he was a serial killer. I managed to turn the tables on him, and I was going to turn him over to the cops. Then he started bragging about how he'd get a good lawyer and be back on the street in a few days. I was pretty sure he was going to drag me into the back of a van and probably kill me at the time, and he claimed he'd done it before.

"You see, I believed him when he said he'd get off easy and two seconds later he struggled and was dead from a bullet up the jaw. I was a P.I. at the time and it *was* self-defense. Or was it justice?"

"You're serious?" Chris gawked at me wide-eyed.

I winked at him.

"You're crazy," he gasped.

"Now you got it." I let go of his balls.

He limped to the door, stooped over and mumbled something to sound tough, but not loud enough for me to hear.

"Don't forget to apologize to Angel."

"You can't threaten me like this."

"Hey, there aren't any witnesses this time. Don't make me come after you."

A minute later I heard Chris mumble something in low voice to Angel outside my door. I lie back on the pillow and somehow felt much better.

Later, I would remember back and wish I could feel this good again.

Chapter 4

The day I left the hospital was worse than the day I had entered it.

My one-week recuperation actually took two weeks. Darrin convinced the doctor I couldn't be trusted to stay down and recuperate properly at home. He might have been right. I had enrolled on COBRA, and I still received the police bureau's extended health benefits, which had a month to go, so I thought I'd make the best of them.

But when I learned the handsome doctor was married, there was no real reason to stick around. Even Chris The Creep abandoned me, failing to show with any information about my assassin.

It was a little after nine Friday morning when my brother Darrin strolled into my hospital room. I sat on the bed, dressed in blue jeans and a white blouse, waiting for the doctor to come and officially cut me loose. I felt good. My wounds healed nicely and I was down to minimum levels on the pain medication.

"I'm glad you convinced me to stay down and take care of myself," I told him. "It gave me time to put things in perspective."

"Really?" Darrin asked.

"Almost dying makes you stop and think. All my life I've been like a guided missile seeking trouble wherever I go."

"You just have an explosive demeanor, Sis, but that doesn't mean you don't do good things," he said.

"I would have run out of here a week ago and hunted down the S.O.B. who shot me if they'd let me out then," I said. "But in the last week, I got to thinking there must be more to life than chasing after criminals and fighting everybody who gets in my way."

"I've noticed during the past few days you seem to have softened," he said. "Does this mean you don't plan to hunt him down?"

"I'm thinking, let the police handle it." I stopped short, not believing those words were coming from my mouth. "I guess I've been re-evaluating my life. What I want from it."

"Have you come to a decision?" he said.

"Not entirely. But I've been wondering what it would be like to get married and settle down. Maybe have kids."

Darrin squinted at me. "You don't think I can do that?" I said.

"Sis, I think you can do anything you set your mind to, but I don't ever remember hearing you talk like this before."

"Dad died in a shootout when I was fourteen. I can't remember his face. I try, but it won't come. Mom passed away two years later. I'm convinced she died of a broken heart after losing Dad."

"I was twelve when Dad was killed," Darrin said. "We all had to grow up sooner than we would have liked. It was worse for Dan. A twenty-one year-old-shouldn't have to raise his brothers and sister."

"I don't want to die young. Does that sound selfish?"

"No. But we shouldn't let fear run our lives," he said. "If we live in a constant state of fear, we can't be in the present enough to truly enjoy life. Dad told me that once and I never forgot it."

"Aren't you afraid you might be killed in action, like Dad?"

"I think about it sometimes," Darrin said. "But I don't let the fear rule me. At age 30 I've had a rich life. I've met some wonderful people and some who weren't so wonderful. But I can usually find something good in most of them. Something I can take and apply to my life, which I hope makes me a better cop and a better person."

"But aren't you afraid of dying?"

"I have my belief in God," he said. "No matter what happens to me, I know it's God's will. I turn my fear over to him so I can do what he meant for me to do."

"What's that?" I asked.

"Be me," he said. "Do whatever I've been put on this earth to do to the best of my ability."

"I love that you see life that way. It gives me hope. But death still worries me. I don't want to miss out on raising a family like Dad."

"What about your job?"

"I'll have to quit it."

"What will you do?"

"I'll be—I'll be a homemaker," I said.

He shook his head and smiled at me.

"What?"

"With you, it's always all or nothing. You don't have to drastically alter your life to get what you want. Leaving *the job* would kill you. You might get married and resent your husband, your children, and your life. You can have both, you know. You may just have to take less risky cases. Maybe go into corporate investigations."

"You think so?" I said.

"Just don't jump into anything right away. Take some time and think it over. This near-death experience could be a good thing if it improves your life, but take some time and make sure you're making the right decision."

"Thanks, Darrin." I hugged him. He made me feel good about myself, but that was Darrin. He knew the right thing to do and, unlike other people, he always did it.

Steve came in a few minutes later and we chatted. I didn't want to scare him away so I didn't tell him about my marriage plans. I was ready to go when a nurse finally showed up.

"I'm tired of waiting for the doctor," I said. "I'm leaving."

"I won't tell anyone," she said. "Besides, he just called and said you could leave. You should have a wheelchair though. It'll only take a minute for an orderly to bring one up."

I got off the edge of my bed, grabbed my purse and started walking. The nurse made noises about hospital policy but they were half-hearted. I think she was glad to get rid of me. I hadn't been an easy patient. Steve picked up my bag of hospital junk while Darrin stuck around to make my apologies.

Steve followed me into the elevator, and I pushed a button as Darrin scooted on ahead of the closing door. "You get any leads on the guys who tried to do me in?" I asked.

"I think we might have an ID," Steve said. He showed me a picture of the little man who fired the big bullets into me.

"That's him!" My heart lurched when I saw him. I felt the adrenaline source of hyper-vigilance course throughout me as the fear returned.

"The little guy is known as Monty, the Jet, a.k.a. Montgomery Bales. He's called The Jet because of his sleek frame and the ability to jet in and out of tight places. We think he may be part of a gang on the East Side, but we haven't been able to run him down. We're still working on the other two suspects."

"Every cop in the precinct is pursuing them," Darrin said. "You have a lot of friends downtown, Sis."

"I've got three patrolmen standing by outside," Steve said. "No one is going to get close enough to shoot you today."

I tried not to smile. It might ruin my image.

"Chris is a no-show as stoolie," I said to myself. "I guess he figured I was bluffing about putting him away."

"Eh," Steve grunted. "How are you going to do that?"

The elevator stopped and we maneuvered around an elderly women coming in as we exited. I spun an elaborate mix of double talk in rushed tones meant to bewilder him and at the same time change the topic because I didn't want Steve to know about the threat and outright lie I told The Creep.

We walked through the revolving whoosh door at the hospital entrance and a chill in the air surprised me outside. It was cooler than I remembered. Of course I had spent a couple weeks in the hospital since the ambush and October was upon us. Although the sun made an appearance, grey cumulus clouds decorated the sky and a cool breeze foreshadowed a turbulent season.

As we stood at the hospital pickup area, I noticed a familiar figure loping across the street, closing fast. Steve didn't see him and mumbled something about getting his car from the parking garage. As he strode away, two uniformed policemen closed ranks around me, Darrin, and Angel, but mostly around me.

A third cop ran up behind the approaching figure and closed the gap as Chris continued to scurry toward us. He looked dapper in slacks and a camelhair sport coat sans tie. His hair was stylish in a spiky gelled sort of way and a big grin belied the fact that he had bad news.

The cop from behind grabbed Chris's arms and pinned them behind his back before he could speak. One of the other cops patted him down as Angel and I watched mutely, amused.

"He's clean," the cop said, and the other officer let go of his arms.

"What's with the police brutality?" Chris said. "I didn't do anything. Tell 'em, Billie. You wanted me to come see you."

I'd have liked to see the act go on. To see him unnerved and roughed up some more. In the end I figured I'd better see if he'd turned up anything.

"What have you got for me?" I asked.

Chris swept at imaginary dirt on the arms of his sport coat and brushed the rough stuff off. "Uh, I hope you don't take this the wrong way."

He withdrew a white envelope from inside his sport coat pocket and handed it to me, staring warily at the two cops. It was a letter-size envelope with a legal document inside. I opened it and read.

"It's a restraining order." He took a step back "I told my lawyer what you said about implicating me in your attempted murder. He said you aren't allowed to be within two hundred feet of me. He also said we're going to sue you for slander and intimidation."

"What?" Darrin and Angel squawked in unison.

I waved them off and gave Chris a steely-eyed glare that unsettled him more than the cops. "Chris, this is a bunch of crap and it's not going to hold up because this time you have no witnesses."

"I don't want any trouble," Chris said. "I went to my lawyer 'cause I was scared. He's the one wants to sue your butt again."

I took a deep breath. My bright idea about frightening him into a confession had backfired. It was a calculated risk to see if he would break, and I had failed.

"To prove I don't have hard feelings, I got something for you."

I waited, expecting him to say he'd settle for half of the twenty million his lawyer was probably going to sue me for.

"That guy who shot you? I know who he is and maybe where you can find him."

"Holy shit," Darrin said. "Spill it, mister." He put my suitcase down and pulled out a notepad and pen from his pocket.

Chris ran his fingers through his gooped hair and alternated his weight from one foot to the other. He gaped around furtively, like he might be seen squealing to Portland's finest.

"I wasn't even asking around much. This friend of mine was at the hospital here a few days ago, visiting a girlfriend. He came out and saw this tiny guy running down the hallway and out the back of the hospital. A minute later he saw two cops searching the hallway asking about this guy. One of them blurted out to a nurse how he tried to kill some lady up on the fourth floor."

"Was he after me?" I cried. "Why didn't you tell me?"

"We didn't want to worry you," Darrin said. "We got a call that a little person burst into a room below you with a gun. He ran out without incident, and we think he thought it was your room."

Another surge of fear struck me squarely in the chest.

"Why didn't your friend tell the officers?" Darrin said.

"Jeff doesn't much like cops," Chris said. "Besides, he might have an outstanding warrant or something against him."

"Jeff who?" I asked.

"I'm sorry. That's privileged," he said, serious like. "I can't reveal my sources."

"You don't have any ethical reasons to withhold information," Angel said. Her face reddened, and I stepped in between them.

"You said you knew the guy," I said, good cop like.

"Well, sorta," Chris said. "I don't really know his name, but Jeff was with me yesterday when I was down near City Hall preparing this restraining order. He said, 'Hey, there's the guy the cops were chasing at the hospital.' He told me about it, and I connected the runt with the guy you wanted me to find."

"Go on," Darrin said.

"So we followed him, and he went into City Hall."

We waited for the punch line. It was slow in coming, mainly because Chris was enjoying the suspense he created.

"Where did he go?" Angel blurted out.

"You won't believe this," he said. "I sure didn't." He paused again for effect, but nobody took the bait. He pouted. "He went into the Mayor's office."

"What?" Darrin said. "Impossible. You're lying."

"He walked in like he worked there or something."

"The Mayor's office?" I shook my head.

"Well, a couple of commissioners are nearby too. So he could have been going to see one of them. Actually he went into the reception area separating the offices. The Mayor's office is to the right and two commissioners are on the left."

"What time was this?" Darrin asked.

"It was noonish," Chris said. "I know because we waited for him to come out and I was hungry, so I sent Jeff for a hotdog."

"What time did he leave?" Darrin jotted something in his notebook.

"Oh, he didn't. At least not while we were there. And we hung around until one-thirty. He either had a lot to talk about or there's another way out."

"Probably went in to steal somebody's purse and snuck out the back," Angel said.

"I'm not so sure," I said.

I could tell Darrin didn't buy it either. That's what I thought at first because he had an odd demeanor on his face, kind of like a snake-bit cowboy in denial. A clammy feeling came over me and I started to sway.

"Something wrong, Billie?" Angel said.

Sunlight flashed off something metallic from the top of the parking structure across the street and hit me in the eye for a second, dazing me more. I gazed to the source and saw a figure hunched over the wall on top of the parking garage. Instinctively I turned to find cover. I saw by the alarm in Darrin's eyes he flashed on it too.

"Sniper," I yelled.

We all moved in one motion toward the ground with one exception. A bullet struck just before the retort from the rifle was heard. I fell and felt a sudden pain tugging at me. But it wasn't from the bullet. Nor did it emanate from contorting my recently aerated torso to avoid the bullet. The pain was in my soul. Darrin had jumped in front of me with his hands stretched outward. I saw him hesitate and slump and fall to the ground like a building gradually yielding to detonation.

"Noooo!" someone screamed, and I realized it was me. Angel and I crawled across the sidewalk and behind a shrub near the entry to the hospital, and I fumbled to get my gun from my purse. Two more shots bounced off the pavement. A bullet ricocheted near my leg. I crawled further behind the bush and another bullet rustled its leaves. I came up with my Glock and fired three rounds at the shadow up high. One of them almost hit him, I thought—even at that range—and the shadow slinked away before I could squeeze off more rounds.

Behind me, Angel held a 25-caliber pistol she normally carried as a backup piece on her upper thigh, under her skirt. "Dropped my damn purse when we dove to the sidewalk," she said. "Otherwise I'd have offed the S.O.B. with my three-fifty-seven."

The cops Steve brought ran around with their weapons drawn, trying to figure out where the shots originated. I knelt over Darrin as the blood gushed from his throat, his body armor useless here. I clamped a towel from my hospital junk bag over the wound and tried to stem the bleeding, but the pooling under his head told me the bullet must have gone clean through. It seemed like forever before Steve rolled up in his blue Crown Vic. He ran to us with a lost look on his face.

"Darrin's been shot," I cried. "He took a bullet meant for me."

I sobbed and let Steve pull me away as he tried to help Darrin. An EMT ran over from the *Emergency* entrance parking lot, radioed someone, and bent over and checked his pulse. One of the cops joined him and he started CPR as the EMT applied pressure to the wound to stop the bleeding. A minute later another EMT joined them and they had tubes connected to Darrin and injected him with adrenaline and something else.

A doctor joined the fracas. They continued pushing compresses against his wound. Steve hovered over the little circle while shouting orders into his remote police radio. Angel kept pulling me away.

"Let them handle it," she said. "You can't do anything."

Her face was white and shaken. I stepped out of reality, watching from above as everything unraveled, not believing the scene. In a moment of clarity I scanned the parking structure. A dark cloud hovered directly above it. There were no glints from the barrel of a sniper's rifle now. No lone figure watched and laughed at me.

I turned back to Steve's somber face. He held my hands but avoided my eyes.

"I'm sorry," he said, flatly. "Darrin's dead."

Chapter 5

"Darrin's dead?" I said. "How can that be? Only a few minutes *before* he'd told me not to make any rash decisions. So he steps in front of a bullet and now he's dead?"

The reality and irony of the situation set in like storm clouds at a weathermen's golf tournament. Darrin protected me. I was the target. A*gain*! Darrin stepped in front of the bullet and saved my life.

The doctor, who tried to resuscitate him, still on his knees, spotted me and shook his head. I wiped a stream of tears from my eyes onto my blouse's blood-stained sleeves, choked, and watched helplessly as patrol car after patrol car screeched to a stop at the turnaround in front of the hospital. Steve barked orders and the cops charged the parking structure. I heard squad cars' tires squeal inside the garage area.

The only ammunition I had to unload now was a barrage of cursing, and I found plenty of targets to vent my anger. I cursed Angel for not seeing the sniper, I chastised Steve for leaving my side to get the car, and I yelled at a couple of bewildered policemen for not spotting the assassin. I told the doctor, who tried to save Darrin's life, he was a quack.

But mostly I spewed this venom at myself for letting my little brother take the bullet meant for me. Someone wanted me dead so badly they killed Darrin to get to me. I wished I'd never survived the bullets two weeks prior. Somewhere in my collection of grief I thought of going after the killer. But tears blurred the images around me, and I realized I was more of a target than a threat in my current condition. I dropped to my knees and wailed.

In minutes there were scores of earnest-faced, blue-suited cops running around. Most of them paused and searched Darrin's lifeless eyes, as if expecting to find a clue to their own mortality. I know what each one of them thought. *It could have been me.* Each cop stopped and wiped his or her eyes before running off in search of the killer.

Somebody finally decided it would be a good idea to get me the hell out of there, and Angel and I were whisked into a squad car. A patrolman hopped in and we sped off without a siren or blue and red flashers.

My thoughts began to clear, and I wondered what happened to Chris Johnson. On the way out, I surveyed the scene of cops, medical staff, rubberneckers, squad cars, police tape, and police photographers, but there was no Chris. He wasn't the kind of guy to stick around when shots were fired.

"I'm so sorry," Angel said. "I should have been watching for trouble. I feel so bad."

"It's too damn late to change things." I took a deep breath and shuddered. "I'm going to find the guy who pulled the trigger on my baby brother and he won't ever go before a judge, I can promise you that."

I wiped some tears with a handkerchief the patrolman handed me over the seat. Angel nodded and grabbed at the handkerchief. I leaned toward the officer I had seen a few times while still on the force.

"McGraw, isn't it? I want to go home."

"Yeah, Ms. Bly, I'm McGraw." He eyed me through the rear-view mirror. His mustache twitched as he talked. "But Lieutenant Thomas said I should take you to the precinct for your own protection."

"That's B.S.," I said. "Hell, there's no one to protect me at the precinct. They're all at the hospital. A killer could walk in and help himself to Danish in the break room."

McGraw mulled this over and radioed back to the crime scene. I heard Steve nix the idea of my going home, and I reached over and grabbed the mike from McGraw.

"If you don't want another homicide on your hands, you'd better tell McGraw to take me home."

"Billie," a voice cracked over the radio, "you'll be safer at the precinct until we get a handle on this."

"You have no right to hold me against my will."

"You're a material witness," he said. "I need to have you some place safe where I can interview you. What you might have seen can help us find the killer."

"I'm not feeling too well, and I've got Darrin's blood all over me. I need to go home and wash up and maybe lie down." I coughed laboriously into the mike. "Angel will be with me and you know she packs an arsenal."

"Darn right." Angel pulled her Smith & Wesson out of her purse. "Let them come. I'm just itching to put some lead in the low-life that killed poor little Darrin."

"I'll even let Officer McGraw stay with me until you can get reinforcements if you like."

"You'll let me station a few officers at your place?" Steve said.

"Suuure," I said.

"That doesn't sound like you, Billie."

"It doesn't, does it?"

"Okay," he said. "But on one condition. You've got to let the police handle this. I don't want you going around messing up our investigation."

"No way," I said. "This is my brother you're talking about. I have just as much a right as anybody to investigate his killing." I realized that my new outlook on life would have to be put on hold for a while until I found Darrin's killer.

"Officer McGraw?" he said. "Take them down to Central."

The Central Precinct is located inside the Justice Center, a concrete 18-story monolith, with a few eye-pleasing architectural shapes and stain-glass art in the main entrance to make up for the otherwise dreary grey color and unimaginative design. Once they got me into the building I might never get out, since five floors are dedicated as a maximum security home to nearly 700 inmates.

"Okay, I promise. I'll let you guys handle the investigation. But you gotta keep me informed about what's going on."

Steve was silent for a minute. He knew I was lying about staying out of his way, but maybe he was hoping I might be a good girl. The dope. I heard his sigh over the radio.

"Take her home," he said. "Stay with her until I get there. It'll probably take me about three to four hours to get things taken care of here. Under no circumstances do you leave before I get there."

"Affirmative," McGraw said.

We crossed the Burnside Bridge, only a short ride to the Central Precinct, as he finished talking to Steve. I told him to keep going up Burnside and to take a right on Northwest 23rd. He nodded and a few minutes later, we turned off Burnside and traveled past three Starbucks and a dozen yuppie restaurants and stores.

At Lovejoy Street, McGraw turned left and we pulled into the drive of a brown Victorian house with purple trim situated next to a bookstore. The house had been left to me a few years back by my uncle, and it was only a hundred feet from Northwest Twenty-Third Avenue, the hub of Yuppyville.

Not the place I might pick to live, but it was free, except taxes, so I lived in it and ran my business from the main floor. A purple, badge-shaped sign adorned with a scrolled wrought-iron frame hung on a pillar. It read, *Billie Bly, Private Investigations.* I wanted it to say P.I., but Angel said Private Investigations sounded more professional.

I didn't feel like climbing the stairs in the two-level Victorian, so we congregated in the lobby area on a sofa and loveseat normally reserved for my clients. I think someone sat there once two years ago. Angel's desk is across from the furniture and when clients come to visit me, it's always an emergency. *No time to sit down. Must see her right now.*

At the moment, I felt the same urgency but my side hurt, and I was drained emotionally and physically. I lowered myself gingerly to the loveseat. McGraw remained standing where he could watch the street through the windows.

Angel went upstairs and brought me another pair of blue jeans and a matching blouse. I took them into the bathroom and changed clothes after washing the blood from my hands and face. The bathroom has a rather large window and I considered it for a minute or two, wondering if I could squeeze through.

When I finished plotting, I steered toward Angel's desk and slid into her chair. I wanted to do anything but think about Darrin. "What's been happening since I've been in the hospital?"

"You can't talk about work," Angel said. "Your brother has just been killed."

I felt myself shudder. "I need to keep busy and until we find Darrin's murderer, I can't grieve."

"Can't or won't," Angel said.

"What's the difference? I won't rest until I find out who is trying to kill me and who killed Darrin. There must be something in one of the cases I'm working that ties in with all of this."

"The case files are on your desk," Angel said.

"The Lieutenant is not going to like hearing this," McGraw said.

"So don't tell him!" I snapped.

Angel got up and went through a mahogany door into my office. I heard frantic rustling of papers and used the time to measure my chances of squeezing through that bathroom window. Angel returned and caught me staring toward the bathroom. She handed me the files.

"Oh crap," I said. "Mrs. Fleming's lost husband."

This was the case that had caused me so much anguish and lost sleep just prior to the day The Jet ambushed me in the warehouse. It involved a Mrs. Fleming from Pocatello, Idaho. Her husband, Art, left for a business trip in Portland three months prior and she hadn't seen him since. He disappeared while in town for an insurance convention.

"She's called me six times while you were in the hospital," Angel said. "She wants me to keep her updated and didn't want to hire another P.I. because she says you worked so hard. She cries a lot."

"That's why I dodged her calls," I said. "The only solid lead I've turned up was he had a pal at City Hall he was going to see." I sighed. "I couldn't find anyone down there who knew him."

"Hey that's a coincidence," Angel said. "Chris The Creep's friend saw that Jet guy who shot you walking into the city councilor's offices."

"You made the connection too, huh? I don't believe . . ."

"In coincidences?" She nodded. "But you had another case with connections to City Hall."

"The child custody case," I said. "I talked to some of the employees in the records section who used to work with Jack Jenkins before the city let him go. He's got one of those Daddies' Rights' lawyers and was trying to get custody of Martha's two kids, Jacob and Eliza. The guy's a rat. I already got statements from six of his former co-workers to that effect."

"So you have two cases with links to the city," Angel said. "Another coincidence?"

"I don't know," I said. "On that case, I was mostly in and out of the records and archives offices, and they've been moved to a new location at Portland State University on Sixth Street. I didn't spend any time at City Hall on that one."

"You never know," Angel said. "Jenkins might have friends there. I'll bet someone told him you were snooping around and talking to people about him. Maybe he has connections at City

Hall."

"People who might be in a position of putting a hit on me?" I said. "That's not likely. Who's going to go to the city to hire a killer?"

"I spent a couple years detailed at City Hall," McGraw said, from the window. "You'd be surprised some of the people that go in and out of those clerks' offices to file restraining orders or pay fines, get married, or file for divorce. You even get junkies and dealers wandering in and out."

I nodded, taking it all in. I knew what McGraw was talking about. As a former cop I saw the dregs of humanity and they're not all blue-collar criminals or nasty appearing people. Some of them wear business suits and include women as well as men.

"So what about this other case?" Angel asked. "Any ties to the city?"

"The corporate fraud case? Nah. I was brought in as a part-time auditor supposedly to work on minor aspects of the company's accounting system. Another insurance company scam. Someone's been siphoning off millions. They want it solved before the federal regulators get wind of it. Also they don't want the publicity."

Angel scowled. "They got another investigator, Billie. But they said when and if you get healthy to check in with them. They liked what you had turned up before you got shot."

I wiped a tear from my face with a Kleenex. I didn't really care about losing a client. I was thinking of Darrin again. I had been ever since he was gunned down.

"I think I'd better use the ladies room again," I said.

"Are you sure?" she said.

We've played this game before, but she still appeared surprised. Officer McGraw was mildly interested too.

"Oh dear, yes," I said. "I'm not feeling too well. I might not make it upstairs."

"I can help you," McGraw said.

"I'll be okay. I'm a little queasy, that's all."

I picked up my purse and walked to the bathroom door, opened it a crack, and offered a demur smile. McGraw nodded and scrutinized the street for any unannounced assassins. I closed the bathroom door, opened another door as he turned his head toward the window, and closed it behind me.

It was a risky move. McGraw could easily have turned back and seen me stepping out the back door. But I couldn't see myself climbing through the bathroom window without moaning and grunting loud enough to stir his attention. As I walked down the back steps, I wondered if I could start my car and get by the not so sharp-eyed McGraw without his hearing.

I checked my purse for my Glock and realized I left it with the Crime Scene Investigators. I went to the side door to my garage to get a backup piece from my car.

The door stuck, like it always does, and I twisted the knob and heaved my weight against it. A pain spasm hit me in the chest like a heart attack. I clung to the door handle until the pain subsided and then used my back side against it.

A few minutes later, with my Colt semi-automatic tucked in my jeans and half a box of shells in my purse, I stood on the corner of Northwest 23rd Street and Marshall, waiting for a streetcar to take me to City Hall. I glanced nervously over my shoulder expecting McGraw to pounce on me. Finally, a blue trolley rounded the corner a block away, and not a moment too soon.

I spotted McGraw, a block down the sidewalk, searching earnestly in all directions. The only reason he didn't see me was because I was in the middle of a small crowd attempting to climb onto the trolley. I crouched and managed to get inside, sat behind a portly gentleman, and prayed McGraw wouldn't come aboard.

An eternity later, the car jerked forward like a roller coaster catching on the uphill track to start the ride. I peered out the window. No McGraw. It wasn't until the streetcar turned east I spotted him through the rear window. His flushed face turned toward the trolley for an instant before he ran into a nearby cafe searching for me.

I breathed a sigh of relief and rubbed my breastbone where it throbbed from my battle with the garage door. I grabbed a couple of pain pills from a bottle in my purse and gulped them down without water and wondered if they would ever make a pill to soothe my aching heart. Then I let myself cry.

Chapter 6

As the snub-nosed trolley rolled down Lovejoy Street, I measured my chances of beating the cops to my brother's killer. The tram stopped abruptly and some hip young people got on and off. I'm probably the same age, but don't go in for the 'being seen at the right restaurant scene' which seems to be the mantra of some of the people who live in my area. By contrast, a street person tried to get on at Broadway and a Max ticket checker turned him away.

I thought about Darrin and figured by now every cop in Portland would be chasing after his killer because they take it personally when one of their own is killed. I squinted at the blurred image of my watch through tears and made a vow not to let my emotions deter me until I found Darrin's murderer.

The MAX streetcar turned up Fifth Avenue and middle-class workers on their lunch hour joined the young hip passengers. It was twelve-thirty when we stopped at Fifth and Main Street, and I scampered off with five other riders. I walked the two blocks to City Hall and entered from the picturesque side on Fourth Street, featuring Italian Renaissance architecture and a portico supported by granite columns.

Inside, I passed through a makeshift security station manned by a smiling gentleman in uniform with a shock of white hair and dentures. He waved me through and across the yellow marble squares where I mounted a circular marble stairway to the city offices. Each step I took aggravated the tightness in my chest.

After reaching the third floor, I searched for the office Chris The Creep said he saw The Jet enter.

Beveled lead-glass doors led into the commissioners' offices and an intimidating mahogany counter inside with a sign announcing the offices were closed until one o'clock. I ignored the sign and passed by the imposing front desk into a more relaxed reception area fronted by a 50's oak counter. In a corner in the back of the room, a clerk tapped away at a keyboard behind an oversized computer screen.

"Hello?" I said. "Can I talk to you for a minute?"

A lady with frizzy graying hair and bifocals perched on the tip of her nose seemed to shrink further behind the computer screen. I repeated my greeting a bit louder.

She continued to ignore me, probably hoping I'd go away. The end of the counter had one of those swinging doors that latch from the opposite side. I reached over and unhooked it. The frizzy-haired lady grimaced, got up, and walked over to me.

"Please close the gate. You're not supposed to be in here. How did you get in anyway?"

"Just walked in," I said.

"They're supposed to lock the door on the way out to lunch," she said. "Half the time they don't, though. What can I do for you?"

I flashed my P.I.'s license at her. "I'm working on a murder case. The suspect in the case was in here yesterday. He's Asian, very short, slim."

She displayed a bland air of indifference.

"He looks like a child almost. He came in about this time of day."

"Sorry, Hon, we're closed between noon and one. The commissioners are in their offices sometimes, but I doubt they'd be meeting anyone like that."

"The little guy could have crawled under the gate." I said.

She shrugged. "You've seen for yourself the door's not always locked. Anyone could come in here, but I doubt they'd get very far without being noticed. There's always someone in here at lunch and we got a security camera that records everyone who comes in the office."

"Has anything been stolen or gone missing from any of the offices here in the last couple days?" I asked.

"If there was, we would have checked the tape," she said. "The support staff here doesn't make enough for anyone to bother to steal anything. Couple years ago someone zipped in and made off with a purse. Guards found it in the trash can downstairs with the thirty-seven cents still in it. Nothing's happened since. Word must be out on the streets that there's nothing worth taking in here."

"Were any of the commissioners in the office during lunch yesterday?" I asked.

She hesitated. I figured she was thinking of a way to get rid of me.

"Listen, a cop was killed a couple hours ago," I said. "We think this guy might have pulled the trigger. If anyone here saw him, it might help us find him."

Her eyes flashed a look of sadness, but her demeanor held firm. "I thought you were a private cop. Why are you involved in a cop killing?" Her eyes peered over the top of her bifocals at me. "Shouldn't be involved in an active police case, should you? Especially if it's a cop killing case."

"I was on the force up 'til a couple years ago," I said. "The cop who was killed was my baby brother. Please?" I don't like begging. Heck, I don't even like asking for help. I wondered how many more times I was going to have to do both.

"Who was killed?" she asked.

"His name was Darrin. Darrin Bly."

"Oh my, one of the Blys. My God I know a couple of them. Darrin? I don't think I've met him. You must be the sister. What's your name again?"

"Billie."

"Billie Bly? Oh, you're the one that jammed the guy's head in the revolving door?"

"Guilty," I said.

"Gee, you're some kind of folk hero around here. Not with the commissioners and Mayor. They pretty much wish they never heard of you. But the rest of us think you're great. What do you want to know?"

I was relieved to finally have an ally in the city government. "Well, if there's any way I can get hold of yesterday's security tape . . ."

"I really shouldn't." She glanced over her shoulder. "It's probably down in the security office. I'd have to wait until four when Larry starts his shift." She removed her bifocals and her face lit up with a conspiratorial smile. Her placid blue eyes came alive and sparkled. "Larry will do anything for me. It might not happen until tomorrow. Is there a number where I can reach you?"

I handed her my business card. "Call me as soon as you get it. I'll pick it up any time, day or night."

She eyeballed the card and smiled at the cute little image of a woman in a trench coat. "I'm Eileen Richford," she said. "Is there anything else I can do to help you find your brother's killer?"

"It would help me to locate anyone who might have seen this guy or might know anything about him. Can you tell me who was in the office yesterday?"

Eileen stroked a finger across her chin. "Not a lot of people. Election campaigns are in full swing for the Mayor and a couple of the commissioners. And we had that terrorist training exercise that's kept some of our office staff away. Yesterday, I think it was at the convention center."

I retrieved a small notebook from my purse and scrounged a pen that was chained to the counter. "Think hard. I need to know anyone who came into the office. Even if only for a few minutes."

"Well, there was Mayor Clemons. He was leaving when I got back from lunch. Said he stopped in to check his messages. None of the commissioners came into the office that day. Except Commissioner Tuttle. He popped in at four o'clock and left with me at five. He claimed he was hitting the campaign trail again."

"What do you mean claimed?"

She made a tipping motion with her fingers to her mouth.

"You mean he likes to drink?"

"I never see him drinking during the day, but it's common gossip that he makes up for it in the evenings. Chases the women too. Still, he's pretty much of a straight arrow during campaign season. That's why I was a bit surprised."

"At what?"

"I could smell him across the office. He'd been hitting the bottle pretty good, I'd say. He was slurring his words and he staggered ever so slightly when he walked. I figured he was heading to the bar to finish what he started."

Eileen paused for a moment and became anxious. "Billie, please don't tell anyone you got this tidbit from me. I shouldn't have said anything. I could lose my job."

"I'll treat it confidentially," I said, scrutinizing the camera above. "What about that?"

"Oh, it doesn't record voices," she said. "Still, I might see if Larry could make the recorder malfunction during your visit. It gets really political in here. A tremendous amount of backbiting goes on in these corridors."

"What about other staff?" I said. "Are there any secretaries or other people who might have been here yesterday?"

"The only other people were Bob Blaney, the city auditor, and Commissioner Tuttle did stop in for a few minutes during the lunch hour, but they were in their offices. Hmm."

"Did you think of something?"

"Yes. I just remembered. Blaney went into Tuttle's office for about ten minutes. I heard some yelling and when Blaney came out in a huff, he was all red-faced. I've never seen him like that. He's usually so calm and unflappable."

"Any idea what they were arguing about?"

"Not a clue. I couldn't hear what they were saying and it only lasted a couple of minutes." She paused. "I try not to pry," she said, absently.

"Let me know if you think of anything else, Eileen. I'll be around."

"Oh sure," she said. "I'll call you later this afternoon or first thing in the morning about the tape."

I glanced back and caught her perching her bifocals on her nose and smiling to herself. "When will Commissioner Tuttle be back in the office?" I asked.

"Maybe tomorrow for a while. Oh, tomorrow is Saturday. But I heard a few people say they were planning to catch up on some work in the morning. The office will be closed. I'm afraid it might be a bit difficult to get in."

I frowned and started for the door.

"Billie?"

"Yes?"

"There's a side door on the South end of the building. It's where the recycling bins are located. The gate is unlocked between nine-thirty and eleven on Saturdays. That's when they pick up the recycling. If somebody knew the routine, they could get inside the building."

I gave her a half-smile. "Thanks."

"And if I get the tape tonight I'll call and arrange where we can meet tomorrow. I don't want to be anywhere around City Hall when I give it to you."

"I live on Northwest 23rd," I said.

"Perfect. I'll call you."

Maybe by then, I thought, I'd know more about what was going on with Tuttle and Blaney. I walked out of the office door and right into my big brother. Dan is six-foot-three inches tall and has the girth of a bear. At the moment his face was as ashen as mine must have appeared.

"I heard about Darrin," he said, choking. "I can't believe it. I was in the middle of my patrol when the news came over the radio." We sat on a stone bench in the empty hallway and held each other and cried for a while.

"Angel told me about The Jet being seen here," Dan finally said. "I knew I'd find you nosing around." He examined me with a stoic demeanor I couldn't read. Was I in trouble or was he here to help? "Did you learn anything?" he asked.

"No one is here but a secretary," I said. "She gave me the lay of the land the day he was sighted, but I've still got people to talk to. Are you here to help?"

"Yep," he said and snapped a pair of nickel-plated bracelets on my wrists. "You're going home to bed. "We'll find the guy who did this."

"But I've got to do *something.*"

"Dag is already chasing down Chris The Creep. He had a line on The Creep's apartment, but he gave Dag the slip. Landlady told Dag a couple places he hangs out. We'll find him. Brother Jason is with the investigative team. He'll have all the info we need. The three of us can do more than you can right now."

I knew he was right but I wanted to be in on it. "Will you guys keep me informed?"

"We'll report to you first time we get anything if you'll stay home in bed for a day or two."

I twisted my wrist to see if there was enough room to slip the bracelets, but Dan had a good fit going for him. "Where's Steve?"

"He's still at the crime scene."

"Does he know I'm here?"

Dan snorted. "He knows you're not home. He sent me after you. Said he didn't trust himself. You really can rankle him."

Dan's squad car was in a loading zone. He opened the passenger side door and, out of habit, put his hand on my head and pushed me down so I wouldn't bump it in the doorway. I guess I'm lucky he didn't put me in the caged area in back.

Chapter 7

I lay in bed and tried to act sickly when Dan and Steve came in after Angel helped me into my nightgown. She had given me the once over and stopped to take a drag from her phantom cigarette.

"You look terrible," she said. "If things keep going like this, I'm going to have to start smoking again." She looked at the space between her fingers reserved permanently for that missing cigarette, sighed, and stormed out of my room.

To tell the truth, I didn't feel so good either. My little escapade downtown had taken the starch out of me. I grabbed a hand mirror and realized my face looked as pale as an unused powder puff. When Steve came into my bedroom ready to read me my rights for escaping while under a house arrest, my stomach didn't feel too good either.

I really did care about what Steve thought of me because I guess I've always had a crush on him. For some reason he's never tumbled, so I've had to continue to play it cool. Easy to do when we hadn't seen each other much during the past two years. It wasn't until he visited me in the hospital, that I realized how much I missed him.

"Billie, what in the hell were you thinking?" Steve said, as he entered the room. "Running off by yourself when there's a killer out there hoping for a chance to finish the job."

It felt good to see him worried about me. The feeling lasted only a few seconds.

"If you're killed on my shift, do you know what it would mean? I'll tell you," he said, not waiting for an answer. "I'll be walking a beat again for letting a cop and his ex-cop sister both get murdered on the same day. Why do you always have to be so irresponsible?"

Okay, I kept telling myself, under all the yelling I know he must have feelings for me. He just doesn't know how to express them, so he yells. He isn't really mad; he's scared I might get hurt.

"I can take care of myself," I said. "Some weasel killed my brother, and I've got to find him. It's my fault he's dead. If he hadn't taken the bullet to protect me, he'd still be alive. I'm the one who should have died."

I broke down crying. First a sob, followed by more sobs and before I knew it I'd sprung a leak in the dam I'd built to keep my feelings submerged. Angel hugged me and Steve stood back like I might spill on him.

Dan came through the door and glared at Steve. "What did you do to her?"

"I didn't do anything," Steve said. "She started blaming herself about Darrin's death and began blubbering."

Dan gave me one of his teddy bear hugs and held me until the rhythm of my sobbing slowed, and I managed to dial it down to sniffles.

"It's okay," he said. "It's nobody's fault. Darrin did for you what you would have done for him if the situation were reversed."

"Except I didn't." I started on my jag again, and Angel joined Dan with a hug. I thought I would have felt better if Steve would have given me a hug too, but I knew he wouldn't.

"Crap," Steve said. "What I meant to say is, I can't find your brother's killer if I have to go chasing after you all the time. The best thing you can do is to stay in bed and take care of yourself. If you do that, the rest of us will be able to concentrate on finding the scum that killed Darrin."

I sighed. He was doing what he thought was best for me.

"Promise me you will do that," he said.

"I can't promise you anything. If my health allows it, I'm going to be a part of this investigation."

"I already told you we'll keep you informed," Dan said. "You'll be in on it all the way if you stay down and take care of yourself."

A low rumbling sounded from Steve's gut and finally erupted in a god awful grunt. "You told her what? You can't do that. It's like waving a red flag in front of a bull. The first time you tell her something, she'll be out following up the lead. She's out of the loop. Not only that. I want her handcuffed to her bed with a twenty-four hour guard. And I want the guards to be up on all her tricks and where the damn bathrooms are in this house. So you and your brothers are on permanent duty protecting your sister as of now."

"You can't do that," Dan said.

"I just did it. I'm going to have dispatch call Dagwood and Jason and get them over here pronto. And if any of you so much as step outside the house, you'll be suspended. That's it. Round-the-clock protection for your sister. I'm not going to have anymore Blys interfering with my investigation."

"This is bull," Dan said. "This is our brother you're talking about. We aren't going to stand on the sidelines while you guys muck things up."

"I'll let that comment slide because I know you're hurting. You know this is standard procedure. If any of you leave the sidelines you'll be suspended. You're all too close to this. I don't want to worry about vigilante justice being wreaked upon unsuspecting citizens by the Bly family."

Dan was speechless. I couldn't believe it either. Steve smiled, like he had done something clever, and walked out of the room leaving the three of us dumbfounded.

"You aren't going to stand for that, are you?" Angel said.

"What can I do?" Dan said. "If we disobey his orders we'll be suspended, and we still won't be able to be part of the investigation."

He studied me for a moment, and I thought he was going to cry. Except he didn't, and I realized that for the first time in our relationship Dan was relying on me for an answer.

"What?" I said.

"Darrin wouldn't want us to get ourselves kicked off the force on account of him," Dan said. "You know me. I'm by the book. But you've never gone by the book."

"So?"

"It's up to you, Sis. I hate to say it because you're all banged up and look like death warmed over, but we need you to think of something."

"I'm beat," I said. "Let me sleep on it. When I'm done napping, you can bring Dag and Jason up and we'll talk."

"That's my Billie," Angel said. "You want I should fix you a snack for when you wake up?"

"Yeah, chicken soup sounds good. Maybe a bowl of soup and a salad."

"Soup? Salad? I was going to make a run to the *Jack in The Box* and pick up a Jumbo Jack."

"For some reason soup and salad sounds good to me. My near-death experience and Darrin's murder makes me think it's time I started taking care of myself."

As I mentioned earlier, I had been Vegan for a while, about two weeks before I had been shot. They must have forgotten, because they both stared at me.

"How about French fries?" Angel said.

"A salad!" I realized for the first time how precious life was and now I wanted to take care of myself so I could live longer and have the strength to find Darrin's killer. They closed the door softly. My eyes became heavy, and I tried to force myself to dream about how to carry on our investigation.

When I awoke I found myself back in the hospital somehow. The possibilities twisted through my brain. Maybe I hurt myself with all the running around I did downtown. I felt all doped up so I figured maybe I suffered some kind of setback. But I didn't remember being taken to the hospital. I glanced at the sun setting outside of the window and the colors splashed against the wall in my room, creating a mosaic of crimson, mauves and muted pinks. The effect was the oozing of blood from a twisted body. I shivered and tunneled under the hospital blankets, pulling them around me to create a safe cocoon.

When I peeked from under the blankets, the colors on the wall melded into a kaleidoscope of dark storm-like clouds. I shuddered, feeling cold and exposed. I peeked through my door into the hallway and was relieved to see a cop standing outside. No one could get at me with him on guard.

A wonderful thought occurred to me. Maybe it was all a dream. Maybe I never left the hospital. What about Darrin? If I was still here, Darrin must be alive, I thought. The sniper, his death . . . was it all a bad dream?

A dark shadow stretched across the room as if trying to grab me. Large and elongated, it slowly took shape. It had frightening wings, a slim body and twitchy ears. Its wings beat against the mosaic in front of me. My adrenaline kicked in, or what was left of it after being weakened by too many doses of drugs to help me sleep, eat, and combat the pain.

I tried to turn toward the figure making the shadow. The object was behind me at another window. My blankets held me tight like a straightjacket. The tangled IV tubes and monitoring wires, attached to my body, wriggled like snakes on Medusa's head. A surge of fear boosted my anemic adrenaline—to a hundred-fifty-proof—and I felt high.

I flashed back to a time as a baby, when I had slipped from my mother's grasp in a swimming pool and spun like a corkscrew underwater until she plucked me from the depths. It's amazing I still remember that traumatic event.

Now the shadow is on the ceiling too. I'm in a god-awful Disney Fantasia nightmare and my dry mouth can't cry out. An improbable squeak from my lips occurred as I completed my turn toward the window. I couldn't believe what I saw next. It must be the drugs, I thought. I shook my head and glanced back to the wall, the ceiling, and then back to the figure in the window.

As its huge black wings fluttered against the backdrop of crimson blood on the wall, a hideous creature sat in the open window, sneering and plotting. My eyes slowly focused and the shape transformed from a giant black bat creature to a less formidable ugly . . . crow.

"Miss Bly? Are you okay?" It was the cop assigned to my room. "I thought I heard a cry."

My contorted body relaxed and I fell back against the mattress. A stupid crow. My imagination at work overtime. "Yeah. I saw that shadow on the wall and it spooked me."

He stepped into the room and laughed at the shadow as the crow flew off. "I can see where it might startle you." The communications Rover on his shoulder squawked and he tilted his head toward it and pushed a button. It squawked again and a screechy voice screamed with urgency.

"We've got a situation on the floor below, and I'm needed. Will you be okay if I go investigate?"

"Sure." I was still shaken from the bat incident, but I couldn't admit it. I reached under my pillow and was pleased to find my Glock. Instant security.

"Thanks. I'll be back in a couple minutes."

He ran out of the room as he said this, so I knew something important must be going on. For some reason--maybe it was the drugs, maybe I crashed after the adrenaline rush—I dozed off. I wanted to see what happened downstairs and something inside told me to stay awake. But I couldn't. I drifted in and out of consciousness and finally awoke to the shadow on the wall again.

The damn bird was back. Its wings were huge against the wall. Then the shadow changed shape. More like an orangutan or some kind of monkey, at least. The breeze from the open window wafted over me and it seemed hot for an October day. I brushed away some matted hair from my cheek. The room grew dark and I wondered why the nurse hadn't switched on the lights. The waning sun elongated my sinister shadow.

I turned on my side to get a panoramic view of the wall and the bird in the window. The move seemed easier this time because I wasn't freaking, knowing my imagination had gotten the best of me before. The cop should have been back by now, I thought.

I saw him as I reached for the nurse's button on the bedrail. Slipping in through the window, which swiveled open enough to let a breeze in but supposedly keep a child from falling out. But The Jet squirmed through easily like he'd been doing it all his life. Behind him, a rope dangled outside from above.

"Hi, Billie. Remember me?"

I felt for the bedrail on my left and it was down. *Thank God!* In one motion I slid my left hand under the pillow while pushing my right hand hard against the mattress. The rubber lifelines untangled as I twisted and the last thing I saw before I rolled out of bed was the little man with the toothy grin and evil eyes raising a semi-automatic at me.

The first shot whizzed by my ear as I gripped the Glock in the wrong hand. *Pop, pop, pop, pop*, four shots searching for me. I wriggled off the bed, but hadn't quite made it to the floor. *Pop, pop.* More shots ricocheting off the floor.

The IV lines held me suspended slightly below the mattress, the gun in my left hand pinned against my waist by the rubber tubes. I pawed frantically at the plastic snakes with my free hand. Finally, I managed to stretch some tubes enough so I could point my gun in his general direction.

"Where the hell are you, Billie? Playing hide and seek?" He squatted to peek under the bed and I managed a shot at the floor.

Sparks flew at his feet and he jumped back. "Damn," he said.

I thought the same thing. His gun had a silencer, so my shot echoed the first warning to hospital staff and that damn cop, still missing from action. I squirmed like an antsy pug dog trying to twist out of its collar and two more shots zinged at me under the bed. One of them tore into my arm and sent me into a shivering fit. I fell to the floor and lifted my gun with my left hand about the time The Jet decided to see if he hit me.

Bam, Bam, Bam -- and this time my bullets found their target. The Jet left his feet and bounced a couple of times before collapsing in a heap on the floor. I straightened to a prone position on the cold linoleum floor and waited for him to get back up. He didn't.

I heard shouts and people scurrying in the hallway, but the door was closed now for some reason and apparently no one was brave enough to open it. I debated on whether or not to shoot if someone did enter the room. I smelled my blood and saw it oozing from my arm onto the floor. And then, in my weakened state, I did something most embarrassing to me. I fainted.

Chapter 8

When I awoke, I was back in my own bed at home. It took me several minutes to get my bearings. Angel stood over me, with a bowl of Caesar salad cupped in her hands, talking in a soft voice.

"Your brothers are here. They're waiting downstairs to see you."

I turned toward her and gradually realized I was not in the hospital. "How did I get here?"

"You've been taking a nap," she said.

"Where's Darrin?" I sat up in a panic.

"Oh Honey, Darrin's dead." Her eyes widened. "You remember that, don't you?"

"A dream? The whole damn killing The Jet thing was a dream?" I said. "That means Darrin being alive was a dream too. Shit!"

"Oh, you had a nightmare. I'm sorry, Honey. Are you ready to see your brothers or do you want me to make an excuse? They've been waiting for over an hour."

"Shit, shit, shit!" My heart was in my throat. The dream seemed so real. I could touch the cop. I could feel the heat from the barrel of my Glock.

I reached under my pillow now for my gun. It was my .38, not the Glock, which probably occupied space in a police evidence room. The revolver's cylinder revealed no empty chambers. A hint of cleaning oil permeated the gun, meaning I hadn't shot at anyone recently. I witnessed the fear in Angel's eyes and realized she'd seen me twirl the chambers and sniff the gun. Of course, she took that ubiquitous phantom puff from that invisible cigarette between her fingers. Did she think I was going to kill myself?

"I'm not crazy. I just had a dream."

"I'm sorry." She put the salad on my nightstand. "You want me to tell them to come back another time?"

"Them? Oh, my brothers. No, give me twenty minutes to freshen up."

She smiled, turned, and walked out the door, closing it softly.

I waited until she stepped out of range and my breast heaved as I sobbed. I clutched at my chest wound and reached for some pain medication. I missed Darrin so much. I blamed God for letting him die and then giving me a false hope. I cried some more, not caring how red my eyes appeared when my brothers arrived. I would cry for them too, and they should know it now. Maybe it would make them more careful.

I nibbled at my salad as I cried, forcing myself to eat to gain strength for what lie ahead. Finally, I wiped my eyes and face and walked to my bathroom. All the makeup in the world wouldn't help me, so I worked on the worst areas of my reddened face. Soon after I finished, my brothers entered and found me sitting up in bed in a martial arts kimono I use as a robe.

"Hi," Dag said. I noticed his eyes, like mine, were red and puffy as he bent a bit to clear the low-framed doorway and brushed his sandy curls with his fingers in case it got mussed coming through. Dag has lots of muscles and I think Angel has a crush on him. He gave me a bear hug, and I yelped at pain in my chest from the still-healing bullet wounds.

"Hey, sorry," he said.

Dan, Jason and Angel trailed in and they all managed stiff smiles and kept a distance, in case my crying was contagious. Jason maintained a stoic pose and roosted on an old-fashioned iron radiator. He stroked his pencil-thin mustache with a finger. Dan sat on a window seat and Angel picked a chair near him. I could see the thinning hair on Dan's head. His fatherly demeanor was replaced by tightness on his round face.

"How are you feeling?" Dan asked.

"I won't lie to you. I'm in a rough patch. I never felt so bad in all my life."

"None of us feel all that good," Jason said. "I don't get why Steve's blackballing us from this investigation. No offense, Billie, but being sent to babysit you is a slap in the face."

"Why don't they just put us on leave or give us a desk?" Dag said.

I rubbed at my swollen eyes. "My guess is Steve knows us well enough to head us off from any unofficial investigations we might be able to start from home or behind a desk."

"Yeah, but why you?" Jason said. "He can't keep you under what amounts to house arrest." Jason's always been quick to temper. Contrary to what most people believe about me, he's the hothead in the family.

"He says I'm a material witness in protective custody," I said.

"It just isn't fair. I'm going to quit." His rugged facial features hardened. "Then he won't tell me what to do."

"You won't do any such thing," Dan said. "None of us will. Darrin wouldn't want us to lose our jobs over him. We've just got to find a way to get around Steve, and Billie's an ace at that."

My older brother was asking for my help. It was a milestone for a man who raised us after my parents' untimely deaths. I tried to appear modest, but I probably looked like the Cheshire cat grinning at the world.

"You got any ideas?" Jason shifted his weight on the radiator and grimaced.

"Yeah, I got a few," I said. "But Dag, I'm getting vertigo with you standing over me."

Dag smiled sheepishly and sat on a wooden chair next to Angel, and I had to laugh at the easy-going giant sitting next to my diminutive, brash secretary. Maybe they *weren't* such a good match.

"Okay, shoot," he said.

"The way I see it, you guys are all grounded. That leaves Angel and me to do the dirty work." I adjusted the bed pillow behind the small of my back and settled in for the battle ahead.

"But you're supposed to stay here," Dan said. "We're responsible for watching you."

"You always go by the book, Dan. That's why you wanted my help, remember?"

He nodded.

"Okay, so first thing we need to do is to put a bug on Steve so we know where he's going and what he's doing. This will be especially helpful if he decides to check on me here at the house."

"A bug, oh my Lord," Dan said. Dag, Jason, and Angel chuckled. I thought it a bit unseemly to be so light-hearted, with Darrin killed a few hours earlier, and then I realized it was a nervous release for their feelings of loss.

"Don't have a heart attack, big brother," I said. "If you want to leave the room so you can say you didn't know about any of this, we can excuse you."

"No," Dan said. "This is a drastic measure. We've got to find out who killed our brother."

"Good. So the next thing is to get copies of all the police reports on the case so we know where we stand. Jason, didn't you used to date that clerk in records downtown?"

"Yeah, Samantha."

"Did you treat her right? Or did you dump her and leave her hating you, you slime ball of a man?"

"I had to cut it off with her," Jason said. "She was getting too bossy for me, so I suggested we take a break for a while."

I rolled my eyes. "Can you go to her for a big favor?"

"I should be able to get all the preliminary reports turned in so far. It's going to cost me though."

"You're a big boy," I said. "You can handle it. While you're sweet talking her, see if you can get her to e-mail you any future reports too."

"You might not get as much as you think if Steve's working the case," Dag said. "He keeps all the info close to him until the case dries up or he makes an arrest. I've worked with him. He's pretty secretive, and he doesn't seem to care much about department protocol when it comes to filing reports."

"Really?" I said. "That's not the Steve I know. Mr. 'Did you finish that report, yet, Billie?' He used to ride me to get the reports in ASAP when we were partners. Of course, he always *was* good at delegating work."

"I worked with him on a couple of cases last year and he's become real tight-lipped about things." Dag shifted his weight on the unpadded chair. "I think he wanted to move up the ladder and maybe made some enemies. He's always expecting someone to screw him."

"I think he blames me for not making lieutenant earlier," I said. "He got called on the carpet a couple of times because of some trumped-up improper use-of-force charges against me."

Everyone laughed out loud. "What?" I asked.

"You did have a reputation for being somewhat tough with some of the guys you arrested," Angel said.

"Yeah," Dag said. "Remember that perp who asked if you were really a woman?"

"I didn't hurt him."

"No," Jason said, sliding off the radiator with laughter. "You just flashed your boobs."

"Normally, I would have shoved his face against a brick wall, but he was kind of cute."

"The guy was so shaken, later when he went before a judge he said he didn't remember being read his Miranda rights," Dag said.

"I read 'em."

Jason's eyes opened wide. "I heard the judge's face went beet red when he questioned the suspect further and learned that Billie had flashed him. The judge threw out his confession and agreed that given Billie's stature, he probably *was* too distracted to concentrate when she read him his rights."

"Steve hit the ceiling on that one," Dag said. "He got called on the carpet by the Captain. I never figured out how you avoided suspension."

I felt my face flush at the recollection of my meeting with the Captain.

"Oh, no!" Dan squirmed in his chair. "Tell me you didn't."

"Didn't what?" Angel asked me. I could tell she'd already guessed, and she wanted to hear me say it.

"Well, hell," I said. "He was going suspend me. I asked him if there was anything I could do to change his mind. He ogled me. I asked him, 'would you like to see what I did instead of running the suspect's face into the wall?' The Captain, he shook his head sheepishly, but I knew he did. So I showed him. In the end he agreed that although my behavior was not strictly becoming an officer of the law, I might have been provoked, and given my situation, I showed remarkable restraint to the point of having a sense of humor."

After the laughter died down, Dan became serious. "In a way, I think we're to blame for some of your problems on the force. We treated you like a brother instead of a sister. All of our macho bull rubbed off on you, and I'm sorry."

Jason and Dag nodded in agreement.

Shit! Darrin would never talk crap like this. He knew I have a feminine side. But I can't show the soft side of myself on the job because I'm a woman and because I'm also a blonde, men think I'm a pushover, and they can walk all over me.

"Let's get back to business," I said. "Angel, see what we've got downstairs that we can put in Steve's car. How about using one of those Pro Tracker GPS systems? If we can get somebody to plant one, say, under his seat, we can follow him in real-time. Then we would know if he's heading here to check up on me."

"Do you think he will?" Angel said.

"Oh Yeah," I said. "Probably twice a day. He knows me too well. If I'm not here when he visits, we're going to have to find a way to make him believe I am. Angel can be helpful in that area. She's a lot more devious than you guys."

"I can plant the tracker," she said. "I'll go downtown and tell them you left something in Steve's car when they brought you home."

"No. Steve will hear about it and he'll get suspicious. We need to find out where he's going to be. Then you can use a Slim Jim and plant the bug."

"But it's illegal," Dan said.

"It's okay, I'm a certified locksmith," Angel said. "I got my degree in the mail last month."

"Maybe we could plant it tonight at his house," Jason said.

I shrugged. "I think it's better to do it when he's out and about."

"I'm going to be at the mortuary tomorrow to finish making arrangements for Darrin's funeral," Dan said. "I could call Steve and ask him to help with the departmental aspect of the funeral."

"Will he go with you?" I asked.

"Sure. I'll tell him I need someone for moral support. How can he say no?"

"Let me know when and where if he agrees to it," Angel said. "I'll bring my Slim Jim. Try to get him to park out on the street away from the mortuary office. The fewer witnesses the better."

"Oh, I want to come, too," I said.

"Do you think that's a good idea?" Dan displayed his patented scorn of disapproval.

"Why not?"

"If you go, Steve might not come. I plan to use your illness to guilt him into coming to support me. And if he finds out you're coming along, he might think I don't need him."

"This sucks." I gave him my five-year-old pouty face.

He ignored it. "I'll go downstairs and call him now."

"Just as well he's gone," I said, as Dan closed the door. "Being a *by-the-book* guy, and as nervous as he gets, it's probably best he doesn't know every little thing we do."

"So what's my job?" Dag said.

"I'm going to need a little help tracking down Chris The Creep and his buddy, Jeff, who saw The Jet at the hospital and again downtown at City Hall."

"Yeah, I'm already on that," Jason said. "Dag and I rousted his landlady earlier today. She said he packed up his clothes and stuff and bugged out. I got her to cough up the name and address of his sister and mother. She's a tough old broad. Told me to get a warrant. I told her the cons would really like her down at lockup."

"We've got to find him," I said. "He said he knows where The Jet can be found and The Jet's the one that killed Darrin. I know it in my gut."

"You go," Jason said to Dag. "I need to call my friend in records and someone should stay close to Billie."

"What happens if I'm spotted away from the house?" Dag cast his eyes about the room nervously.

"Tell them you're filling my prescription." I handed him a slip of paper the doctor gave me. "You just better damn well know where the nearest pharmacist is in whatever area of town you visit."

He scrutinized the script. "I feel like I'm back in school with a hall pass."

Dan returned and passed Dag on his way out. "Where's he going?" he asked.

"To fill my prescription."

Dan's forehead developed furrows deep enough to plant corn. "Well, I guess it's okay. Steve's going to pick me up at my house tomorrow at a little before eleven. I told him I had to go home and change first. I wrote down the address here for Angel. It's

Thompson's Mortuary on Northeast 81st off Burnside."

"Right," said Angel, taking the slip of paper. "Maybe, I'll wear black so as not to stand out."

"So what did I miss?" Dan said.

"Not much. Tomorrow I'm going down to City Hall."

"On Saturday?" Jason said. "It's closed."

"Not if you know the secret handshake," I said. "A new friend of mine in the city commissioner's office said the back door would be open for me. I plan to be there to find out who The Jet stopped in to see yesterday."

"What?" Dan's face became animated. "He was in the City Hall to see a city commissioner?"

"Or the Mayor. My friend is trying to get a security tape showing The Jet's visit and maybe who he was there to see."

"My God, that's incredible," Dan said.

I nodded. "Maybe with a bit of luck we can nail Darrin's killer and find out who wants me dead."

"Who else knows about this?" Jason asked.

"Just we four and, with the exception of Dag, I don't want anyone else to know. If there's someone inside City Hall involved, it could be very dangerous for all of us."

"Amen," Dan said.

"Mum's the word," Jason said. "Until we catch the son-of-a-bitch. Then all bets are off."

"I think we should lay low, not make too many inquiries to our partners and fellow cops," Dan said. "We don't want Steve or the Captain getting any tips that we're investigating."

"Okay," Jason said. "But I want to be there for the finish."

"You will be," I said. "All of us will." The room grew quiet.

"I've got to call Mary," Dan said. "She's really shaken over this."

"That's a good idea," Angel said. "Billie needs her rest. I'll fix you each up with a bedroom. Lieutenant Steve told me that you guys are houseguests here until he says differently."

"See if you can set up a command post in the laundry room," I suggested. "It's out of sight if anyone comes snooping and big enough to set up a table and a couple of chairs." I pulled a comforter over my weary body. "Oh, and use your personal cell phones, not the city-issued ones. We don't want anyone listening in or checking email or texts. You can use my laptop, and we have a wireless network so you should be set."

"I'll stop and get some throwaway cell phones after I bug Steve's car," Angel said.

"For God's sake be careful," Dan said. "Does she know what she's doing?"

"She's done it hundreds of times," I said.

"Hundreds?"

"She's exaggerating," Angel said, and escorted him out to give me some rest, but popped her head back in through the doorway. "I'm thinking maybe I could wear that hot new red miniskirt tomorrow. I've got some matching three-inch heels and a new avant-garde blue hat with white lace that covers part of my face."

"Stay with the black," I said.

"I can wear sheer black panty hose."

"You won't be able to run in those heels, and you might get arrested in that outfit," I said. "How are you going to bug the car from jail?"

She seemed puzzled. "Save it for a more formal occasion," I said.

"What better occasion is there than tailing your boyfriend? I don't want to stand out wearing Jeans or something around a funeral home."

She winked at me and bounced out the door. I felt what I was sure were some remaining interior stitches tearing inside my chest as I laughed. For a moment, Angel helped me feel a bit lighter, but my good mood quickly gave way to thoughts of revenge. I made a promise to myself to avenge Darrin's death. His killer would never see the inside of a courtroom.

Chapter 9

I slept fitfully because of nightmarish dreams. Rickie Lee Jones mercifully belted a tune on my clock radio at eight o'clock and I responded by groaning and wrapping my pillow around my ears. The radio alarm played for half an hour before it stirred me again. I was behind schedule, so I took a sponge bath to avoid wasting time changing my wet bandages.

The redness and puffiness in my eyes had subsided so my makeup went on smoothly. I slipped into a black dress and viewed my reflection in the mirror. I filled the dress out pretty good upstairs, but it was obvious I'd lost a lot of weight during my stay in the hospital. The skirt was a little short for mourning attire, but it was the only black dress I owned, and I figured it might help me with the questioning of any male suspects I might run into. Men are such dopes.

I packed my .38 into a good-sized purse. That's the problem for a woman carrying a gun. You have to have a large enough purse to hide it and still be properly accessorized. And where can you put a backup piece in a dress so short it barely hides your modesty?

I wanted to avoid my brothers asking about my feelings, so I snuck down the stairs hoping to get away unobserved. Voices carried from the laundry room in the back of the house, where I figured Angel and my brothers were sorting bugging equipment. To avoid them, I'd have to exit by the front door in plain view of potential witnesses or cops.

I shut the front door softly and scanned the street for cars to see if they belonged in the neighborhood. Right away I saw one looking too much like it belonged. It was a BMW with a fresh wash job. With the rehab of three homes on my street, a car wash would last for a couple of hours, at most, because of all the dust stirred up by workmen.

The Bimmer's occupants, two men, were busy talking and didn't notice my exit. Steve didn't trust me. He set up a stakeout to watch me. I legged it, as ladylike as possible, over the rail at the side of the front porch. As I slid down, trying not to rip a stitch in my dress or my chest, I noticed the driver and his partner were still oblivious to my escape.

I cut through old lady Shelly's back yard and stopped to straighten my skirt, en-route to an alley leading to Northwest 23rd Avenue. I walked half a block down the alley with plans to get a Venti-sized cup of Cinnamon Spice Mocha at Starbucks.

Once inside the coffee shop, I purchased my drink and sat and waited for the trolley to make an appearance around the corner. I also watched the opposite direction for two harried cops or their blue Bimmer while I sipped the coffee.

About five minutes passed before the trolley chugged around the corner. It was nine-fifteen and I cursed the surveillance in front of my house which made it necessary for me to rely on public transportation. I had no idea how long it would take to get downtown and later out to Northeast 82nd Avenue to meet Dan and Steve at the funeral home. Too long I imagined.

I got off the Max, two blocks from City Hall, at nine-thirty and walked to the rear entrance. An eight-foot wrought iron fence protected the garbage bins and the gated entry appeared to be locked.

I stepped closer to examine the chain wrapped through the gate and gatepost and noticed the catch on the padlock was ajar. I unwound the chain from the gatepost, lifted the latch, and pushed the gate open. A few furtive moments later I strolled into a small storage room and peered through a glass window in a door. The lobby was empty.

I opened the door, put on my cop persona, and marched confidently up the stairs. It was Saturday. The front door appeared locked and apparently there was no security guard on duty, unless he was making his rounds.

The door to the Mayor's office was locked, but I saw a shadow further back in the office. His Honor appeared to be in. The door to the public reception area where I'd met Eileen was unlocked and it made me wonder when she was going to call me about the security tape.

Only half the lights were on in the empty clerk's office. I observed a security camera pointing at an angle to the door and a little red light blinked at me, meaning I was likely being taped. To get to the Mayor I would need to pass through the gate with a buzzer. After my painful step over the porch railing, I balked at a repeat performance. The buzzer barely chimed and shut off as I slid through, the noise almost unnoticeable. In a minute the Mayor would know I was there anyway, and I hoped he wouldn't call security on me.

I tapped on his frosted glass door with my knuckles and opened it. Mayor Marshall Clemons, a medium-sized, middle-aged man with perfectly combed white hair, peered over his bifocals from behind his desk. He held a pen over several pages of legal papers.

"Mr. Mayor, I'm Billie Bly, and I was hoping I could speak with you for a minute."

"I know who you are."

Clemons didn't act surprised to see me. He removed his square bifocals and laid them on the papers. "It hasn't been that long since you brought a multi-million dollar lawsuit upon the city."

"I guess I don't get any leniency for a death in the family." I tried to act sickly and instead came across as pathetic.

"Not at all. Sit down. Didn't you just get out of the hospital?"

"Yeah, the day my brother was killed."

"I'm sorry." He said all the right things, but his eyes glanced behind me, possibly watching for a security guard. "How did you get in here?"

"Back door," I said. "You shouldn't leave it unattended, even on a Saturday."

"Mmm. I'll check into that. You look pretty good for someone who was gunned down in a warehouse a couple of weeks ago."

"You heard?" I said.

"Well, of course. It was front page news. We were all worried about you. The commissioners, the police department. About your dismissal, well, we just didn't have much choice. We had to take action because of the lawsuit against the city. We appreciate the fact you didn't appeal the decision through the union." Again, Clemons peaked behind me.

"I don't like the city's style of justice," I said. "Now I'm my own boss and I can work by my own rules."

"I see. And what are some of your rules? I must say, I'm curious."

"Things really aren't that much different. Just not so much politics. For instance, when a brother catches a bullet in the line of duty, everything comes to a halt, and I concentrate on finding the killer."

"So that's why you're here?" he said. "You're searching for your brother's killer?"

"You catch on quick."

"Why come to me?"

"The day before someone shot Darrin, a short man, a dwarf actually, was seen entering the reception area outside your office. He's been identified as Monty Bales, also known as The Jet. It was during lunch, and I think he might have come into your office. I'm wondering what you two had to talk about."

"I don't remember seeing him. What did he look like?"

"I told you, he was short. Shit, Mayor, are you jacking me

around, stalling me until a security guard gets here? Maybe you're going to have me arrested. I can see the headlines now. 'Mayor busts fallen police officer's sister.'"

"Take it easy." Clemons appeared horrified. "I'm expecting someone and I don't know how much time we have to talk."

"Well, answer my question and I'll get out of here." I wondered who he was waiting for. The Jet?

"Nobody of that description came into my office."

"Who else did you see Thursday?"

"Nobody while I was here. It was lunchtime. I stopped in to check messages and made some calls. Eileen was the clerk working. None of the other commissioners were around, except, wait, Tom was here. He had somebody in his office, so I didn't bother him."

"Tom?"

"Commissioner Tuttle. He and the other person were arguing about something."

"Did you see the auditor?" I asked, remembering that Eileen said he and Commissioner Tuttle argued that day.

"Bob? No. He left a message saying he wanted to go over some figures with me, but then he took yesterday off. I haven't had a chance to get back to him."

Clemson fidgeted with his pen, manipulating it through various fingers. Beads of sweat permeated his brow. I wondered whom he expected. As if he read my mind, he responded.

"I'm the only one here today so far. Commissioner Tuttle said he might drop by, but I think the rest of the commissioners are wiped out between campaigning and the terrorist drills we've been running this week. Is there anything else?"

"No, I'll get out of your hair."

"Let me know if there's anything I can do," Clemons said. "I knew your brother, and I'd like to help if I can."

"I think The Jet was the one that killed Darrin." I leaned over the desk and dropped my business card. "If you hear anything, call me. I've got to go now to make plans for Darrin's funeral."

"I'll see you there," Clemons said.

I exited through his secretary's office and opened the front door, but closed it without leaving. Footsteps marched toward me from down the hall. I scooted around the secretary's desk, pushed the chair out, crawled under the desk on my hands and knees, and nearly cried out from a sharp pain radiating in my chest. I pulled the chair into me just as the front door opened. Long feminine legs strolled past me into the Mayor's office.

"Hello, Marshall. Have you been waiting long?"

Her sulky voice permeated the office, as did a vibrant rose-scented perfume. From my low vantage point, I spotted her hot-red high-heel pumps. Angel would approve, I thought.

"No, you timed it just right," he said. "No one's in today so we don't have to put on airs."

It was quiet for a long minute, except for smooching sounds I associated with busy lips.

"Billie Bly was here," Clemons said. "Did you see her leaving?"

"I didn't see anyone," the woman said.

"She's asking about a dwarf. She said he killed her brother."

I heard a sharp intake of breath followed by silence. "I thought she just got out of the hospital," the woman said.

"I told you how stubborn she is," Clemons said. "She's determined to avenge her brother's death. She was asking about who was in the office Thursday, the day before her brother was killed. She said someone saw this dwarf come into my office."

"That's ridiculous," she said.

It was quiet for a moment. I thought maybe they'd heard me.

"*Was* he here?" she asked.

"Hell no! I never saw him."

"Christ, if she's snooping around, we've got to be careful," the woman said. "We don't want her messing up everything."

"You're not suggesting . . ."

"Nothing of the sort," she said. "But she *has* been a pain for you and your re-election. We should just lay low until this thing blows over. That idea we talked about? Maybe we should put that into action."

"I'll take care of it," Clemons said.

"Let's get out of here and you can buy me some brunch," she said.

"I thought we'd go someplace quiet," Clemons said.

"Like a motel with separate adjoining rooms. I don't think so. I'm tiring of meeting on the sly. You can buy me something to eat and then we'll go back to my place, and I'll rock your world."

"What about your husband?"

"He's out of town all weekend."

"Where?"

"Seattle. Some kind of seminar."

"That's nice of him."

The lights went out and I felt a slight breeze as they whisked by the desk I hid under. I carefully dislodged myself after the door closed. By the time I managed to get on my feet and to the stairs, all I could see was the back side of a tall brunette, in a red miniskirt and heels, walking down the stairs with Clemons.

I wanted to follow them, but it was past ten o'clock and I needed to catch Tuttle if he was in his office. I walked down the hallway to his door, but the office was dark. I jiggled the knob and it was locked. I went in through the reception area and tried his side door, also locked.

I exited on Fourth Street and made for the bus stop to go to the funeral home. As luck would have it, the Mayor and his girlfriend stopped at a light only 30 feet in front of me in his white Mercedes.

I recognized the Mayor's hottie in the red dress. I'd seen a picture of her in one of my many trips to City Hall when I fought my lawsuit against Chris The Creep. I needed all kinds of records and documents and public policy manuals to support my case and I'd met with her husband, Bob Blaney, a few times.

Blaney, the city auditor, was a laid back, unassuming man with a friendly demeanor and average looks. Who would think he would have landed a trophy-wife like Gloria? I wondered if he had been yelling at Tuttle and maybe others because he suspected his wife was cheating on him. If so, apparently he hadn't figured out it was the Mayor she was boinking. I wondered with whom else she was playing house.

Gloria appeared animated as she talked to the Mayor. I tried to get closer to hear what she was saying. I stood on the edge of the sidewalk curb ten feet behind them when she twisted her head in my direction.

Instinctively I stepped behind a pole displaying the *Walk* and *Wait* pedestrian signals and held my breath. I heard one word uttered from her lips as I hid.

"Shit!"

The light changed, the Mayor drove off, and I shifted my angle to stay concealed. Did she see me? If she did, she must have wondered why I hid. Why did I hide? It was then I remembered something I'd heard in their conversation. Gloria's words wafted incoherently into the air, jumbled by traffic noises and people talking around me, and magically realigned when I began breathing again.

"That bitch is going to cause trouble."

Chapter 10

I walked up Fourth Avenue to Madison Street and found a sign displaying the options for catching buses. The number 19 would drop me off within three blocks of the funeral home on Northeast 80th Avenue and Glisan Street. Ten minutes later I climbed the steps up the bus mindful it was time for some pain pills.

I dropped a bus ticket in the box and a couple of pills into my dry mouth and sat on a side seat where I could stretch out. The acrid taste of the pain pills reminded me how bitter life can be. I thought about Darrin and tried not to cry.

I got off the bus, thankful for the short walk. The medication had kicked in, but I felt so tired. When I stepped through the doors at the funeral home and found Steve and Dan talking to a mortuary counselor, it wasn't "it's good to see you up and around" or "how do you feel?" Steve said to me.

"What the hell are you doing here? You're supposed to be home."

"I came to help plan Darrin's sendoff, Mister Thomas. Do you have a problem with that?"

"Well, no. It's just . . . I mean, I came because I didn't want Dan to be alone. I thought your brothers were back at your house watching over you."

Dan grinned like he was expecting me to show up.

"They think I'm in bed asleep. Oh, come on, Steve. Do you think I'm not going to be a part of my own brother's funeral?"

"I guess not." He sulked. "Maybe I'm not needed here, then. You can drive Dan home, can't you?"

"Me? I took the bus. I didn't want to alarm your surveillance team in front of my house. They were having such a good time swapping stories."

Steve's face flushed and he motioned for me to sit at a table.

"Thanks, Stevie." It turns me on when I get his goat.

I sat at a table covered with samples of prayer cards to be handed out at the funeral, picked one and asked the counselor to include a copy of Darrin's favorite prayer as an insert. Arrangements were made for a newspaper story even though the department had flooded the local media with press releases and the television news had already run several stories on his death. I gave the counselor a brief history of his rank-and-file accomplishments, a list of his volunteer activities, and suggested a donation to a children's charity in lieu of flowers.

"We were thinking of this stainless steel casket," Steve said, pointing to a display.

I recoiled. "Oh God no, it looks like a bullet."

"I think it looks nice," Steve said. "And it's moderately priced."

"I'll pay for the damn coffin," I said.

I got out my credit card and thought unkind thoughts about the cheap bastards at the police bureau. Steve must have read my mind because he excused himself to make a phone call. Dan grinned at his retreat and winked at me.

"Let's go with the nice mahogany model," I told the counselor.

After the decisions had been made, I noticed Steve pacing back and forth outside the window with his cell phone to his ear. When Dan and I completed the paperwork, we joined him in the parking lot as he finished one of many calls.

"I've got someone at the city working on compensating you for your expenses," Steve said. "You shouldn't have to foot the bill. Hell, he was killed in the line of duty."

I nodded and searched the street to see if Angel lurked nearby. Sure enough, a block down the street I spotted her pastel green Volkswagen Beetle parked behind a rusting orange pickup truck. I fought the urge to feel under my passenger seat for Angel's bug after I sat next to Steve in his car. Dan fidgeted behind me, likely also fighting the need to check.

"Any leads yet on who killed Darrin?" I asked.

"I told Dan what we've learned so far, which isn't much," Steve said. "The Jet is nowhere to be found. I think your friend, Chris, was pulling your leg. And, by the way, he's skipped out too."

"He probably thinks the shooter is after him," I said. "Maybe he's right."

"You figure someone might try to keep him from talking?" Dan said.

"I don't know. Chris sure isn't going to talk now and the pressure must be building on whoever hired The Jet to kill me. He bungled the job twice and the person who hired the hit has got to be nervous because he knows I'm coming after him."

"Not to mention the entire Portland Police Bureau," Steve said flatly. "Aren't you the modest one? Did it ever occur to you that this Chris character might be lying? He probably doesn't know anything at all."

"Do either of you think it's possible the shooter was after Darrin?" Dan asked.

"It's possible," Steve said. "He's a cop. He's probably made enemies. Maybe it's payback for some con he arrested."

"Darrin didn't have any enemies." I snarled at Steve. "He treated everybody square. Even the people he arrested liked him. Heck, a few of them probably wrote him from jail."

"She's right," Dan said. "You haven't had the chance to work with him, but he would give you the shirt off his back. He didn't judge people. He had this way of putting himself in their shoes. He respected the people he dealt with and they respected him."

"Everyone makes enemies," Steve said. "I'm just saying it's a possibility."

"If you want someone who makes enemies, I'm your woman," I said. "I step on people every day to get to the truth."

"I know I've thought about taking a shot at you from time to time." Steve chuckled. "Uh oh."

"What's wrong?" Dan said.

"We picked up a tail. I noticed it back at the funeral home."

Dan peered over his shoulder, but not me. I figured that damn Angel followed too close while testing her tracking devise.

"Which car?" Dan said.

"It's the blue Honda two cars back. The one behind the green bug. It pulled out the same time we did at the funeral home."

I almost choked. He'd made Angel and didn't know it, watching a car behind her.

"I'll radio dispatch and have a car intercept it. Then we can double back and find out who's following us."

But before Steve had a chance to make the radio call, the blue Honda accelerated past Angel and pulled up to the left of us. Steve cussed over his shoulder, hit the brake and veered behind the Honda. "We got him now. Did anyone see the driver?"

"Are you kidding," Dan said. "I'm still trying to find my stomach."

"It happened too fast," I said.

Steve clicked on the radio and called for help. He was answered by static.

"What's wrong with the radio?" I asked.

"I dunno. It's not working."

"Great. Let's get the hell out of here," Dan said.

"I'm with you," Steve said.

"Make your first available left," Dan said, pointing with his Sig Sauer pistol.

Steve slowed his car in anticipation and now the erratic driver in the Honda switched to the right lane and hit his brakes. The blue car moved on our right now and sitting behind the driver was The Jet. He pointed another very big gun right at me.

It all happened quickly. I faced the driver directly across from me, a wiry-looking Asian with coal-black hair. I recognized him as one of the three guys at the warehouse who shot me. Monty Bales, behind him, had a nice angle to blow me away. His yellow teeth sneered as his green malevolent eyes sighted down the barrel pointed at me.

"It's The Jet!" I screamed.

"I'll get him!" Dan yelled from behind.

I fumbled for my gun but the angle through my window was entirely wrong. I reached over and pulled the car's automatic gear-shift lever into the lowest gear and the car lurched as if braked. Glass exploded and tiny shards from my passenger window sprayed onto my lap as I watched holes appear in the front windshield.

"Shit, unlock the window, Steve," Dan cursed.

The Jet missed me, but the driver had time to line them up for another shot. I tried to slink down in the seat, which is hard to do when you have your safety belt on and an aching upper torso.

As my mind raced to keep up with the events at hand, it occurred to me Steve was the only one wearing a Kevlar vest. I thought back to the phone calls he made outside the funeral home and how the Honda mysteriously appeared soon after we left. I wondered why the radio to call for help didn't work and why Dan's maneuvering allowed the Honda to swing close enough to take what should have been the fatal shot.

These thoughts were interrupted by a loud metallic crash and the Honda veered off the road and down an embankment.

"It's Angel," Dan said. "She's pushed them off the road."

Sure enough, the Honda careened off the shoulder of the steep Mt. Tabor road and plummeted down the side of a hill. The Volkswagen took its place outside my window. The driver, a fashioned-challenged woman in a white laced cobalt blue hat, took a puff from that damn missing cigarette and wrestled the steering wheel with her free hand. The green Beetle shuddered and spun out behind us and, as I squinted into the passenger-side mirror, Angel followed the Honda down the ravine.

"Stop the car! Stop the car!" I cried.

Steve pulled over to the shoulder and we all stumbled out of the car. I spotted the Honda about two hundred feet down the cliff. It was bent around a thick Douglas fir.

"Where's Angel?" I yelled. "I don't see her."

"Over here," Dan shouted. "She's over here."

About a hundred feet down on the left and near some blackberry bushes, Angel's Beetle was nestled at the base of another fir, which had stopped its descent. The Beetle obviously was totaled and there was no sign of Angel.

"Angel, oh God, not Angel too," I cried.

"Dispatch! This is Officer Dan Bly," Dan shouted into his direct-call cell phone: "We have a possible Code 49 at East Seventieth and Burnside. This is a Code three. Do you hear me? Code Three. Our radio is out and an attempt made on a person in protective custody. . . The perpetrators may still be in the vicinity at the bottom of a cliff. I need backup to create a perimeter and EMT personnel capable of descending a steep hill. Yes, an injury accident involving two cars. Both went over the cliff."

Steve grabbed me before I could start down the hill. "There's nothing you can do," he said. "We'll have to wait for help."

"I don't want to wait for help. My best friend is down there, and she needs me."

Dan tugged at my other arm, and they wrestled me back onto the street.

"She saved my life. Did you see what she did? She rammed that Honda before The Jet could fire a second shot. She saved my life."

"Yeah. Where did she come from?" Steve asked.

"Angel's never too far behind Billie these days," Dan said.

Thank God for Dan. I was too rattled to lie, and I didn't really care at this point. "I have to find out if she is all right."

In three minutes the ambulance and rescue squad showed up from their station ten blocks away on Burnside. The first squad car arrived a minute later followed by five others in rapid succession. More squad cars secured the bottom perimeter on neighboring side streets and Steve directed the cops as they worked their way to the Honda about a hundred feet from the bottom.

"I don't see how anyone could have survived," Dan said of the crashed Honda. "It rolled three or four times and the roof is crushed flat. Maybe, if they jumped out on the way down?"

The side of Angel's car resembled an accordion. I watched hopefully as the first firefighter, supported by a lifeline, approached the Beetle.

"Can you see her?" I yelled.

The firefighter tugged at the door and put his face to the driver's shattered door window. "She's unconscious," he yelled.

A crowbar materialized from his belt and he wedged it into seam of the door. The firefighter gripped the door handle with one hand and strained against the crowbar with the other. He mouthed something through the window and put both hands on the metal bar, trying to *will* the door open. I heard a metallic crack as it resisted his efforts.

Another firefighter repelled down the hill and joined the first and together the two men yanked at the door and it creaked open about six inches. The first man wiped his brow with his arm and said something to the second man, who nodded. They yanked again and the Beetle shifted from its perch.

"Stop!" I yelled.

Both men scrambled to brace themselves against the VW, as it teetered away from the tree.

"Dan, get a tow truck here, pronto." I pounded his shoulder with my fists like a little girl. "We need to attach a tow line on the bumper to secure the car."

Dan called dispatch and a senior firefighter radioed the rescuers at Angel's car and told them to sit tight. I waited helplessly for fifteen minutes until a white tow truck rolled up. A balding potbellied man, with a naked lady tattooed on his forearm, hopped from the rig and marched toward us. He pulled a toothpick out of his mouth and smiled at Dan.

"Where's the car you want towed?" He eyed Steve's squad car.

I pointed down the hillside. "It's the Beetle against the tree."

He stuck the toothpick back into his mouth. "Okay. What about the other one? I can get that too. I might need more cable though."

"Let's just concentrate on this one," Dan said.

A radio popped behind us. "These two are both dead. We're going to need some help getting them out. Can't tell where the car ends and the bodies begin."

This wasn't the news I wanted to hear. If they didn't make it, was Angel dead too? She lay unconscious and nobody could get close enough to learn her condition. My heart started beating irregularly and I felt a little faint.

"You better go sit down," Dan said. "Your face is white."

The tow truck driver approached me. "Cop said a friend of yours is in that car, Miss."

"Yeah," I admitted.

"Don't worry. I'll get the car up for you."

"Thanks," I said.

I noticed he held a heavy wire cable around his thick waist.

"Name's Earl," he said. Then he jumped backward down the hill and the cable unwound from a pulley on the truck. It was a startling sight to behold. Earl backed down the hill like a seasoned mountain climber, holding a remote control unit in his free hand. The cable continued to unwind with him as he descended.

Eventually he arrived at the Beetle, then crawled under the bumper and wrestled with the cable. He returned from under the Beetle and stopped to admire his work. He pointed to the tow truck and the cable whirred until the slack was gone. The winch stopped and Earl spoke to the firefighters. They argued about something, and I saw Earl go to the driver's window and speak through the broken glass.

The two firefighters followed him, talking in his ear and the next thing I knew the winch on the tow truck cranked again. The Beetle lurched forward and slipped around the side of the tree before jarring to a stop. The big tow truck didn't budge because the driver had put blocks under the rig's back wheels.

"You're crazy!" a firefighter screamed at Earl.

Earl shook his head and pointed at the truck and the Volkswagen seemed to march up the hillside. The firefighters tried to reach for Earl's remote, and he said something that stopped them cold.

"It's coming up." I said. "Angel's coming up." My heart was in my throat each time the Beetle's flattened front wheels hit a bump in the hill. The truck jerked occasionally, but the Beetle steadily and slowly climbed the hill. A minute later it was on the side of the road. The potbellied man hooked the cable to the driver's door, clicked his remote, and the door popped off the Beetle's body.

"She's okay," Earl said when he was done. "Your friend is awake, and she doesn't seem to be hurt too bad. I told her the ride up might be bumpy, but it's better than spending three hours sideways while they try to get that door open. She said to get her up here. All the blood was rushing to her head."

"Bless you," I said.

"That's one tough dame," he said. "Those firefighters didn't want me to try it, but I've done this a few times before. Not with people in it, but it's safe enough. And she wanted to come up."

"Billie? Are you out there?" It was Angel.

I ran to the car as the EMT's eased her onto a stretcher. "I'm here, Angel. Are you all right?"

"I'm a little sore. Probably be worse tomorrow."

Her face held little color and blood seeped from a small cut on her cheek, but the damn blue hat with white lace sat erect on her otherwise disheveled black hair. She was more shook up than she would admit, but she looked great to me.

One of the firefighters joined us, shaking his head. "That was a crazy stunt, mister."

"Earl said he could get me out," Angel said, "so I told him to go for it."

"We're going to have to take her to the hospital," a paramedic said. "She appears okay, but they'll probably want to keep her overnight for observation."

"I don't want to go to the hospital," Angel squawked. "Take me home. A good night's rest is all I need. Well, that and maybe a good man."

She winked at Earl and he winked back.

"I'll come with you," I said.

"You go home and rest," she said. "You look like the walking dead. I'll be all right."

I peered down the ravine at the crushed Blue Honda and felt a sense of well-being, daring to hope there was no way anyone walked away from that mess.

My luck hadn't run toward hope lately.

Chapter 11

The morning after The Jet tried to kill me, I almost murdered Steve.

I had overdone things Saturday. I awoke in pain but was just glad to be alive after Angel ran The Jet and his pals off the road. I fetched my Kimono robe from the closet and wrapped it around me on the way downstairs. Jason sat at the dining table sipping coffee and Dan and Dag hunkered over a laptop trying to make it track Steve's car.

"Any news on The Jet?" I asked.

"Same as yesterday," Jason said. "No one survived the crash at the bottom of the hill, and Steve won't talk. Says he wants to update you in person."

"That's nice of him, but I'd rather know now," I said. "Any coffee?" For the first time in weeks I felt somewhat at ease.

"Just that rotgut stuff Dan made," he said.

I trudged into the kitchen and poured some rotgut into a Stephanie Plum mug I picked up at the local bookstore and returned. "Any calls?"

"A couple yesterday," Jason said. He flipped through a stack of torn out message memos Angel used to track my calls.

"Here's one from a Mrs. Stella Fleming in Pocatello, Idaho. She said she got a call from the coroner's office. They found her husband's body in a marsh along Terminal Six of the Willamette River."

"Great," I said. "My crying client's husband is dead. Why are so many people dying all of a sudden?"

"She's going to be in tomorrow and wanted to know if you can meet her at the airport," Jason said.

"Is that tomorrow or today? The message was left yesterday."

"Uh, not sure. I accidently erased the message this morning."

"I need Angel here. Did Mrs. Fleming say how her husband died?"

"She didn't know," Jason said. "She wondered if you had heard."

"Did you tell her about the lady from the city?" Dag stole a sip of my coffee and made a bitter face.

"Eileen something, from City Hall called." Jason said.

"I'd almost forgotten about her," I said.

"She didn't want to talk to any of us cops," Jason said. "But she did leave a message earlier on your recorder. Somehow I managed not to erase it."

I got up and switched on my answering machine: "*Billie? It's Eileen. I've got the surveillance footage you wanted. I'm a little nervous. I think I'm being followed. I'll call back later.*"

"Did she leave a number?"

"Nah, and the caller ID listed it as a private number," Jason said.

"Anyone else?" I asked.

"Steve called twice last night and once this morning," Dag said.

"Checking up on me?"

"He said he's worried about you, but each time he called, he wanted an exact account of where you were. Dan and I got the GPS tracking system working, and he appears to be heading here now."

"He's on Northwest Seventeenth and Burnside," Dan said.

"Maybe I should go back to bed and play sick," I said.

"You don't have to go back to bed," Jason said. "Have you

looked at yourself in a mirror lately?"

I walked into the hallway toward a full-length mirror. It took me a minute to realize the unwieldy yellow-haired frump with hairy legs and faded makeup was me. "Eeek! I can't let him see me like this."

I left them laughing and went to my bedroom to call Angel. The phone in her hospital room rang unanswered. I called the main number again and asked for the nurse's station. A tired voice told me she was walking the hall with a male friend. *A male friend?* Who in the heck was she seeing that she hasn't told *me* about?

The doorbell rang downstairs. Rats. Steve was here and I had to take a shower. I disrobed, removed my bandages and gazed at the stitching on my chest. The two bullets probably created holes about the size of nickels. But the surgeon's exploratory surgery to get at the slugs was much more invasive. Most of the wound was on the mend, but a few stitches had reopened and displayed the reddened tell-tale sign of infection, so I cleaned the area with antiseptic wipes and took my antibiotic medicine.

I grimaced at the puffy tissue just below my breast. If it scarred, I planned to return the favor to my surgeon. I redid the wound with large waterproof bandages the hospital sent home with me.

Fifteen minutes in the shower, and I almost felt like a new woman. I combed my hair back and it just touched my shoulders wet. I liberally applied my makeup over my sallow features with some extra touchup on bags under my eyes.

"Billie? You out of the shower?" It was Dag out in the hall. "Steve's here. He's been waiting. Are you decent?"

"Tell him to hold his horses. I'll be down as soon as I get off the phone with Angel."

"You better make it soon. I don't think he believes you're here."

I hopped onto the bed in my nightgown and called Angel again.

"Hello?" A husky male voice answered.

"Ah, is Angel there?"

"I'll check . . . some broad wants to talk to you," he said.

"Billie? Is that you? Are you okay?"

I laughed. "You're the one who got run off the road."

"I know. But I'm all right. I've been worried about you, but they had me all doped up last night. I would have called you this morning, but I've been slightly distracted by my guest."

"Yeah, who answered the phone?"

"It's Earl," she said. "He walked into my room a couple hours ago, saying he was worried about me."

"Oh, that's nice."

"Yes, he's a very nice man. Very charming in his own way. Not what you'd expect at first sight. I like him."

Earl said something in the background I couldn't make out and the sound was muffled when Angel responded to him.

"He's going to give me a ride home," Angel said. "The doctor will be in soon and then I'll be cut free."

"Good," I said. "Did they find anything wrong with you?"

"Just some bruises on my chest and legs. Oh, and some face burn. Those airbags might save lives but they leave hellacious marks."

"Well, I can come and get you."

"You stay there and rest. Earl's going to take me to lunch, and I don't want to tire you out. Did your brothers get the GPS tracker working?"

"Yeah. Steve's here now. The boys have been tracking him all over town. I'm letting him cool his heals for a while."

"You shouldn't treat him that way," Angel said. "He's probably worried about you. Maybe you can play it to your advantage."

"He doesn't think that way about me, and I'm not so sure I have feelings for *him* anymore. He seems distant. Besides, he almost got me killed yesterday, and he seemed more concerned about where you came from than he did about me."

"Sweetie, I know you still like him. What's not to like? He's tall, handsome, and muscular and his voice could put me to bed anytime. He likes you, too. But you have to come on softer with him. He wants to feel he's a man. Show him your feminine side for a change."

I decided to change the subject. "By the way, I have this message on my machine from Stella Fleming saying she's flying in on flight three-forty-three on Alaska Airlines. My dumb brothers erased the message so I don't know if she's coming today or tomorrow."

"She's supposed to be here today at two-thirty," Angel said. "I checked the messages from the hospital last night and called her before they doped me up. Earl and I will meet her. She's going to stay at a hotel near the airport."

"You're just getting out of the hospital. You should go home and rest."

"I'm fine. Besides, Earl has offered to do all the driving. All I have to do is give directions."

I learned a long time ago you can't argue with Angel. "Did Stella happen to know her husband's cause of death?"

"Not yet. The coroner's being mum on it until she arrives."

We argued for a few more minutes about Steve, and I hung up the phone receiver and wondered about Angel's new man. It was obvious she liked him. Maybe she was right, I thought. Maybe I *did* need to be nicer and softer with Steve. I went into the bathroom to apply some perfume. After I finished drying and combing my hair, I slid into a playful dress with fall colors and found some sandals.

Jason met me at the bottom of the stairs and eyed me suspiciously.

"Steve's here. What's with the getup?"

"Nothing. I just felt so good after my shower I thought I'd celebrate by sprucing up."

"This is the second day in a row you've worn a dress," he said.

"Yesterday I can understand. You were going to arrange Darrin's funeral. But today there's no reason. Is there?"

"Where's Steve?"

"He's in the kitchen getting some more coffee." Jason glanced at me sideways.

"Ask him if he'll get me a cup too and meet me in the living room."

"I'll be glad when you get better so I don't have to wait on you hand-and-foot."

I winced, sauntered into the front part of the house, and sat on the only piece of furniture, a white wicker settee with plump yellow cushions. Steve entered a minute later with a coffee mug in each hand. He looked yummy in his brown slacks and an Argyle vest sweater under a brown sport coat.

He gawked at me for a moment. "Uh, how you feeling this morning?"

"Surprisingly good," I said, patting the cushion next to me. "Sit down."

He approached the settee from a couple of angles before deciding on a course of action. "I'll just stand. Here's your coffee."

"Come on, sit down. I don't want to strain my neck peering up at you." I took the cup and forced myself to sip the bitter stuff with a smile. He glanced around the room for another place to sit, and seeing none, squeezed in next to me.

"This is cozy," he said.

"Isn't it? I find it's nice sometimes to slow down a bit and appreciate what we have. Don't you?"

"I guess. The job does get wearisome. Are you telling me you plan to let us handle the investigation on your brother?"

"Well, yes, I think so." I fidgeted on the settee a bit. "I mean, who is better qualified to find Darrin's killer than you?"

He blinked. "I'm on top of things. You really mean you're going to butt out?"

"Of course. Why do you act so surprised? I have every

confidence in you, Stevie."

"Stevie?"

"I mean, I've always thought you were extremely capable." I think I overplayed my hand. I'm not a good flirt.

"Really?"

"Sure. Why would you think otherwise?"

"It could be because you always tried to override my ideas when we were partners. Or it could be because you went around my back when we didn't do things your way."

"I know. And I feel terrible about it. But this brush with death has softened me. I don't want to go through life alone anymore. Do you know what I mean?"

"I'm not sure," he said. I put my hand on his wrist and his coffee cup rattled on the saucer. I could see I made him nervous so I changed the subject.

"Why don't you tell me about yesterday? I'm sure you have it all sorted out by now. Did you ID The Jet? Do you know who hired him? I bet that's why you came to see me. You can't wait to give me some good news."

Steve put his coffee cup down on the wicker coffee table in front of us. "We identified one of the two who died in the crash. He was known as Sammy Nygyen, a known Laotian gang member in the San Francisco area about ten years ago. He was believed to be a Portland recruiter for the Irving Street Boys, a hard core gang specializing in murder, extortion and street shootouts with rival gangs."

"Are you telling me this is gang related?" I asked.

"I don't know," Steve said. "Maybe the local gang set up a murder-for-hire business. We don't know for sure yet if Nygyen was even still in the gang. We're still trying to piece that together."

"Well, The Jet looked Asian too. Did you get anything on him yet?"

Steve's face reddened. "I don't know how to tell you this."

"You haven't found who hired him yet? That's all right. I'll wait. It's a relief just knowing he won't be gunning for me anymore."

"Yeah, about that."

"What? You know you can tell me anything. I won't bite. Unless you want me to. Ha, ha." Steve didn't laugh at my awkward attempt to flirt. In fact it went right over his head.

"There was a bit of a mix-up," he said.

"Oh?"

"Yeah. The two guys found in the blue Honda were dead all right."

"Yes?" I waited for the other shoe to drop.

"But The Jet wasn't one of them. It appears there were three people in the car. Things happened so fast, we didn't realize it. The car door was open when we got to the scene. The Jet must have gotten out on the way down the hill."

"What? But you've got him in custody, right?"

"Not exactly."

"What do you mean *not exactly*?" The sweetness was gone from my voice and the phrase came out like an interrogation.

"I mean, he got away. It took a while for us to respond and set up a perimeter and there was confusion about what had happened. Somehow he just slipped through our net."

"What do you mean there was confusion? Dan told the dispatcher what the situation was. He was clear and to the point. We were nearly run off the road and shot at. The cops should have detained anyone they came across. How could he get away?"

"It seems one of our officers came across a boy wearing an oversized baseball cap at the edge of the crime scene and he . . ." Steve displayed a crooked smile. "Well, he told him to go home, that there could be trouble."

"Are you telling me one of Portland's finest shooed a hired killer home?"

"That's just about the size of it." He tried a wry grin at his little joke.

"I can't believe this. Weren't you in command of the situation? Didn't you give a description of the suspects? Shit, Steve, this is dumb even for you."

"I didn't have a radio until the first unit arrived at the top of the hill, remember, mine was broken. By then the officer already sent what he thought was a boy, enamored with a dangerous crime scene, on his way."

"It's still a colossal error," I said. "Cops are supposed to be trained observers."

"If I remember right, his little boy act fooled you too," Steve said.

I flashed back to the empty warehouse, where the evil grinning childlike man sat up with his wicked smile and gunned me down, and I shuddered. He waited out there somewhere now for another chance.

"Damn it. You're supposed to be in charge of this investigation. Are you screwing it up on purpose?" I jumped up from the settee and stormed out of the room. When I turned back, his face was an angry red.

Shit. So much for showing my soft side.

Chapter 12

Steve nearly knocked Dan to the floor with an elbow and slammed the front door on the way out. Dag and Jason, who had been tracking Steve's car on the computer in a back room, joined Dan and me at the dining table a few minutes later.

"What in the heck did you say to Steve?" Jason said. "He clocked the first three miles in under a minute. He must have blown five stop lights to get that far."

"Not now," Dan said. I saw him make a cut-it sign with his hand at his throat out of the corner of my vision.

"Um, okay I think we need to upgrade Billie's security," Dag said.

"What security?" I asked.

"Exactly," Dag said. "When you go out sleuthing you're an easy target."

"Yeah, I wonder how The Jet and his gang always seem to know where you are," Jason said.

"Let's stay with what we know," Dan said. "I've drawn up a list of everyone who might have a reason to hate, maim or kill her."

"Jeez, how many pages is that thing?" Jason pinched at his thin mustache and chuckled.

"Yeah," I muttered. "I can't have that many enemies."

Dan peered up from the hand-scrawled pages. "Relax. I've separated them into categories. The first category is arrests. These are all the people you arrested the last two years before you ah, retired."

"It's been two years since she's even been on the force," Dag said. "Do you really think someone would harbor a grudge that long?"

"Well let's see," Dan said. "Joe Buckowski was arrested by our dear sister in commission of a convenience store holdup. She knocked out most of his front teeth, handcuffed and hobbled him, and threw into him into the back of the squad car that way."

"I remember that one," Jason said. "When they got to the station, she bowled him across the parking lot on his stomach, hands and feet cuffed behind him."

"He shot that little store clerk," I said. "If I had been there a minute earlier, I could have stopped him."

"We don't need to go through all of these," Dan said. "I've already been through the list quite a few times and I've narrowed it down to a manageable group of suspects. First there's The Jet. I'd love to get a hold of that guy and find out who put the contract out on you."

We all nodded.

"Then there's Chris. My money's on him at this point."

"You've got to be kidding," I said. "He's done nothing but small stuff. Murder would be too big of a jump." The suspicions I tossed at Chris in the hospital were imaginary. After his initial bluff in my hospital room, he had proven to be harmless.

"Not according to some of his associations in the state prison," Dan said. "He spent half his time telling anyone who would listen he was going to get even with you for the way you roughed him up. And he wasn't talking about financial payback. He meant physical harm. He talked to some of the inmates to see what they would charge for a contract kill."

"That clicks with what I've turned up so far, which wasn't much," Dag said. "I talked with Chris's mother and she hasn't seen him since he went to prison. 'Good riddance to bad rubbish,' was what she said. Claims if he shows up she'd shoot him herself. Apparently he's burgled her place a few times."

"What about the sister?" Dan asked.

"Maribell? She spent most of the time trying to put the moves on me," Dag said. "I was lucky to get out of her apartment with my shirt on."

"A real uggo?" I suggested.

"Nah, she was alright. Blond, nice figure, smart. I have a hard time believing she was related to that creep brother of hers."

"He could be handsome," I said. "He's just slimy and crude and not very smart."

"Hey, big brother," Jason said. "If his sister is so well put together, why don't you like her?"

"She's too aggressive for me," Dag said. "And she's short."

I stretched my neck to view my six-foot-seven-inch brother's face and asked? "How short?"

"I'd said about five-one."

"Ouch," we all said in unison.

"You could use her head for an armrest," Jason said.

Dan snickered. "She's shorter than that redhead who used to kiss you on the navel when she had to leave in a hurry."

They waited expectantly for my retort. "Oh, no. That's as low as I go."

"Anyway," Dag said, anxious to change the subject, "she did give me one lead. He likes to hang out at a little club in the Old Town area. I stopped by, but no one wanted to talk to me."

"Well I can understand that," I said. "You've probably made a few arrests in that neighborhood. Anything else turn up?"

"Not yet," Dag said. "Maybe Jason would have better luck at the club. He's more of the playboy type that would hang out there. It's called *The Boiler.*"

"Yeah, I've been there a few times," Jason said. "Pool, loud music at night, some card games in the back room. It's a little too seedy for me. But Chris would fit right in. I think they have some rooms for rent upstairs. Maybe he's hiding there. I could check it out sometime when Steve's not around."

"You don't want to wait," I said. "We need to find him ASAP. Bring him here and sit on him if I'm not here. I don't think he's involved, but he knows something and he's scared."

"Okay," Dan said. "The other suspects are either involved in the city's lawsuit or in one of Billie's cases. This Fleming guy who's dead: What were you supposed to be doing on this?"

"I was supposed to find him for Stella Fleming, preferably alive," I said. "He was in Portland three months ago for an insurance convention. His wife said he planned to renew an acquaintance with an old friend who made good here in Portland. That's all he told her. Not who, not where, not how he made good. He just told her it would be quite a surprise when he showed up."

"Then what?" Dan said.

"He disappeared. He attended the convention for two of the three days and went missing. I talked to a couple of insurance agents who saw him. One of them said he bragged during drinks that he was going to see an old friend who owed him some money. He said he thought this friend of his had died years ago. That was supposed to be Saturday night. Sunday was half a day and he was supposed to drive back to Idaho."

"No one saw him Sunday?" Darrin said.

I shook my head. "He never called his wife Saturday night like he promised, and she never heard from him again. Here's the interesting part. One of his convention buddies said he told him he saw this friend's picture in a news article in his local newspaper. It was some kind of election picture of somebody running for a local government office."

"In Portland?" Dan shook his head "That narrows it down to three county commissioners, four city counselors, the Metro board, judges, congressmen, senators and the state legislature."

"I know. I went to City Hall and checked with a community relations person to see all the press conferences during a six month period leading up to the May primary. Do you know those damn politicians sometimes have three news opportunities a day? And most of them are out in the community not at City Hall. I stopped at the security checkpoint just on the off chance someone might remember seeing Fleming at City Hall. No luck there either. I was set to fly to Pocatello to research the news story and interview his wife when I got shot."

"This one has possibilities," Dag said. "Probably not connected, but we have to follow up on it. Fleming's death smells like foul play. Terminal Six is an odd place for an out-of-town insurance agent to turn up dead."

"Okay, this next suspect's name never leaves this room," Dan said. He wrote the name on a yellow legal pad.

Jason let out a shrill whistle. "Mayor Clemons? That's ridiculous. Where did you get this theory?"

"Clemons hates Billie," Dan said. "Her incident with Chris Johnson made him appear foolish. It happened right after he launched his community policing model."

"Yeah, he took a lot of flak from our rank-and-file about it being a waste of time and too soft on crime," Dag said. "Billie's incident made it seem like a rebellion among the ranks."

"Hey, I was community policing," I said. "I stuck up for a community tired of purse snatchers, carjackers, and home invaders. What I did falls into the category of a crime deterrent, which is certainly within the community policing model."

"You really think Clemons would stoop to murder?" Dag said.

"He has a hair-temper," Dan said. "He doesn't like to look bad, ever! He threatened to do things worse than firing her to some of his aides. He has the power, the money and the clout to do away with her and maybe even get away with it."

"It's hard to imagine the Mayor hiring a slipshod operation like these stooges," I said. "These guys not only missed me, but killed a cop. Pros they're not."

"Well, Clemons is up to something," Dan said. "Jason, show

her what you found."

Jason dropped a thick manila folder on the table. He opened it and turned several sheets of paper over one by one. Each page had scores of words and lines blotted out by a thick felt pen.

"This was what Samantha turned up for me. The records she had were skimpy, but she knows where the homicide detectives keep their working files and she managed to find a sympathetic investigator who let her copy them for us."

"This is useless," I said, turning over page after page. "Names are missing, paragraphs and even whole pages are blacked out. I've never seen anything like it."

"Samantha's friend said someone above was censoring the police reports until an arrest is made," Jason said. "Steve told his investigative team the unmarked report is kept by the Police Chief. The Chief also warned Steve not to talk to anybody about the investigation, especially the Bly's.

"They're determined to keep us out of it," Dan said. "Even with all the blacked out areas, it's clear they don't have a firm suspect. They're mucking the whole thing up."

Jason stood up and went to the window to check on our assigned surveillance team sitting in their now dirty sedan across the street and turned back to me.

"Samantha said Steve told his team pretty much the same thing," he said. "She suggested there was too much interference from above. Steve claims he's being directed from higher ups as how to handle the investigation. He told Samantha it wasn't right the way he had to treat the Bly's. Apparently it's not making him popular with his fellow officers."

"Oh, crap," I said. "And I thought he was being a jerk."

"Still, I think we have to add Steve to our list of suspects," Dan said.

"Why?" Dag asked.

"Did you see him when he left? Steam poured from his ears. If anyone has a strong motive to kill Billie, Steve does."

For one of the few times in my life, I didn't have a comeback. I remembered the questions I had about the attempt on my life coming home from making funeral arrangements and how Steve seemed to be more hindrance than help. I had my own suspicions about *Lover Boy*.

Chapter 13

Coffee Maestro is one of those dingy shops where the hip people hang and the rest of the world avoids. The tables are Goodwill rejects, made of old doors, wooden crates and even a cardboard box. All the wood chairs are splintered or just plain uncomfortable.

The coffee smells good though, the pastries are adequate, and the prices are much lower than the Starbucks up the street. It took a moment for my eyes to adjust to the darkness upon entering. The walls were adorned with jute objets de'art and the only light in the establishment seemed to be emitted from half a dozen laptops humming on tables with young people hovering over them. The barista called a number and a familiar figure stepped from a dark area near the wall into the window light.

Eileen McIntire was not the same frumpy woman I met at City Hall. Her frizzled hair was straight now and the dishwater gray transformed to sandy blond. She wore a brown pantsuit and a floral wrap around her neck, and her eyes sparkled more than I remembered.

She picked up her coffee, nodded at me to follow her, and we drifted back into the gloom.

"Thanks for coming on such short notice," she said. "I'm on a tight schedule today."

"You look nice," I said, as I sat down.

"I've been meaning to get my hair done for months now. I have a date tonight and it's my first in a couple of years. I needed a makeover."

"You pulled it off in a big way. Who's the new boyfriend?"

"Oh, he's just a customer who comes in on a regular basis. We always chat, and I know he's single, but he never manages to get beyond the chit-chat."

"And you like him and wanted him to ask you out?"

She sipped her coffee delicately.

"Well I hoped he might, but he's very shy. So I finally asked him."

"That's nice. Where are you going?"

"Just to a movie and dinner." She noticed her hand trembling. "Cripes, between the date and this mess I got myself into with you, I'm a nervous wreck."

"What mess have I gotten you into?" I asked.

"That's what I'd like to know." She reached into her purse and pulled out a DVD disk in a clear plastic case. "This is a compilation of a few of the cameras in the office area between noon and one o'clock on the day you asked about."

She reached down by her feet and hefted a small laptop from a briefcase stashed under the table. I watched her open it and tap some keys. A minute later she had it humming and slid the DVD into its player slot. I scooted my chair next to hers and watched as she searched through various scenes labeled on the screen.

The first clip was from a camera facing the door entering the reception area where Eileen worked. We watched intently and nothing seemed to happen so after about a minute.

"What are we supposed to be seeing?" I asked.

"Watch it again, carefully," she said. "I'm going to zoom in on the video."

The movie went from postcard size to filling the screen. I watched again and saw only a slight movement.

"Oh, the door opened a bit," I said.

"Yes, and that's all you're going to see. Now look at this."

She opened another file and we watched from a side angle as the door opened and the The Jet's sinister face peered around the door. He scooted across the floor hidden from sight by the counter, still in a crouch, and snaked under the swinging gate. Because the camera pointed toward the Mayor's office we could see the side door to his office open and a slight flash of The Jet sliding through it.

"Oh my God," I said. "He went to see Mayor Clemons."

"We don't know for sure. There's no way to tell if the Mayor was in or out. He was checked out that day, but he often comes in unannounced during the lunch hour to get work done. He might have been there or maybe not."

"Are there any cameras in his office?" My eyes were glued to the video.

"No," Eileen said.

"Did you catch him leaving?"

"Keep watching. Security sped the time frame up. It's been five minutes now."

My jaw dropped as the Mayor's door cracked open again and he pirouetted around its edge like a ballet dancer. He slunk down below a table and disappeared. Seconds later the camera caught him scooting under the gate. He was out of sight for a while.

"What happened?" I said. "Where did he go? I didn't see the lobby door open."

"There's a gate on each side of the counter. My friend in Security thinks he slid under it and now he's heading for the auditor's office."

"Bob Blaney? Are you sure?"

"As sure as I can be," she said. "Security didn't have this angle. He could have gone into Commissioner Tuttle's office, but he'd have to go right down the aisle past me, and I didn't even have a clue that slimy little guy was crawling around. Damn, this represents a big breech in our security. The guard who made this video for me is going to have to report it. Then he's going to have to explain why he viewed the video. He's going to tell his superiors I felt uneasy, like someone was in the office watching me, even though I never saw anyone. I don't know if that's going to hold up, but I've got to watch out for myself too."

"What kind of trouble do you expect?" I asked.

"My friend said the Mayor is really paranoid about this kind of stuff. He told Clemons about it Friday and said the Mayor will probably want to talk to me Monday. Word must have leaked out because late Friday afternoon I felt like my co-workers were avoiding me."

"I'm sorry if I got you into trouble, Eileen. But this is the guy who tried to kill me twice, and he is probably the person who killed my brother. If it means pissing the Mayor off or one of us risking arrest so be it. I'll do my best not to incriminate you."

"I'm not complaining," she said. "I offered to help you, and I've been through more administrations than most of these elected types. I've got a good union and a good work record. The thing that creeps me out most is that this guy was skulking around the office, and I was alone."

"Hey, what ever happened to him? Does he show up again on any of the cameras?"

"No. I think he went into Blaney's office because Blaney has a second door that opens to a side stairwell. I thought it didn't work, but maybe someone fixed it or this thief jimmied it or something. He could have slipped out unobserved and walked down the side stairs and no cameras would have caught him."

"That might explain why Chris and his friend didn't see him leave when they staked out the reception door," I said. "Was Blaney in his office?"

"Like I told you before: that was the day when he went into Tuttle's office and they argued."

Do you remember the approximate time?"

"It was about twelve-thirty. I remember wondering if I should go to lunch so I wouldn't have to listen to them scream."

"Could Blaney have been in his office when The Jet entered?"

"I don't think so," Eileen said.

"It would make sense if he was," I said. "Maybe The Jet tells Blaney something nefarious about Tuttle, and he charges into Tuttle's office to confront him."

"I guess it could happen that way," Eileen said. "It wouldn't take much to upset him. Bob's been short with a lot of people lately. He yelled at me the other day because he was out of paper clips."

"Why do you think he's so testy?" I said.

"I don't know if I should say. It couldn't have anything to do with your brother's death."

"Does it have something to do with his wife?"

"How did you know?" Eileen asked.

"I get around. Does he know who she's fooling around with?"

"No, I don't think he does." Eileen glanced at me sideways and a slow grin revealed itself. "I don't either in case you're wondering. Maybe he thinks its Tuttle."

"It's not," I said. "There must be something else between Blaney and Tuttle."

"How do you know? I mean, that it's not Tuttle. Do you know who she's seeing?" Eileen's grin was huge now and she gulped her coffee and waited expectantly.

"You don't want to know, believe me. I'm almost sorry I know."

She wasn't paying attention anymore. Her face was taut and even in the dim light I could see concern in her eyes.

"What's wrong?" I asked. I turned to the door and saw a familiar figure, slim and young, with a department approved mustache and a day's beard growth. Eileen tried to hide behind her laptop.

"The man who just came in," she said. "I saw him down the block earlier. I think he's following me."

"It's Officer McGraw in plainclothes," I said. "He's one of

Steve's men. He's probably searching for me."

Eileen ejected the DVD from the laptop and clumsily jammed it into the plastic sleeve. "Take it. I don't want him to see us together. I need to get out of here."

"Well, I don't want him to see me either. I'm supposed to be under house arrest." I slipped the DVD into my purse. "Is there a back exit?"

McGraw scanned the room. I hoped his eyes hadn't adjusted to the darkness yet. We stumbled over each other, juggling our purses and Eileen's laptop and briefcase.

"The ladies room is open," she said.

I followed her through the door into an unlit bathroom and fumbled for a light switch. It took a minute for me to realize the web brushing across my face actually was a string connected to the overhead light. I flicked it on and we stared at each other in a frenzy. Seeing each other's worried faces made us laugh.

"We've got to stop meeting like this," I said.

Eileen turned and cracked the door open in the one-toilet, one-sink, one-mirror bathroom. "He's coming this way."

"What are you doing?" I said.

"I'm locking the door."

"Don't." I snapped off the light and we were in the dark again.

"What are you doing? He'll come in."

"If he sees the door is locked, he'll wait to see who's in here," I whispered.

"What if he comes in?"

I shrugged, but she couldn't see it. "We'll have to take that chance."

A minute went by and someone pushed the door open a couple of inches. We squeezed together against the wall behind the door. A hand fumbled for the light switch and Eileen jabbed me with a knuckle in the small of my back as if to say *I told you so.*

"What are you doing?" a shrill voice said.

"I'm looking for a friend," McGraw said.

"In the women's bathroom? Why don't you wait for her to come out?"

Officer McGraw was being busted by a woman outside the door.

"I guess nobody's in there," he said. "I was just looking."

The door whooshed open and suddenly there were three of us in the dark. The light flicked on, and I clasped my hand over the mouth of a young black-haired girl in dark pants and a halter top.

"Shh," I said. "We're hiding from him."

The alarm in her eyes told me she was about to scream.

"He's my boyfriend and he's very jealous," I said. "He follows me everywhere. He's very possessive and he thinks I'm stepping out on him."

She relaxed a bit, but when she turned and saw Eileen, the concern came back to her face.

"She's the one I'm out with. We can't let him find us here, he'll go ballistic." I took my hand away from her mouth and held my breath.

"Okay," she said. "You almost gave me a heart attack."

"Will you check and see if he's still out there?" Eileen said.

She nodded and cracked the door open.

"He's going out the front door," she said. "He's not bad looking, but he seems mean."

"Thanks," I said. "Do you mind waiting a few more minutes? We need a place to hide until we're sure he's gone."

"Well, I don't seem to have to go any longer so I guess I can wait. I'll come back and tell you when I'm sure he's moved on."

"You certainly know how to show a girl a good time," Eileen said when the girl had gone.

"I think your guy tonight is going to have to go some to top our little date."

"If he tries to get me in the ladies room, I'm scramming out on him," she said.

"So, tell me about him." I said.

"Oh, he drives a tow-truck. He drops off paperwork across the street once a week in the city records department and then he stops by to talk with me. I used to fill in at records over there. That's where we met. He said he misses having someone to talk to, sitting in the truck alone all day."

"Oh, that's interesting," I said. "I've got a friend who . . ."

"He's gone," the black haired girl said through a crack in the door. "He's walking up Twenty-Third towards Lovejoy, looking in all the store windows on this side of the street."

"Thanks," I said.

Eileen and I left the tiny bathroom and went to the barista counter. A red-haired girl wiped the countertop with a wet cloth while the dragon tattoo on her bicep breathed fire at me.

"Is there another way out of here, aside from the front door?" I asked the dragon.

She looked at me blankly and waved the cloth over her shoulder. "You can go out through the storeroom. It opens into the alley."

We walked behind the counter and down a narrow aisle filled with shelves of rich smelling coffee beans to a metal door at the end. I opened it and Eileen and I stood out in blustery fall air. My eyes dilated and it took me a minute to focus against the bright sun. The alley was graveled and by heading north we could exit a full block from where Officer McGraw was last seen.

"I'm going home," I said, walking toward the end of the alley.

"Me too," she said. "I'll walk down to Twenty-First to catch the bus."

"Be careful," I said. "And have fun on your date tonight."

"I will," she said. She walked away from me and waved back. "Earl is fun to be around."

I was busy plotting my elusive path home to make sure I didn't run into McGraw, and I had walked a full block before what she said hit me. Earl? She has a date with a tow-truck driver named Earl?

Chapter 14

Since I first caught sight of the two watchers across the street Saturday, I'd been using the back alley. I entered the side yard between my house and garage and scanned the street, but saw no sign of the familiar sedan. What I did see was a huge white tow truck with half its wheels up on the sidewalk so it wouldn't stick too far out in the street.

It was Earl's tow truck. That meant Angel was home. I hurried out onto the front lawn and climbed two steps at a time up the porch. Inside, Angel sat at the dining room table, with the familiar space between her fingers where a cigarette used to rest. Around her were Earl, Dan, Jason and Dag.

"Angel!"

"Billie!" She jumped up from the chair and gave me a bear hug in the middle of the room. The top of her brunette head butted against my chin.

"I was so worried about you," I said.

"Me too, about you," she said.

She looked great, although I noticed she had a bruise on her forehead from the car accident. She wore a too-short dress with black, white and yellow colors in it, black pantyhose, and three-inch yellow heels. She reminded me of a bumblebee flitting from flower to flower—in October. Like I've said, Angel isn't a slave to fashion.

"How are you feeling?" she asked.

"Much better now that you're here, and I can see you're all right."

"I got some bruises." She pushed her blouse sleeve up her arm and displayed a monstrous black and blue mark, which traveled from her bicep up to her shoulder. I got a nasty one on my hip and my legs. That's why I'm wearing dark panty hose."

"I'm so sorry. Thanks for saving my life."

We hugged again and she broke it off.

"I bought something for you," I said. I handed her a pack of her favorite cigarettes. "I've noticed you seem to be yearning for them more than ever since I was shot. I know I talked you into quitting, but now I feel guilty."

She looked at the cigarettes and back to me. Then back at the cigarettes again. She opened the pack and tamped one out, nestled it between her fingers and sighed. "Nice to have you back." She didn't try to light it.

"It's not like I need to smoke," she said. "For some reason there's this gap in my life and it seems to fit between these fingers." She sighed again and put the cigarette back into the package. "No, this doesn't fill the gap any longer."

The tow truck driver reached from his chair and slipped one of his pudgy fingers into the gap between her fingers and she smiled.

"You remember Earl. He's been with me all morning. He's such a dear. He said he was worried about me and brought me the most beautiful Stargazer lilies."

Earl, in a blue and white checkered button-up shirt and khaki slacks, got up from his chair and tugged at his shirt to make sure it covered his belly.

"Pleased to meet you, Miss Bly." He extended a beefy paw to shake my hand and his gentle grip surprised me.

"Thank you for getting Angel out of that mess," I said. "You were great, the way you pulled her VW up the hill."

"It was nothing. I rigged up the remote control thing myself a few years ago. My rig didn't come with remote control, so I made one using a garage door opener and some spare electronic parts."

"It sure came in handy yesterday," I said.

"Earl showed us how it worked earlier," Jason said. "He has a remote for the back side too. We were going to hook it up to the surveillance car across the street, but they were gone so we connected it to Dan's car and raised and lowered it from the front porch."

"Until Dan took the remote from us," Dag said.

"You probably bent my frame," Dan said.

"You make an interesting point, Dag," I said.

"What? Dan's a party pooper?"

"No. What happened to the car across the street with the two cops in it? It wasn't there when I got home, and I don't remember seeing it when I left about one o'clock. I know they were there earlier this morning."

Dan scratched his head and glanced toward the window. "What's the concern, Sis? They probably got called off. Or maybe they only work half a shift on Sunday."

"You'll never guess who almost busted me a little while ago," I said. "Officer McGraw."

"Did he see you?" Dag asked.

"I don't know. I hid in the ladies room at Coffee Maestro. I don't know if he saw me go in. I was meeting Eileen McIntire." I watched carefully as I spoke her name but the two-timing Earl didn't react. In a few minutes, we all sat at the table and Jason fired up his laptop. I loaded the DVD into a slot and played the various scenes for the group.

"Hey, that's City Hall," Earl said. "I've been in that office before."

I didn't comment on why he might have been in Eileen's office, and we continued watching the video with me dissecting The Jet's routine. I froze the frame the few times he could be seen on camera.

We discussed theories, which ranged from *he was hired by*

someone in the office to kill me versus *he's blackmailing someone*, to *he was robbing the Mayor and the commissioner's offices.* At the end of our discussion we were no closer to a solution than when we started.

"We're not getting anywhere," Dan said. "Let's revisit this later. What else have you got going, Billie?"

"I'm going to meet Stella Fleming tomorrow morning at the Medical Examiner's office," I said. "When are we supposed to be there, Angel?"

"She meets Sergeant Jackson at ten o'clock. I've arranged for her to meet with us at a nearby coffee shop at nine."

"I'm going with you," Jason said.

"Do you think it's a good idea?" I said. "Steve wants you at the house."

"Yeah, but he also wants me with you. I'd rather lose my job than my sister. There have been three attempts on your life. Someone seems to always know where you are. I think you need protection and I'm volunteering."

"I agree," Dan said.

"Me too," Dag said. "Someone needs to watch out for her."

I sulked. "Sergeant Jackson is investigating the case and he'll be there when we meet at the medical examiner's office. He'll tell Steve."

"Won't matter if he sees you," Jason said. "I'll tell him I'm your bodyguard. How are you going to explain *yourself*?"

"I'll play on his sympathy." I winked at him. "I'm on a case. I'll say I'm trying to keep my mind off poor Darrin. Oh crap. I need a hanky."

"Then it's settled," Dan said, handing me a Kleenex. "I'm going home for the night to be with Maria and the kids."

"You're getting a bit rebellious too," I said.

"Steve knows." Dan said. "I mentioned it to him when he was here earlier."

"You're lucky," Dag said. "It's bad enough we have to stay

here, but my bed is too short by about a foot."

"Uh, I was wondering if I might stay here tonight," Angel said. "I brought a change of clothes. Earl has to be somewhere soon, and he doesn't really have time to run me home."

"Of course," I said. "You can have Dag's room. Dag, since Dan isn't here tonight, you can join Jason. The beds in that room might be a little bigger."

"Great," Earl said. "I *do* have to get going."

I turned at him, defiantly. "That's too bad. You could have had dinner with us. What do you have planned tonight?"

"I have a prior engagement with a friend I couldn't get out of." He smiled sheepishly.

"Is this friend a woman or a man?" I asked point blank.

"Well, it's sort of a woman. Somebody I work with. No big deal. I would just feel bad canceling on short notice."

Angel didn't even seem curious. She smiled and hugged him and followed him to the door. Maybe I misread the situation. On the phone she sounded as if she really liked him. I wondered if he had already told her he was going out on a date with Eileen.

All right, I didn't know for sure he was Eileen's Earl, but what were the odds he wasn't. Astronomical if you ask me.

Chapter 15

Angel, Jason and I were about to leave for our meeting with Mrs. Fleming Monday morning when the phone rang. I left them standing in the doorway and picked up the telephone at the reception desk.

"Billie? It's Chris," a frazzled voice said. "Chris Johnson. I need to talk to you."

"Shit, Chris. Where have you been? We've been looking all over for you."

"Hey, I'm sorry. I've been on the lam since that shooter tried to cap me."

"Are you crazy? He was shooting at me."

"I know you think that's what happened, but I'm not so sure. Hey, I'm sorry about your brother. If he hadn't got between me and the shooter, well you know . . . I'm sorry."

It's the last thing I needed. A neurotic witness who thinks everything is about him.

"Chris, I haven't got time for this. Tell me where you are and I'll send my brother for you."

"Oh, no. I can't trust anybody except, maybe, you. We're kind of in the same boat with someone trying to kill us and all. If you'll come and talk to me and help me, I'll drop this lawsuit thing. I need help, Billie."

He was a nut job all right. I didn't have time for this with my world unraveling at warp speed and things spinning out of control.

"Okay Chris, where and when?"

"In about 30 minutes. Stand outside Two Tarts Bakery on Northwest 23rd and Kearney. If you come alone, I'll send word on where the meet is."

"I can't. I've got a meeting with a client in 30 minutes and the medical examiner afterwards. Come to my place at one o'clock. If I'm not here, wait. My brother, Dan, will keep you safe."

"No cops," Chris said. "Meet me at the bakery at one. If you come alone, I'll take you to the guy who shot you. His name is Monty. He goes by *The Jet*. If you bring the cops, I'm skipping town."

Well nuts or not, I couldn't turn down a chance to find The Jet. I agreed to his terms and decided to keep the details to myself lest my brothers or Angel might want to tag along.

Jason drove around the block and picked Angel and me up in the back alley in case Steve's surveillance team was lurking nearby. Angel sat in front and I elected the back seat to be able to stretch out a bit. As they talked about their gun collections, I puzzled through some scenarios. How did Chris find The Jet? Did he ask around or did his friend from the hospital tip him off? It never occurred to me The Jet might have found Chris.

Up until a few years ago, the state crime lab was located on Northeast Third and Knott Street. The medical examiner's office used to be located across the street from where I had been hospitalized.

Emanuel Legacy Hospital is a central triage facility in North Portland for violent crimes against gang members and transients. It is close to the downtown and the Central Precinct and so the location was perfect for a ME's office.

But in 2005, the state crime lab was whisked away from Multnomah County into Clackamas County. The new facility houses medical examiners for the state and the two counties. We took Interstate-84 to the 205 and got off twelve miles later on Sunnybrook Road.

I thought it ironic as we passed Costco, literally a stone's throw from the medical examiner's office, because the discount store sells coffins now. My morbid thought struck me hard when I remembered Darrin and how he also rested at the medical examiner's office.

Jason escorted me from the car, grabbing my elbow and looking furtively for bad guys, into the Clackamas Town Center shopping center where we found Mrs. Fleming in a Starbucks inside.

She sat alone sipping a plain black coffee. She was short, maybe five-feet-two in heels, with red hair clipped short in ringlets hugging the side of her face. She was in her late-thirties, with a nice petite figure and a generous bust line. Her eyes were not red or puffy like mine. I supposed she had long since done her crying. She watched as we approached and managed a half-hearted smile.

I introduced her to Jason and Angel. Jason, although in plain clothes, drifted off to stacks of books a few feet away so he wouldn't intimidate my client with his intense demeanor.

Stella summarized her life story for us. Her husband worked for a few years for the Pocatello City Council on various land-use, budget and other volunteer committees. Eventually he was hired on by the city as an auditor. He had been accused of theft of city funds, and although most of the money was never found, he was convicted and served time in prison. When he got out, most of his friends shunned him.

Unable to get a job, Art Fleming started a small insurance company a few years ago. He found a loophole in the state's lax laws and was allowed to apply for and get an insurance license. Still, he struggled because of his past record.

During the last few months her husband grew distant. He also became restless and mentioned many times he would like to move onto something more lucrative. He talked of relocating to Seattle or San Francisco and starting over. He had pitched several get-rich quick schemes to her.

He planned to network about some of these opportunities at an insurance industry convention in Portland in August and seemed excited. About four days before he left, he sat at the breakfast table reading the paper and slammed his coffee cup down hard enough to rock the table, spilling half his coffee.

For crying out loud, he had said. I haven't seen him for eight years. I thought he was dead and there he is, only 700 miles away. When Stella had asked who he was talking about, he folded the paper and tucked it under his arm. *Nobody you'd know, he said. Someone I knew before I met you. Maybe I'll look him up if I get a chance next week.*

Oh, was he in Portland?

Oh, yeah, he said. He's definitely in Portland.

Stella Fleming stared blankly at me after sharing this sad history.

"After that morning Art was a new man," she said. "He seemed happy again. He chatted me up when he got home from work, and we made love three times before he left for the convention. I don't think we'd made love three times in the year before that."

"Did he let on what he was so happy about?" Angel asked.

"He only said this old friend was going to make his dream of leaving Pocatello come true. This friend, he said, owed him and we might be moving to Portland instead of Seattle."

"And he wouldn't tell you who the friend was?" I asked.

"He said it was an old golfing buddy, but that's all. And he wouldn't let me see the newspaper article. He said he didn't want to jinx anything. Art is very superstitious. "But I think he lied to me when he said I didn't know this friend of his."

"Why?" I asked.

"It's just a feeling," she said. "The way he talked about him. I think the friendship was more recent than he let on. And he wouldn't let me look at the paper."

"Didn't you ever get curious and find another copy of the article?" I asked.

"No. Art was always off on some get-rich-quick scheme. I learned not to put much faith in his little notions."

"Do you have any idea who his friend might be?" I said. "It could be important. If this unclaimed body you've been called here to identify is Art, this friend might lead us to his killer. If the man in the morgue is not your husband, this friend might help us find him."

Stella Fleming licked her lips. "It's the strangest thing. I'd forgotten about his mentioning they played golf together. It wasn't until I was landing at the airport and we flew over this beautiful golf course on our landing approach. It reminded me of Art's fondness for the game."

She stopped talking. I waited for a moment before asking: "So who do you think this friend was?"

"Oh, I don't know. It could have been any number of people. Art was very involved in committees and social functions. He had to network so much in the insurance business."

Her eyes avoided mine as she stirred her coffee. I was sure she knew who this friend was and for some reason she was withholding his name.

"Mrs. Fleming. If you know who this person is, you need to tell me," I said.

"I only know they must have known each other while we were married. Art never told me his name."

"You must have some impression. Maybe a vague feeling or a guess?"

She nodded vacantly. "I do have an impression. Not of the friend, but of Art. I've had the feeling for some time now he was dead. I didn't want to believe it, but there it is. I've been a wreck ever since he went missing. It will be good to be able to finally put this whole tragedy to rest."

She had successfully evaded my question, and I wasn't able to follow up because Jason had rejoined us with a shopping bag in his hand. We left Starbucks, followed by Stella in a black Impala rental car and pulled up to the medical examiner's office a few minutes later.

Inside the square building, consisting of brown brick and red-trimmed windows, a receptionist pointed us down a hallway with a copper-finished concrete floor and contemporary art prints. We pushed through a metal door, next to two large double doors leading into the surgery, and stepped into a waiting room where we were joined by Homicide Detective Bruce Jackson.

The Detective was in his early thirties with a square face and chiseled chin. He had blond spiked hair, which made him appear like a local TV weatherman or rock star, and wore a tight fitting charcoal Henley shirt over muscular arms.

"Hello, Miss Bly," he said. "I'm surprised to see you and your brother here today."

"Mrs. Fleming is a client of mine. I felt I had to be here for her in her time of sorrow. I know exactly how she feels." I dabbed my eye with my hanky and he changed the subject.

"Mrs. Fleming?" he said. "I want to warn you that this person has been in the water for at least a month. He's bloated and damn near unrecognizable. But from what you told me over the phone, I'm hoping you can identify him. Would you like someone to accompany you for moral support?" He meant me.

"Oh yes," she said in a high-pitched whisper of a voice. "Will you come with me, Billie?"

"Of course," I said.

Nothing short of armed restraint would have kept me out. I too, wanted some kind of closure to this case, and I thought seeing Art Fleming might give it to me. Of course I knew it wouldn't. I'd want to know what happened to him and who made it happen.

We left Angel and Jason behind when we walked through the hospital style double doors. Jackson led us to a sterile room with sturdy chrome framed chairs and a body on a hospital gurney. It was cold in the room and on the bed was a body covered with a white shroud. A woman in scrubs with a blue mask nodded at

Jackson and went toward the gurney.

"I'm deputy medical examiner, Cheryl Hanson," she said. Her brown hair was tucked in a bun under a blue scrub type bonnet and she had thin black-framed glasses perched on the tip of her nose.

"You can come as close at that yellow line on the floor, but no closer to the body. Okay?"

We nodded.

"I'm going to unzip the shroud to reveal the upper half of the body. If we need to, I will reveal more. I hope that won't be necessary because the condition of the body isn't good."

Without waiting she unzipped the shroud and revealed a bluish male figure. Its face was bloated and on its chest tread marks in an upside down V-shape were sown in a hurried fashion. The man was a mess. I couldn't make out any facial features or other recognizable features on the body.

"He's been in the water for a month or longer," Jackson said. There's not much left of who he was I'm afraid."

Stella Fleming's face went white, but she forced herself to view the body.

"It's him," she said finally. 'I can tell by the hair. He was balding on top and turning gray at the temples."

"A lot of men fit that profile," I said. "How about his size. Is that about the same?"

She nodded. "Can I see the ring you said he had on his finger?"

"Certainly," Hanson said. She opened a zip lock bag and removed a gold ring. Mrs. Fleming took the ring and examined it carefully.

"It's his ring. See the inscription inside, *Together always*? We had that engraved on each of our rings. I guess we won't be together anymore, Art."

Stella faltered and Jackson guided her expertly to a chair. She sobbed, the ring still in her hand.

"Not anymore," she mumbled.

Chapter 16

After returning from the morgue, I made my excuses to my brothers and went to my room to lie down for an hour before I planned to slip out and meet Chris at the Two Tarts Bakery. I couldn't sleep so I lay in my bed and tried to imagine how Chris found The Jet.

It occurred to me to be more than a coincidence that a friend of his saw The Jet at the hospital and then they both saw him again at City Hall. Another sighting in a city the size of Portland blew away any chance of a meaningful statistic as far as coincidence.

The only logical conclusion? Chris had hired The Jet and his leading me to him meant it was a trap. Was his offer of withdrawing his lawsuit the bait? A chill shot up my spine as I tossed onto my side.

If Chris had hired The Jet, maybe I had been right to accuse him of putting out a contract on me, even though I really didn't think so at the time. I was only trying to get him to withdraw his lawsuit. Although unlikely, I had hoped fear might motivate him to do something noble. How stupid was that? Not only did he want the money from the city, but he was going for the *Daily Double*, meaning he wanted me dead too.

I arrived at Two Tarts Bakery twenty minutes early with a .25 caliber backup piece stashed inside one of my new brown leather boots. I wore jeans and a denim coat, over a light blue blouse, to conceal a holstered revolver.

A few people sipped coffee and munched cookies inside the bakery, but business was slow in the tiny shop. It would be easy to spot someone who didn't belong if Chris had set up an ambush.

He was twenty minutes late, and I was about to head home when a slick olive-colored Jaguar slipped into an open spot in front. I watched through the window as Chris hopped out. He stopped twice to admire the car.

"Sorry I'm late." He took a seat across from me on a lacquered wooden bench and grinned. "I was shopping for a new car. Stopped at my P.O. Box after I talked to you and found I'd gotten my settlement check from the city."

"So you went out and bought a new car?"

"Not yet. I'm trying it on approval. It'll take a while for my bank to release the funds and the guys at the dealership didn't mind. They told me to take this beauty out and drive it for a few days and we'd talk when I brought it back."

"So what's this about you knowing where The Jet is?" Inside my brain I rolled my eyes at this yahoo, but I didn't want to piss him off so I kept my cool.

"Yeah, I can lead you to him, but first I got a few conditions. You see, my life might be in danger here, and I want you to protect me until they catch this psycho killer. Do that and I'll release you from your obligation to pay me on the lawsuit. Of course you'll still have to give my lawyer his cut."

"Why would you want to be so generous?" I asked.

"It's not like you're going to be able to come up with a million dollars. I'd be garnishing your paycheck into my great-grandchildren's lifetime. Even the house you live in is untouchable. My lawyer says it's set up in some kind of trust. I only sued you for revenge anyway."

He offered me 70 percent of a good deal since his attorney wasn't about to give up his fee. Of course, if I was going to be dead he wouldn't be getting any money anyway. Could Chris hate me bad enough to kiss off so much money?

"Why do you feel you need protection?" I asked.

He glimpsed over his shoulder through the café window. "Somebody is trying to kill me. I think it's because of my friend, Jeff, seeing The Jet in the hospital the day he tried to kill you on the wrong floor. Or maybe because we spotted him at City Hall. Anyway, The Jet told me someone wants to kill him now because he's a liability, having failed, and the cops have his description and are hunting him."

"How did you happen to find him?"

"He found me. I was playing pool with a guy over at *The Matador* on Burnside and he walks up behind me and taps me on the back. I just about had a heart attack. But he started talking like we were old friends. He said I was in danger and he was too. He was going to get out of town, but he had to talk to you first."

Chris rested his elbows on the table and cradled his chin with his fists, watching me expectantly, like I must know why The Jet wanted to see me. But I didn't know why, other than he wanted to get up close when he put a bullet into me.

"So how did he find you?" I asked.

"Well, that's a funny story," he said. "He spotted me and Jeff tailing him at City Hall. He snuck out a side entrance and waited for us to leave. Then he followed us. I guess he trailed me home and was watching me when I went to see you at the hospital, and I guess he put two and two together. He said he met your brother's killer and if you want to know who it is, you're supposed to come with me to see him."

"The Jet shot my brother!" I yelled. "And you just put him on the scene when it happened if he followed you the day you came to see me."

"He said he didn't do it." Chris directed his eyes around the bakery to see if my yelling attracted any attention. "He says he tried to kill you at the warehouse and inside the hospital and in the car. But he swears it was the other guy who shot your brother. He didn't know you would be there."

"And why would he want to tell me who killed Darrin? It's just a lame excuse to lure me into a trap."

"You think so?" Chris's face flushed. "Oh my God. He's probably going to kill me too. You know. No witnesses."

"I wouldn't doubt it."

"He said because he messed up trying to kill you that his higher-ups want him dead. They're afraid he'll talk. He told them about me following him and they were real upset."

"Who are these higher-ups?"

"I don't know. He talked to a handler and whoever it is tells him, 'great now they got two witnesses to dispose of' and hangs up. Oh my God. The witnesses are me and you."

"Maybe," I said. "Or maybe they *are* going to get rid of The Jet. Maybe he knows who hired him and now they want him dead."

"Billie? Where are you?"

"I'm on my way to meet a witness. What's going on?"

It was Dan on the phone and he sounded worried. We were riding in Chris's Jaguar westbound on Lombard Street in North Portland heading toward Cathedral Park, the meeting place The Jet had picked. I had spent fifteen minutes talking Chris into taking me to meet him.

He acted scared now, and I knew he wanted to rabbit again. He kept checking his rear-view mirror to make sure we weren't being followed. I felt a bit edgy too. I thought I spotted a plain clothes cop down the block when we left the bakery. It looked like McGraw.

My telling him to take various turns and double back routes made him even more nervous. I explained it was better to be safe at this point, but I didn't tell him there might be a cop following us.

"Well you better get home fast," Dan said. "Steve's coming this way, and I'm sure he's coming to the house to check on you. If you can sneak in the back door, I'll keep him distracted in the front room."

There was no way I could ever get back in time, and I didn't want to miss this chance at The Jet. I also didn't want to tell Dan because he'd have a fit and probably haul all my brothers over to Cathedral Park. I knew going in alone without backup wasn't smart, but if I brought reinforcements The Jet would be scared off.

"Can't make it, Dan. We're too far away. You're going to have to think of something."

"Jeez, you've got to try. If Steve finds you aren't here, he'll blow a gasket, and I'll be pounding a beat in the 'burbs."

Chris turned down a side street just before the entrance to the St. John's Bridge and coasted downhill toward the park.

"I can't help it. You guys will have to think of something."

"Cripes, we don't have much time. The GPS tracker shows he's almost here. What am I going to do?"

"Tell him I'm with my client consoling her after she identified her dead husband."

"But we're not supposed to let you out of our sight."

"Shit, Dan. Have Dag disappear and tell Steve he's with me."

"That's not going to work. You're supposed to be here."

"I don't know what to tell you. I can't possibly get there in time. You'll have to think of something on your own."

Chris grinned at me as I turned off my cell phone. He had parked a block away from the park on a side street and we were lucky to get that close. Cars cluttered the streets for several blocks in each direction.

"What's going on here?" I asked.

"Some kind of Pirate Festival, according to a sign," he said.

A banner on a fence with a skull and crossbones and the words *Portland Pirate Festival* announced the festivities. We stood in a line of about twenty people and eventually got to a cashier.

"Fifteen bucks for the two of us to get in?" I said. I fished in my purse and came up with thirteen dollars, including change. "You got any money."

"Nah," Chris said. "I'm still waiting for my bank card."

A plump teenage girl, wearing a serving wench's dress and a black and white checkered bandana, looked at us sympathetically.

"Arrrrr, we take credit and debit cards as treasure at that thar table," she said.

I went to that thar table, pulled my debit card out, waited as she put a blue wristband on my wrist, and we walked into a world of pirates. I thought at least The Jet would be easy to spot in a crowd. Then I saw six giant blowup pirate slides, kid bouncers, and obstacle courses being pursued by hundreds of miniature pirates. They were children actually, but many were in some sort of pirate garb.

They wore black pirate hats, eye patches, swords and sabers, toy pirate pistols, and plastic hooks dangled from hands. Scores of roaming adult pirates roamed the grounds, dressed to the hilt with authentic swords and holstered antique firearms. One of them wore a faux parrot attached to his shoulder.

I closed my eyes when a middle-aged bearded man walked in front of me carrying a spear, his huge pot-belly sticking out from an unbuttoned toga-like robe. Another sheet was wrapped around his waist. It was like watching a fat, old man parade around in diapers.

"Where are we supposed to meet him?" I asked.

"He said down by the river at two-thirty. We better get going or we'll be late."

We weaved around various pirate games in an open field and past tents with pirates and wenches selling costumes, eye patches, swords and food. I almost got run over by two kids racing back and forth carrying gunny sacks of pirate cargo as a crowd cheered them on. A loud gun blast bellowed throughout the festival. It came from the river and I started to run without thinking, instinctively reaching inside my jacket for the handle of my gun.

Chris caught up to me, and I could see he was scared too. A thunderous boom shook everything, and I felt the compression in the air. I thought *bomb* at first and remembered where we were. A crowd gathered behind ropes along the river and a huge smoke ring floated out above the Willamette River from cannon on a sailing pirate ship.

We found a spot on the edge of the crowd with a good view of the battle and not too many bystanders. A small cannon fired toward the pirate ship from shore. The boom was as loud as the ship's gun and was followed by more explosions as buccaneers touched off five miniature land cannons near a boat landing. When the cannons went silent, a female pirate hoisted a French-style flintlock pistol and fired it into the sky.

"Ahoy there," a shrill voice said over the din. "It's only fitting a Bly be attending a pirate festival, don't ya' think?"

I turned and faced a short pirate holding a derringer on me.

"Aye, it's a pirate gun," he said. "Only this one doesn't shoot blanks. It's loaded for real so keep it in mind if you're thinkin' of reachin' for yur gun."

When I saw The Jet, adorned in the full regalia of a pirate costume, complete with authentic miniature sword threaded through his belt, I realized why I was fooled on the day he first shot me. He was young, maybe 30, and his face was thin and youthful. He stood less than four and a half feet tall.

"You're pretty clever," I said, realizing at first glance people would think he was a child. "I thought you'd be easy to spot, but you blend right in."

"Aye," he said, staying in character. "I saw an advertisement for this and figured it was a great way to meet an old seadog friend of mine."

"Friend? You tried to kill me." Another cannon blast clipped off whatever response he made. "What do you want? To finish the job in front of all these witnesses?"

"That would be sweet. But it doesn't get me what I want. Even if I kill you now, I'm a marked man. I'm here for some revenge, and then I'm skipping town to leave you to untangle this mess."

"You mean, you're going to kill me?" Chris sputtered.

"He's not too bright is he?" The Jet smiled. "I'm here to tell you who wants you dead, Billie. They've decided I'm a liability now and already tried to dispose of me once, just yesterday. I doubt if I killed you now, they'd forgive me my failures. They want to be rid of any witnesses."

I waited for him to continue. I learned a long time ago that when a perp starts talking, you just have to let him unwind the story in his own way. If you interrupt, you usually don't learn as much.

"They were to pay me half up-front, and I was to get the rest when I finished the job. But they stalled me on the *up-front* part and I never saw a dime. They made me wait to see if you were going to die. I'm pretty sure they never meant to pay me. When you got better, they wanted me to go in the hospital and finish you off. I screwed that up because they gave me the wrong room number, and I became expendable then probably. It didn't help when this moron, here, spotted me at City Hall."

The cannon fire started again as the pirates on land fired land cannons toward over the river at a replica pirate ship with 40 foot masts and full sails in full battle, and we struggled to hear each other.

"My handler is a cop with a tattoo on his arm. His name is . . ."

Another cannon erupted, jarring me, and I didn't hear what he said.

"What?" I asked.

"I said you probably know him. After my last meeting with him, I followed him to City Hall. He went upstairs where the Mayor and city councilors are. But I didn't see which office he went into."

"What is his name?" I asked, over another boom. The Jet

cupped a hand to his ear, indicating he hadn't heard me.

"That's why later I went back to City Hall. I went in through the clerks offices and snuck into a couple of offices, trying to get a lead on who hired me."

"Did you find out who the dude was wants her dead?" Chris said.

"Man, you can't trust anyone these days, you know." The Jet grinned. "You'd better watch your sweet backside, Honey. These people will skin you alive."

"Who?" I hollered over more cannon fire, my hands outstretched as I pleaded for an answer. "Who was the cop and who gave the orders?"

A cannon boomed from the ship. I shuddered because it shook the air so. The rotten smell of sulfur drifted over us in a cloud of smoke. When I noticed The Jet again, he had a startled countenance on his face. I'd seen that surprised expression on my brother's face.

"Oh no," I cried.

The Jet sank to his knees and grimaced. His body lurched foreward as another bullet sailed into him. I wanted to shake him to get him to tell me who set me up, but my instincts prevailed. I faded back, found Chris, and pushed him to the ground, stumbling over him.

We rolled down a sandy slope. "Stay put!" I yelled. "Sniper!"

Pings of dirt chirped up from the ground, spitting sand into my eyes, as a high-powered rifle searched for us. The smell of dirt replaced the sulfur as I buried my face in the ground. I counted eight slugs either whistling over my head or digging into the sandy slope above us. If there was a sound from the gun, it was muffled by the cannon fire and resulting echoes.

When the cannons ceased, and I was sure the other shooting was done, I raised my head to see The Jet lying on his side with blood trickling from his mouth and a maroon pool gushing from under his body. I crawled over to him, staying low in case the sniper lurked nearby waiting for another chance to kill me.

"Who was your handler?" I pleaded.

He craned his neck to me and tried to smile through the pain. "It was . . ." His last words hung in air and disappeared like warm breath exhaled on a frosty morning.

The crowd still watched the battle so I went through his pockets. I found a ragged wallet with some money and a California Driver's License. His ID said his name was Montgomery Bales. He had a Los Angeles address.

Chris crawled over beside me and watched as I went through The Jet's pockets. "You saved my life. Thanks. If you can get me out of this alive, were even. I'll give you back all your money somehow."

Chris wasn't very intelligent, but he had a loyal quality, and I believed him. I stuffed the wallet back into The Jet's pocket and stood up.

"Let's scram."

"I'm with you," Chris said.

We meandered behind bushes and tents along the Willamette River and later snaked up through the other side of the park, zigzagging between the crowd and tents to avoid being easy targets. We exited the park and somehow made it to his Jaguar. Chris started the engine and slunk down in his seat to where he could barely see over the dashboard.

And that's how we left the Pirate Festival. Cowardly pirates, lying low and without any booty to show for our trouble.

Chapter 17

Our welcoming committee was in a sour mood when Chris and I stepped through the front door.

I knew I was in trouble when we drove up and saw two marked police cars and Steve's unmarked squad car parked in front of my house. I counted six cops in my living room, my three brothers, who were in plain clothes, two uniforms, and Steve.

Jason met me at the door. "Careful. Steve's on the warpath. I want to hit him real bad."

"Don't," I said. He stormed out the front door, and I watched him walk to Steve's car and start letting the air out of one of his tires. I chuckled and wandered into the hornet's nest.

"Well, look who decided to pay us a visit, boys." Steve's face flushed against his green sport coat. "It's Princess Billie. And who is this you've brought in with you, ex-P.I. Bly? I believe it's our star witness, Chris Johnson?"

"Uh, hello, Steve." I fingered my blonde hair, hoping to soften him. "What's going on?"

"That's what I'd like to know. I showed up here and Dan tells me you're out with a client. You and your brother, Dagwood. Then Officer Johnson finds *said brother* in the alley. So where have you been?"

"I've been with Chris. He's my new client. He wants me to protect him from someone he says wants to kill him. That wouldn't be you, would it?"

"Right now I'd like to tar and feather all of you. I'd like to suspend all of your brothers and get them kicked off the force. You lied to me. You've been out investigating Darrin's murder against my explicit instructions not to."

"I don't know what you're talking about," I said. "I got a call to meet Chris over at *Two Tarts*. You can call the bakery. We were there for a while and then Chris took me for a drive in his new car and then we came home."

"Why did Dan say you were with your client, Mrs. Fleming?"

"I told him I had an appointment. He must have thought I meant Mrs. Fleming." It should be noted that I'm a very good liar under pressure.

Steve sneered at Chris. "Is any part of this true?"

Chris didn't miss a beat. I guess lying to cops is some kind of prerequisite training for a thief.

"Sure," he said. "I hired her to protect me. Rumor on the street is somebody's out to get me. I guess word's out I came into some money."

"Oh man," Steve said. "You're the one who sued Billie and the city."

"Yeah, and right now I wish I'd never done it. It's causing me a lot of misery."

I heard the gears mesh as Steve contemplated the repercussions of another lawsuit if he didn't tread carefully.

"We'll still need to talk to you about the shooting," he told Chris. "So, Billie, explain why you were supposed to be with your brother and you weren't."

I noticed Dag's expressionless face as he sat in a wooden chair by the reception desk. "Did you ask *him*?"

"He didn't have an excuse," Steve boomed.

"They wouldn't listen to me at all," Dag said. "Told me it would just be a lie anyway."

"I see." I glared at Steve. "Dag was inside with us at the bakery. I talked him into letting me go on the drive alone because

Chris wouldn't talk freely in front of a cop. I'm sorry, Dag."

"That's okay," he said.

"This is all bull," Steve said. "Your brother was found walking away from the house."

"I lost my sunglasses," Dag said. "I was going back to find them."

Steve's face became beet red. "Tomorrow is Darrin's funeral, so I'm not going to take disciplinary action on your brothers at this point in time."

"Damn right you aren't," I said. "It wouldn't play well in the media, would it?"

And it was then I got one of my more devious ideas.

"Maybe not." Steve's tone was lower now. "But there are going to be some new rules. All of you are going to stay here. And I'm adding two patrolmen to the party, Officers Johnson and McGraw."

As if on cue, McGraw walked in the front door. He was in plain clothes, dressed as if heading to the beach, maybe.

"I checked the hotel where Mrs. Fleming was staying, and she hasn't seen them," he said.

"As you can see, she's turned up," Steve said. McGraw turned in my direction and grinned. "He's been searching for you ever since you gave him the slip at the bakery. Did you see Officer Bly anywhere near the vicinity when you were watching Billie?"

"No sir. She went in alone and about 40 minutes later Chris Johnson, here, showed up. They left soon after. Her brother was nowhere to be seen. Then they made a bunch of evasive turns and I lost them."

"You're blind," I said. "Dag was there with us. He went in a minute before me to make sure it was safe."

Steve grunted. "McGraw, make arrangements for a couple of cots to be delivered. Have another officer pick up whatever clothes and toiletries you may need. I don't want this bunch left alone for a second."

"Yessir," McGraw said. He pulled out his cell phone and walked into the kitchen. A few minutes later he returned with a sober face. "Lieutenant Thomas? We just got a call from Homicide down at Cathedral Park. Lead detective thinks you should come down and see for yourself. The victim might be the guy you think shot Bly and her brother."

I played along with the boys after the urgent call came in, asking questions and even becoming a bit emotional for them. Steve refused to let me go with him to the crime scene, but promised to update me later. I had mixed feelings about going. I wanted to see what the cops found, but I was afraid a witness might remember me.

A few hours after Steve left, Angel arrived with Earl on her arm. She wore a hot short black skirt with black lace stockings and gold killer heels. Earl, in khakis and a yellow knit shirt, completed the odd couple ensemble.

She offered to help me cook beef stew and after dinner, she, Earl, and I cleaned up in the kitchen while Chris, my brothers and the two assigned officers played penny-ante poker at the dining room table. Occasionally McGraw would peek into the kitchen to check up on me.

I updated Angel on the events of the day, including our meeting with the now dead Monty Bales, alias The Jet. She peppered me with questions while Earl listened attentively and nodded.

"What a terrible thing," Angel said. "To be so close to finding out who killed your brother and knowing it might be a cop or a politician. It sounds like one of those conspiracies you read about in books."

"Except this is real," I said. "Earl, you need to keep your mouth shut."

“Don’t worry. Nobody would believe me anyway.”

I must have been crazy to let Earl in on what happened, but he refused to go in with the boys, and he *did* save Angel’s life. I prayed he was trustworthy. One word from him would get us all in more hot water.

“My brothers don’t even know about this with McGraw and Johnson staying here,” I said. “They don’t give us a chance for any private conversation.”

I grabbed my phone and started tapping its keys.

“What are you doing?” Angel asked.

“Texting my brothers. They can read my updates at the table while they play poker with their watchdogs. Steve is just dreaming if he thinks he can stop *me*.”

“What are you going to do?” Angel asked when I’d finished. “I mean if a cop was responsible for killing Darrin and is trying to kill you, well, you can’t trust anybody.”

“I never do,” I said. “We’re going to have to find out who shot The Jet.”

“Maybe it’s the policeman who hired him,” Earl said.

“The Jet said his handler had a tattoo,” I said. “I’ve been wracking my brain all afternoon trying to think how many cops I know with tattoos. Shit, Steve has a couple, and I noticed during dinner McGraw had a small tat on his wrist. And the shooter would have to be a marksman. Whoever shot The Jet used a high powered rifle, probably with a scope, and he nailed him from at least a hundred yards away.”

“You said he.” Angel shook her head. “It could have been a woman. There are plenty of lady cops on the Bureau, and I’ll bet a lot of them have tattoos. Did The Jet say the cop was a man?”

I scratched my head. I couldn’t remember him differentiating the sex. Surely he would have mentioned a woman. I realized that he didn’t have time to tell me much of anything. If he had said *he* or *she*, I wouldn’t have heard it anyway over the canon fire.

“I guess not,” I said. “And I’m wondering how he knew it was a cop who hired him if the cop was out of uniform when they met."

Chris walked into the kitchen and grabbed a beer from the fridge.

"What you guys talking about?" he said.

"We're trying to figure out the identity of the cop who tried to have Billie killed," Earl said, also helping himself to a beer.

"Billie couldn't remember The Jet ever referring to the cop as a man or a woman," Earl said. "Do you remember if he said anything about it?"

Chris took a long swig from his beer bottle. "Not that I can remember. I always assumed it was a guy. I mean, The Jet was afraid of him and he didn't seem the type to be afraid of many people."

"I guess The Jet would have to be tough, to kill a cop and stick around to face the heat." Earl chugged on the bottle and smacked his lips.

"He didn't kill Billie's brother." Chris put his beer on the counter. "He told us someone else shot him."

"That's right" I said. "I didn't believe him at the time, but there obviously *is* someone else in the game. It could be another hired contract killer, or it could be this cop. Things must be unraveling if his handler did the killing."

"Hey," Chris said. "When I first met with The Jet at the pool hall, he wanted to play a game to settle his nerves. He said someone just tried to kill him. And he blamed some broad for all his trouble. He was ranting about it between shots. 'That damn bitch got me roped into all of this,' he said. 'I wish I never met her.'"

"So maybe the cop *is* a woman," Angel said.

"This doesn't make any sense," Earl said. "Why is someone out to kill Billie in the first place? Who do you know at City Hall who wants you dead?"

"Aside from the Mayor, I haven't a clue," I said. "But I don't think he hates me enough to have me killed. I've got to get out of this house and stir things up. Starting with Clemons, I guess."

"He'll probably be at the funeral tomorrow," Angel said. "You could corner him then."

"The funeral's tomorrow?"

Steve mentioned it earlier and it went over my head because I was busy hatching a plan to get him off my back. Immersed in finding Darrin's killer, I'd lost all track of time. *No time to think. No time to feel. No time to grieve.*

"What are you guys up to in here?" Officer McGraw stood in the kitchen doorway. "I hope you aren't plotting another escape for Billie. I'm in enough hot water with the Lieutenant as it is for letting you get away so many times."

How long had he been standing there, listening? "We're not going anywhere. You don't have to check on me every five minutes." Soon his snooping would stop if things worked out the way I anticipated.

"I'll feel better if I do," he said. "I like my job. But that's not why I came in here. You have a phone call in the living room."

"Who is it?" I asked.

"Someone named Eileen."

I passed by the poker game and could see they were gabbing more than playing.

"Hello, Billie? This is Eileen. How are you doing?"

"I'm fine," I said. Inside I felt wobbly and tired.

"I wanted to call and wish you well. I know you've been under a lot of stress, and I've been thinking about you all day."

"Thanks, Eileen. I appreciate your concern."

"I just wanted to take a minute to chat. I know your mind will be on other things tomorrow. Is there anything I can do for you?"

"Not that I can think of. But thanks for offering." It was quiet for a minute on the other end of the phone. "Eileen? Was there something you want to say?"

"Oh pooh. I don't know if this is the right time, but here goes. I was just wondering. I mean, when you feel up to it. I had such a good time with you at the coffee house, and I was wondering if we could get together again sometime and get to know each other better. It was so much fun hiding out from the law together."

I don't know what I expected, but I sure didn't expect this. Did she want to be my friend? I remembered what The Jet had said. Some broad had gotten him involved in this mess. But Eileen wasn't what I would call a broad. Still, this was sudden.

"I, uh, I guess we could get together sometime."

"When would be good for you?" she asked.

"I don't know when I could get away. I'm being watched very closely and they're restricting me to house arrest."

"Who are they?"

"The police. They say I'm a material witness."

But at that moment I knew it was more than that. I was being confined because someone was worried I'd find out who killed Darrin. The only person I could think of was Mayor Clemons. He'd used my brothers to keep me away from the investigation and when it didn't work he'd called in reinforcements.

"I should be able to get away tomorrow if you don't mind a chaperone," I said. "Let's meet after the funeral."

"Won't you have a lot of guests? I know how cop funerals are. Everyone will want to pay their respects. Probably lots of drinking too."

"The reception's is at Jakes Grill. Two o'clock. I'll be leaving at three after making my appearance." I figured Angel would be with Earl, and Steve had pretty much ignored me since our last tiff, so why not make a new friend.

"I'll be at the funeral and then I'll go to Jakes," she said. "In case you need someone."

We talked for twenty minutes about trivial things and after we hung up, myriad feelings surfaced. The conversation with Eileen was nice, but felt odd at times. Why did she call me out of the blue? What did she want? I could always use another friend aside from Angel and my brothers and now that Angel was seeing Earl we likely would have less time together. But the timing of Eileen's call -- the night before Darrin's funeral--seemed off.

I was too keyed up to mourn my brother. Call it denial, but I didn't feel I could grieve properly until I found his murderer. Maybe that's why I agreed to meet with Eileen. If she was up to something, I wanted to find out what it was. Why was I always so suspicious of people's motives? Oh yeah. It's my job. Still, something about Eileen seemed sincere.

Little did I know that her sincerity was about to cause me a lot of trouble.

Chapter 18

It was an early fall morning on the day of Darrin's funeral. The leaves on the trees were yellow and orange and a blustery wind tried coaxing them from their branches. Unable to sleep, I nursed a cup of coffee in the living room and witnessed the sun make its daily appearance.

I felt a solitary moment's peace at the quiet outside as lights began to flick on in homes down the street. It was the closest thing to serenity I had experienced in recent days. I thought about Darrin and wept gently. I missed the way he would wink and grin after telling me a not-too-funny joke. I missed his smile and his eagerness to help others. I missed our late night talks on the phone and how he helped me through my problems.

In these early morning moments, I felt close to him. Closer than I would feel at his funeral.

The last cop funeral I attended was for my father, William Bly, who also was killed in the line-of-duty, three days after my fourteenth birthday. It seems so long ago and, because of the trauma, most of my memories are nebulous. Of course, I'd heard stories of patrol officers coming from other states and even Canada to support a fallen comrade, but I was not prepared for what happened the day of Darrin's funeral.

The procession started at the overwhelmed funeral home in

Northeast Portland, where it weaved along side streets to the I-205 Freeway and snarled traffic for five miles. Motorcycle patrolmen closed freeway entrances and blocked southbound lanes to the public for the stream of over 400 squad cars, adorned with blue ribbons and American flags, as they moved solemnly along the route.

My brothers and I were in the lead squad car driven by McGraw. The Mayor and city councilmen followed behind us. Crowds stood on streets and overpasses and waved. Car horns bleated their support as their drivers patiently waited. My brothers and I wept openly each time someone honked or waved.

When we finally arrived at New Hope Community Church, I noticed the parking lots were already full. Our procession entered on an adjoining street, and we travelled down blocks reserved for the procession to park on the street.

The hall held three thousand people and it was packed with uniformed police officers from around the country, along with news media, city officials, friends and well-wishers. Dan said more than 330 jurisdictions planned to attend. I couldn't help thinking the person who killed Darrin was inside this great hall pretending to mourn my brother's death. It made me feel angry and frustrated. At the appropriate time, Mayor Clemons walked up to the podium.

"Darrin Bly was a model police officer," he began. "He represented everything good about the Portland Police Bureau. He was kind, patient, and respectful toward everyone he came in contact with. Two years ago he was named *Patrolman of the Year* by his peers."

Clemons looked over the sea of cops nodding their heads at his words and smiled a little. "He was a true hero sacrificing his life for that of another human being, in this case, his own sister." He smiled at me, and I tried to avoid his gaze. Clemons went on for another twenty minutes before finally yielding the floor.

Next, Dan gave a eulogy and we smiled, wept, and laughed at memories Darrin left behind. Dag tried to talk but had to sit down because his voice failed him. Jason shook his head at a chance to talk, the tough guy, probably not wanting to break up in front of so many cops.

Finally, I got up and walked behind the podium. I adjusted the microphone down from my brother's nearly six-foot-seven height to my five-ten stature.

"I want to thank everyone for coming today," I said. "It is truly uplifting to see support like this from ones friends and peers. I know Darrin would have been embarrassed at all this attention, but he also would understand this is more than just a tribute to one fallen comrade. This tribute is for all of our fallen comrades. It reminds us not to become complacent, to respect life, and to love our families.

"Darrin would have been proud of all of you for being here and remembering our brothers and sisters who passed in the line of duty. I speak as one of you because I once *was* one of you and in my heart I always *will be*. I come from a family of cops and when I was shot recently I found I bled blue.

"Now, because of Darrin's death, I am still bleeding blue. The wounds are inside and can't be seen, but they are there. I am no longer a police officer, just a citizen trying to make a living as a private investigator. But when my brother was shot, I swore an oath to myself that his killer would be caught. At this point nearly a week later, his murderer is still at large.

"It feels like the investigators have spent more energy keeping me bottled up as a material witness than pursuing Darrin's killer. I am a prisoner in my own home. My police officer brothers have been appointed as my wardens and told not to let me get involved in my brothers investigation. Surveillance teams are posted outside my home to keep an eye on me."

The great hall began to vibrate with low muttering between cops and citizens alike.

"And only yesterday, because my brothers lost track of me when I managed to duck out . . ." I waited as the audience laughed.

"When I managed to escape and returned to my home later. . . I was told my brothers likely will be suspended pending termination, and I was being assigned two full-time police officers to keep me under house arrest."

"*No, Nooo,*" came calls from the crowd.

"I don't want to ruin my brother's funeral by complaining about this now. I certainly don't want to turn this gathering's attention from paying tribute to Darrin and all of his other fallen comrades. But this is the only way I can see to bring this matter to someone's attention. I *do* want to go on the record as saying I will find my brother's killer if the department can't."

I smiled my most demur smile.

"Darrin is to be respected today. He is the one who made the ultimate sacrifice. Unlike me, he always had respect for everyone he met, and he always tried to help others if he could. I've always been a bit of a rebel, so I could usually count on him to keep me in line. I will remember all the lessons he taught me, and, if I can, I will try to be more like my brother. Thank you."

Tears streamed down my face, so I ended abruptly and stepped carefully down from the stage. The audience took my message faithfully and the grumbling stopped. I explored the sympathetic faces and hoped I hadn't tarnished Darrin's memory. It probably wasn't the best way to handle things, but it would be faster than going to the press—if they even wanted to print things of this political nature.

Dan and Dag grinned ear-to-ear when I got back to my seat. "Only you would pull a stunt like this," Dan said.

"Did I screw up?"

"Nah. The worst they can do is fire us. People should know what's going on. I don't think they're trying hard enough to find Darrin's killer and it stinks."

"You did good," Jason said. "Those sons of bitches think they've shut us up, but now that we're probably off the force anyway, we'll help you find Darrin's murderer."

I glared across the aisle at Mayor Clemons. He stared straight ahead as the minister called for others who might want to speak about Darrin. His face was hard and red. Beads of sweat dripped from his forehead. Next to him sat Gloria Blaney and next to her was her husband, Bob. The Portland city commissioners and their spouses sat further down the row. Gloria seemed confident and relaxed. Her husband seemed agitated. The killer or the person who hired the killer could be sitting in that row, I thought.

I didn't see Eileen at the church and by the time we arrived at the cemetery and finished all of the ceremonial rituals, including me being awarded the flag which covered his coffin, it was past two o'clock and I was emotionally spent.

I wanted only to get out of my sweaty stiff black funeral dress and to have a drink. I changed in an office at the cemetery into a less conservative fall inspired dress I'd found in my closet from the previous year, store tags still on it, and managed to avoid the press on the way out.

Eileen, Angel, and Earl sat at a table away from the bar at Jakes. There were two hundred people crammed into a fifteen-by-twenty-foot room, with overflow onto the sidewalk outside. It took me twenty minutes to reach them. I kept getting stopped by well-wishers, most of whom were police officers, telling me to 'give 'em hell.' Eileen seemed to be getting along quite well with Angel and Earl. I wondered how they could act so mature when Earl had been dating both of them.

"You did a great job," Eileen shouted over the noisy din. "I couldn't believe you called the Mayor out."

"You think I was referring to the Mayor?"

"Who else would have the clout to keep you in line?" Angel said.

"Where's your shadow?" Earl asked.

"McGraw? I think he got called away when I left the cemetery. Another officer drove us here."

"Sounds like the Mayor is regrouping," Angel said. "Maybe he's called an emergency meeting to figure out how to deal with you. Steve got called away just as he got here."

"Maybe I really started something," I said. "Dan and Dag are over there talking to the president of the Portland Police Association."

"So what's the plan?" Angel always knows how my mind works.

"While they're all busy protecting their butts, we start kicking this investigation into high gear," I said.

"Can I help?" Eileen asked.

"Yes," I said. "You can keep your eyes and ears open for anything that might be going on in the city offices. Don't put yourself in any kind of jeopardy. These people may not be beyond making a too intelligent secretary disappear."

"Office assistant," Eileen said.

"Okay. Just do some low-level snooping and report to Angel anything you might find out."

"Can't I call you direct?"

"I might not be available. You can always reach Angel. She knows how to find me."

"If you say so." Eileen frowned.

"I'm going to make the rounds at City Hall and see if anyone is sympathetic enough to leak some information about the investigation," I said. "Somebody has to know something."

"You could dab your eyes with a hanky," Angel said. "That works for me sometimes."

"I got some contacts at the city," Earl said. "I'll see what I can turn up."

"Uh, thanks, Earl."

He stood and grinned. "Anyone else want another drink?" We nodded and Angel got up and followed Earl to the bar.

I snickered at Angel's new boyfriend as he left the table.

"What?" Eileen said.

"It's Earl. I mean, it's nice of him to offer to help, but what contacts could he have with the city?"

"Oh, it's best not to underestimate him. You might be surprised. He knows a lot of people. I've known him for about seven years myself."

"I have to admit he's surprised me a lot already. I'm puzzled how you could have dated him and don't seem to mind now that he's seeing Angel. What is it about Earl that makes women so forgiving?"

"He's a nice enough guy, but I finally realized he's not my type. I like them a bit more . . ."

"A bit more, what?"

"Oh, I don't know. Just different than Earl."

"So you think he might turn something up?"

"If anyone can, it's Earl," Eileen said.

"Why do you seem so sure about him?"

"Well, he's asked me not to say anything to anyone, but maybe you should know."

"I'd love to know more about the secretive Earl. Go on . . ."

"He's a tow truck driver when business is slack for him. It's kind of a fallback job. He fills in for other drivers at different companies."

"What's his regular job?" I asked.

"Promise not to tell him I told you."

"I promise."

"He's the same as you, a P.I."

"What?" My jaw dropped.

"That's right. And he's had a couple of cases with the city. I think he's working on one now. I think that's why he agreed to go out with me. He spent the whole time trying to pump me for information."

I was dumfounded and my cynical brain searched for a rational way to fit Earl into the puzzle. He ingratiated himself with Eileen and now with Angel. And here he was right in the middle of my investigation, even offering to help.

"Who has he worked for at the city, Eileen?"

"I know he worked for Commissioner Tuttle once a few years back. Tuttle thought his opponent in an election mismanaged public-financed campaign donations. Earl investigated and a few weeks later the newspapers reported Tuttle's opponent spent $50,000 on personal non-campaign related expenses."

"I remember reading about it. Earl was involved in that?"

"Yeah. You should have heard Tuttle bragging about Earl's part in it. Earl told me all he did was point him in the right direction."

"So, what do you think he's working on now?"

"I'm not sure. He was asking me questions about Bob Blaney."

"What kind of questions?"

"Did I think he was honest? Did I know if he was cheating on his wife? I think he was just digging for some dirt on the guy."

"Did you give him any?"

"There's nothing to tell. Blaney seems like a decent sort to me. He gets around the office and jokes with all the staff. He works late into the night. Always has his reports ready for city staff and always seems to know what's going on."

"Except with his wife, I guess." Eileen made a wry face. "He doesn't seem to have a clue about her. You never told me who she's fooling around with. Can you now?"

"Not yet. I don't want to make any false accusations. You never knew she was fooling around before I told you that day at your office?"

"I knew it was a strong possibility. She spends a lot of money on wardrobe and makeup and doesn't seem to be doing it for Bob. All he seems interested in is numbers."

"No time for the wife?"

"Oh she comes and visits him at work, but I get the feeling it's always about money. Half the time you can hear them arguing."

"Here are your drinks," Earl said, Angel in tow. "The line at the bar stretched outside. You two come up with any ideas while we were gone?"

"One or two," I said.

Eileen shook her head. Earl studied her and then gave me an equally scrutinizing gaze. "Anything you care to share?"

I lifted a glass of white wine to my lips and looked over the rim. "Just a drink at the moment."

Chapter 19

I slept in until nearly ten the next morning. When I made it downstairs, Angel was on the phone at her desk in the reception area. She wore her orange-streaked brunette hair atop her head in chunks, probably to look taller, and clicked her red-spiked heels together while tugging downward on her purple mini-skirt as she talked.

I went into the kitchen and poured the last bit of coffee to help dull the colors. I toasted a bagel and returned to her desk just as she hung up the phone.

"I'm surprised you're here," I said.

"I work here."

"I know, but things have been so crazy. I guess I'm out of the day-to-day work routine. Where are Dan, Jason and Dag?"

"They were called back to duty."

I lifted an eyebrow "What about their suspensions?"

"Steve called this morning and said he had been venting and not to take what he said seriously. He said the guards and surveillance have been taken off, and he'd like to stop by later today and apologize."

"Wow. That's kind of amazing." I said.

"Yeah, your little speech at Darrin's funeral yesterday caused quite a furor."

"No. I mean, it's kind of amazing Steve is going to apologize. He hates ever admitting he's wrong about anything."

"Maybe the Police Chief or Mayor is making him do it."

"Probably. Any other calls?" I took a sip of the stale coffee.

"Are you kidding? The phone has been ringing off the hook. I have three piles of messages. This one is the 'give 'em hell' pile. The second one is request for interviews from two newspapers and all the television stations. The third pile I'd classify as leads on your brother's murder."

I sifted through the murder leads.

"Gloria Blaney? What did she want?"

"She wouldn't say other than she has some information and she wants to talk to you as soon as possible. I told her you were still recuperating so she suggested lunch at *Meriweathers* at 12:30. I told her I'd call her back and confirm if you wanted to go."

"Yeah. I love their Crab Louie with the chili dressing. And Mrs. Blaney is at the top of my list to interview."

"You think she's involved?" Angel asked.

"I think the Mayor might be. And since Gloria is kicking heels with him, she's in a position to know what's going on inside City Hall. Maybe I can persuade her to open up to me. Who else is in this stack? Who is P. Richards?"

"Oh, he's one of the investigating officers on your brother's homicide. Said he'd like to meet with you and update you on what's going on."

"Another move by the Mayor in the spirit of cooperation?" I said.

"I don't think so. He made me promise not to tell anyone he called. He didn't even want to give his name at first. I promised him you'd call him discreetly. Here's his number."

"I'll call him after lunch. I grabbed at another page of Angel's stack of leads. "Stella Fleming is still in town?"

"Yes, but she sounded kind of agitated. She told me to have you call her as soon as you were up. Said she had something to tell you she should have said before. Something her husband was doing you should be aware of."

I picked up the phone and dialed her hotel room number. The phone went straight to message without ringing. "Her phone's turned off. She called at eight o'clock this morning?"

"That's about right," Angel said. "She was persistent. She wanted to talk to you, but I knew you'd had a rough day, and she agreed she could wait."

"Keep trying. Call me when you get hold of her and give her my cell number."

"Okay. How are you feeling?"

"I've got a double hangover. It's a combination of the funeral and going out and tying one on with Eileen. That girl can really put away the booze."

"Oh? Where did you two go?"

"A bunch of places I've never been before. A couple of nightclubs. A couple of pubs. I think we even went out to dinner. Eileen is really a sweet person and a very good listener. I have to admit I was a little suspicious after talking on the phone with her the other night. I couldn't believe she wasn't after something and she just wanted to be my friend. But we had a great evening and she didn't seem to want anything except my time."

"I hope that's all it is," Angel said.

"What do you mean?"

"Earl told me last night he had gone out with Eileen right after we met."

"Oh, he fessed up, huh?"

She smiled her irritating *you aren't going to get my goat grin* and went on. "We don't have any secrets. He told me about the date when he brought me home from the hospital. He said it was business and I believe him."

"Did he say what kind of business?"

"He *did* say it was another one of his jobs and that he couldn't discuss it because it was of a confidential nature. I told him it was all right with me, and he promised to tell me about it when he could."

I decided this Earl was a slippery character and not to be trusted. He gave out enough information to appear legitimate, but I had a feeling Earl was out for himself.

"He did tell me one thing," Angel said.

"*Oh*?" I said, with emphasis on sarcasm.

"He said after his date with Eileen, she told him she had just met someone else she was attracted to."

"*She* dumped Earl?" I remembered she'd told me Earl wasn't her type.

"Well, he wasn't going to see her again anyway," she said.

"Eileen didn't say anything to me about seeing another guy last night."

"Well maybe, uh . . ." Angel hesitated. "It seems this new love interest might not be a man."

"Well if he's not a man, who is he?" I was confused now. Maybe it was the hangover, I thought.

"It could be a woman. Eileen once told Earl she was bi-sexual."

I gradually began to form coherent thoughts, and I remembered something Eileen had said about Earl. *He's a nice enough guy, but he's not my type. I like them a bit more assertive and. . . .*

I've been called a lot of names, but I've only been called assertive by people who are trying to be kind when describing my "bull in the china shop" methods for dealing with people. It was what she left unsaid that was running through my mind now: *and . . . female?*

"Now Billie, calm down. I'm sure she could have been yanking Earl's chain. It's just, what you two did last night sounds a lot like a date."

A date? Oh my God. My mind flashed on a hundred things we did and said as I searched for confirmation I was the new woman in her life.

"How could this happen?" Angel avoided my gaze, and I knew she was holding something back. "What?"

"I'm sorry Sweetie. It's just that you dress in blue jeans, your hair, although blond and stylish is cut a bit too short, and your brusque way of dealing with people, gives one the idea you might be a bit too butch, if you get my drift."

Meriweathers is on Northwest 26th and Vaughn Street, about a mile from my house so I thought I had plenty of time to get ready. After spending forty-five minutes prowling through my closet for something feminine to wear I settled for a pair of gray slacks, white blouse and flats. Because of my wasted efforts at the closet, I only had 30 minutes to do a slap-and-dash with my hair and makeup and get to the restaurant in time to meet Gloria.

I rescued my cute little red Miata from the garage, pleased with my new freedom to go where I pleased without Steve's storm troopers hovering nearby. It ran a bit rough, I thought, and then realized it had been three weeks since I'd driven it. I parked on the street, the restaurant being in an industrial area and hiked half a block.

When I saw Gloria, I wished I'd found a dress or anything besides what I wore. Gloria radiated opulence in a black sexy dress, which showed off her long curvy legs and ample chest. I couldn't help staring as I sat down at the table with her. Maybe she could give me some lessons in style, I thought.

"I'm glad you could make it," Gloria said. "You like what you see?"

She caught me giving her the once over, and I had been staring at her bosom wondering if she was really that big or used a push up bra. I've never been able to force myself to push the girls out into the open like Gloria seemed to do so effortlessly. Yeah, I flashed that guy and the Captain once upon a time, but I did it on anger and impulse so it doesn't really count.

"I'm sorry. I've been a bit distracted today." My face felt

flushed and I knew it was red.

"That's okay, Sugar. I'm glad you like what you see. It means I haven't wasted my time."

Her voice was all saccharine and suggestive. I wondered what she was up to.

"You said you had something to tell me," I said.

"Oh, you're all business," she said. "Okay, I heard something from my husband and the Mayor yesterday."

She grinned at me and brushed her long, jet-black hair back with her fingers.

"Marshall Clemons says the police are close to making an arrest in your brother's death," she said.

I waited, breathless, for her to continue, but she just sat there gazing at me with half-a-smile and two-parts mischief in her twinkling blue eyes.

"Well? Go on . . ." I said.

"I thought we might do some quid-pro-quo here," she said in a raspy voice.

"What do you want?"

"We can get to that in due time. For now I'd just like to know what you've turned up. Mayor Clemons said you aren't very smart, but I think he underestimates you." She reached across the table and stroked my forearm with her long manicured fingers.

"So you don't deny you're having an affair with the Mayor?"

She drew back her hand and sat erect with a stunned countenance. Her playfulness quickly returned, and I'd almost wondered if I imagined her surprise. I hadn't.

"Oh. I see you like to play rough," she said. "No, I'm not having an affair with him. He's just a good friend. He and Bob and I sometimes go out together. Bob has ambitions."

"Are you sure it's Bob who has ambitions and not his wife?"

"You *are* a regular little firecracker. Let's cut through the crap. You fill me in on what's going on in your little investigation so Mayor Clemons doesn't have to lose any sleep over your shenanigans, and I'll help you find your brother's killer. And for a bonus, you can have a shot at me."

"A shot at you? What have you done?"

"I must be losing my touch. I'm suggesting we might have a little fling together. I saw how you were checking me out just now. I don't normally swing that way, but I have to confess you are a striking woman. You have such firm muscle tone, and I'll bet you are a wild thing in bed."

"Gloria," I said between clenched teeth. I grabbed her wrist and squeezed until she winced. "I . . . AM…NOT…GAY! I'm straight. Why does everyone think I'm gay?"

"You're not?" She seemed amused. "But you're so butch. And Marshall . . . I mean Mayor Clemons said you were gay. Of course, now that I think of it, he was cursing you when he said it. I just thought you *were*."

"Are you so attracted to me that you had to make a pass?"

"Not really. Bob and the Mayor asked me to talk to you. To see what I could find out about what you were doing. Marshall said things would go better for Bob if I cooperated. There's some new deal brewing he's offered to cut Bob in on if I help him."

"What kind of deal?"

"I don't know. That's between them. But Marshall has been talking about a run for governor. I think he's thinking about bringing Bob along with him to the capitol if he wins."

"I must really be making things difficult for him."

"You are, Sugar. Try to see it from his point of view. First you cause him terrible publicity when you roughed up that guy in the revolving door after he just announced his new community policing campaign. Then, your actions bring a lawsuit upon the city. And apparently, you've been skulking around City Hall *which has* everybody nervous. Marshall is worried that you're going to make a big mess of things again."

"So his idea is to keep me locked up in my own home?"

"Could you blame him?"

I knew what she was after. She wanted to know if The Jet had told me anything the day he was shot at Cathedral Park. I wondered how they knew I was there.

"Look, Gloria, I'm nowhere, okay? I haven't turned up one puny little lead. I was supposed to meet The Jet at Cathedral Park in St. John's. But he was killed before he could tell me who hired him. And with him, he took the secret of who tried to have me killed and who killed my brother. I don't know anything. So *if you do*, I pray to God you'll tell me now."

I was in tears. A pretty convincing performance, but I didn't have to dig very deep for emotions.

"You were there at the park when he was killed? Wow! That must have been scary. Did you talk to him? He must have given you some kind of clue."

"Between the cannons they were shooting off I could only hear every other word. And he wasn't very talkative. Just scared. He was going to skip town, and he wanted to tell me something, but it seemed like he couldn't make up his mind. Then he was dead. The only person who could tell me who killed my brother was dead."

I studied her facial expressions. Her lips curled downward and a few lines dared to reveal themselves on her forehead. She was considering my story. Wondering whether or not to believe me.

"It's too bad he didn't say something. It might have put the final nail in the case against the person police think killed your brother."

"And who do they think the killer is?"

"I don't know and that's the truth. Marshall told me to tell you they expect to make an arrest in the next forty-eight hours. He asked me to beg you to back off and give them time to wrap up the case."

Something in my reaction must have tipped her off to my answer.

"He isn't your enemy. He just doesn't want to be shown up as a schmuck in this whole thing. And you just made him one again with your little news conference at the funeral."

"If you could give me something tangible to help me believe you," I said.

"They know where he's going to be at a certain time. Warrants are being drawn up. They plan to intercept him sometime in the next two days, as I said. I don't know any more than that. I'm just the messenger."

"Why didn't someone official come to me? Why didn't Steve tell me this?"

"No one wants to be around you after the fireworks you caused at the funeral. I'm surprised Marshall is even extending this olive branch. Be smart and show some patience."

I thought about it for a minute. "Okay, I'll sit tight. But you have to bring me in on it when the arrest happens."

"I'll ask Marshall about it." We got up to leave and Gloria waited as I paid my bill. "Let me know if you change your mind about getting together. I think you're kind of cute in a pedestrian sort of way."

"No thanks," I muttered as I brushed by her.

"I'll call you," she said and blew me a kiss.

Why, all of a sudden, did everyone think I was gay? I pulled a compact out of my purse and gave myself a once over. Hardly any makeup, my hair was thick and unwieldy, and my lips were chapped.

But to call me pedestrian? Not only was she a sex maniac, but a snob. But I thought I saw her motivation for our meeting. If Clemons had an eye on the governorship and he was single, it might give Gloria ideas. It would certainly explain why she fronted for him.

But what about her husband?

Chapter 20

He stood there, frozen in silhouette, waiting for me to make a move. I didn't pay him much attention.

My thoughts drifted toward why Eileen and Gloria both thought I was gay. If they thought so, how many others were in on the conspiracy. What had I ever done to deserve the label? It's the type of thing which makes you stop and think. Would I ever consider an alternative lifestyle? No, I liked men, damn it. Even if they--meaning Steve--seemed not to like me.

I was feeling sorry for myself. Things had not been going my way. My brother was dead, the only witness to the killing was murdered and Steve was mad at me again. Two women wanted my body, and I was no closer to finding Darrin's killer other than Gloria's vague assurance.

And I was angry. I'd held my emotions in check since the day I woke up in my hospital bed. I couldn't be angry about being shot because I had to put on a positive front for my brothers. I couldn't be angry about Darrin's death because I had to find his killer. Then there was Steve, who remained distant through this whole thing and was mad at me despite the distance.

Did he think I was gay? If I had to be honest with myself, I'd admit he was the only man I have ever cared for.

I decided it was time to be angry. It's why I showed up 30 minutes early on this arranged meeting. It was just me and him now, my Colt 1911 semi-automatic .45 at my side. He was unarmed and I didn't care. I raised my gun and pointed it at the solitary figure 30 yards away.

"You are going to die a terrible death," I cried. He mocked me, not showing the slightest fear.

"This is for killing my brother." I squeezed the trigger and the gun jumped in my hand. Two rounds entered his head.

"This is for shooting me, you asshole!" Three more rounds tore into his heart.

"And this is for thinking I'm a lesbian." Another round into his head and the sweet smell of cordite assailed my nose.

I wasn't close enough to clearly see his face, but I felt his defiant sneer so I put the last two rounds into his groin.

"Need any help?" It was Detective Phil Richards.

"What the hell? Don't ever come up on my blind side like that."

"Sorry. I heard you yelling and I thought you might need some backup."

"Very funny," I said. "You're lucky I'm out of ammo. I might shoot you too."

Richards was young with brown soulful eyes, and a thin face.

"I don't think I would have liked that, especially on our first date."

"Oh? You like to take your dates to the shooting range?" I pondered the sterile grey walls and paper torsos hanging on clips 50 feet away. We were inside the police bureau's new shooting training facility on Airport Way.

"Only my cop dates," he said. "But I didn't realize you were so fine or I would have picked a nice restaurant."

I wasn't in the mood to be flirted with. It occurred to me I'm never in much of a mood to be flirted with. So I smiled at him.

He grinned. "You aren't as tough as I heard."

"Maybe I'm tired of always being tough," I said. "Maybe I'm developing a soft side."

"I'd ask you to go out to dinner later, but after you hear what

I've got to say, you probably won't feel like eating."

"You're on the investigative team with Steve aren't you?" I asked.

"Yeah." He licked his lips and lowered his eyes to a .44 magnum he held. "That's why I wanted to talk to you. A bunch of us think your brother's investigation has been mishandled."

I waited.

"I don't know how to tell you this, but Steve has been taken off the case."

"Why?"

"The Mayor has been micro-managing things since we started. And no matter what Steve does, the Mayor gives him grief for it. The Chief just goes along with everything the Mayor wants."

"There's been a lot of stress and most of it is probably my fault," I said.

"True. But the Mayor wasn't entirely convinced Steve should be in charge of this investigation from day one."

"Why not?"

"Because of his connection to you. Clemons thought it might be a conflict of interest."

"Well, he used to be my partner, so I guess I can understand it if he thinks Steve was too close to the situation."

"Maybe," Richards said. "Steve came on real strong with the Mayor and said he knew you and the family, and he'd be able to keep the investigation orderly and at the same time have an insight into possible motives."

"What did he mean by orderly?"

"I guess he was referring to keeping you in line. The Mayor didn't want you or your brothers to interfere with the ongoing investigation."

"So it *was* Clemons who had us under house arrest."

"No, I think it was Steve's idea, but it's probably why the Mayor agreed to let him head the case."

"I can't believe Steve would hinder me without pressure."

"You think so? I thought he *got off* on keeping you contained."

"Why would you say such a thing?" I asked.

"You *do* know what Steve thinks about you, don't you?"

"At one time I thought I did." I remembered some of the intimate times during our partnership when I hoped he would take it to the next step. "But I have to confess I never understood that man."

"So you don't know what he's said about you?" Richards said.

"What do you mean?"

Richards shook his head. "The man hates you. He's always complaining about how you stopped him from making Captain."

"I never . . ." My face flushed.

"Scuttlebutt says because of all of your screw-ups, and his standing up for you, he was told he would never be promoted. It's a miracle he made Lieutenant."

"Steve told you he hates me?"

"Not exactly. Over the years he *has* complained about you being outspoken and getting into trouble a lot. I mean, whenever he goes down memory lane about you, he starts bitching about it. Eventually he explodes. Says he doesn't want to talk about it. It's in the past. But you can see he's still angry about it.

"Did he tell you this?"

"All the time. You know I was his partner for three months. I asked for another assignment, because he was always griping. A real negative dude."

I reloaded my gun, turned and took aim at the target, firing off four rounds. I missed entirely on two shots and caught the edges of the torso with two. I raised the gun again and took careful aim at the face. My hands shook, and I missed the whole damn target again. Richards didn't say anything about my performance.

"I'm sorry to be the one to break the news," he said. "I thought you knew."

"And he said the reason he wasn't promoted was because he couldn't keep me in line?"

"I don't think I ever heard him said that, but there was a lot of speculation among his fellow officers. You two were always in hot water and people noticed. You know there are no secrets downtown. Most people think he blames you for his situation."

My heart ached. Richards might well as shot me because it hurt as badly as when The Jet took me down in the warehouse. I couldn't believe Steve felt that way. I had always hoped he might return my feelings someday, but now I knew he never would.

"Why are you here?" I said.

"I wanted you to know, I think he's gotten a raw deal," Richards said.

"Then why are you trashing him to me?"

"I . . . didn't mean to. I guess I wondered if you hated Steve too. Maybe it's why you're making all of this trouble for him."

My heart sank. "So why did Clemons take him off the case?"

"Same reason he should never have put him on, I guess. He botched the security detail at the hospital which got Darrin killed. Then he nearly got you killed on the way home from the funeral home when The Jet tried to shoot you again."

"Steve couldn't have done much about the shooting on our way home from the funeral home," I said. "It was my own fault. I was supposed to be home recuperating."

"But it was Steve's responsibility to make sure you stayed home, and he blew it. And I heard a rumor you had visited the Mayor just before that incident. Is that true?"

"I guess I didn't care much about what might happen to Steve." I groaned. "I was mad because I thought he wanted to keep me from finding Darrin's killer."

"Can you see it from his point of view?" Richardson said. "He's trying to find your brother's killer and keep you safe and maybe have a chance to get his career back on track."

"I think I've had enough shooting practice," I said.

Richards nodded.

"Did he ever say . . . to anyone . . . he thought I was gay?" I could tell I surprised him because his face became more animated.

"Are you?" he said. "I mean, I never would have thought it."

"No, I'm not! I just wondered if he ever mentioned it. Even if he was joking."

"I never heard him say anything like that. He called you a bitch a couple of times . . ."

"I can live with that," I said. "I *can* be a bitch when I don't get my way."

I spent the twenty-minute drive to the Central Precinct downtown rehearsing what I wanted to say to Steve. My emotions were raw, and I tried not to cry and ruin my makeup before I saw him. I was still dressed in my black Nike sweatsuit and smelled of gun powder from the shooting range. My makeup was the last bastion of femininity, and I *so* wanted to be more feminine these days.

I walked straight into Steve's office, if you can call it that. It consisted of a small desk in a cubbyhole near the records file room. Not all of the records were in their home, however. A good amount of them were on his dingy walnut desk and they were stacked so high I could barely see Steve slumped behind his fortress of solitude.

"I want to talk to you," I said, slamming the door harder than I intended.

"This is a surprise." He scooted his chair on wheels to the side of the desk and cleared a stack of files from a nearby chair. "Sit down. I'm glad you stopped by."

His appearance shocked me. His face was haggard and defeated. His eyes poised above dark puffy half circles. His rumpled brown suit added to his sad sack appearance. I thought I smelled a faint odor of liquor on him.

"Are you all right?" I asked.

"Me? Oh I'm fine. But I wanted to talk to you before any rumors made it your way."

"Well, they already have; that's why I'm here."

"I'm sorry. I would rather you heard the news from me."

"I would rather you *had* told me yourself too. Why did you keep silent about this for so long?"

Steve's dark eyes fixated on me. "I only found out this morning."

"I'm confused," I said. "You only just found out that you hated me and that I'm a bitch?"

"What are you talking about? I've known you were a bitch since the first day we were partners." He grinned. "But what is this about me hating you?"

I told Steve about the rumors I heard earlier at the gun range, but didn't mention Richards as the source. He listened intently, his face turned redder as I unraveled the facts.

"That was a long time ago," he said finally. "I don't hate you!" He pushed a stack of files off his desk, stood and kicked his chair over. "This is the last straw."

"It's not true?" I asked.

"Shit!" He blew air out of his cheeks and made a moaning sound.

"I owe you an apology. I *have* blamed you for my misfortunes and I did speak badly about you on several occasions. At the time I was venting and it felt good to blame someone other than myself. But in the last year or so I realized I was the only one responsible for what happened to me.

"I stood up for you because more, often than not, you were doing the right thing. Sometimes it got us in hot water, but I could have reined you in more than I did. You see, at the time I had a crush on you so I let you get away with more crap than I should have."

I swayed into the back of my chair and my heart skipped a beat. "You had a crush on me?"

His eyes darted to the floor and gradually rose to see my reaction. “Yeah, but you know. It wouldn’t have done for us to have a physical relationship because we were partners.”

“And later? After I left?”

“You were in hot water with the city and a lot of the heat came back to me. I guess I was distancing myself from you to avoid the flack.”

“But I was off duty when I banged Chris’s head in the revolving door.”

“I know. I know. But I was your superior and I should have had control of you. That was the feeling of the Chief and he was right. If I’d done a better job holding you accountable, maybe you’d still be on the force and I’d be a Captain by now.”

“I think I would have found a way to get booted eventually,” I said. “I don’t like to follow orders. It has nothing to do with you.”

He smiled a bit and leaned forward. “Thanks. But like I said, I’ve figured out I’m the only one responsible for my troubles. I wanted to head the investigation of Darrin’s death to make up for the way I treated you in the past. The Mayor wanted the Chief to put one of his boys in charge, and I convinced him otherwise.”

“How’d you do that”?

“It wasn’t by telling him I could keep you in line. That was his idea.” He grinned. “I told him it might not be in his best interest if word got out he was putting it to the wife of his city auditor.”

“You knew about their affair?”

“I’d seen them together a couple of times. He said I was blackmailing him, and I told him to call it whatever he wanted, but if he didn’t put me in charge I’d go to the media.”

“Steve, that’s so unlike you.”

“Yeah, well it blew up in my face.”

“But why did he take you off the case if you’re holding all this leverage against him. Isn’t he afraid you’ll go to the press?”

Steve slunk in his chair and ran his fingers through his stringy brown hair. “I don’t know, but I don’t like the way things are unfolding. The Chief gave me the news this morning. I got called into his office along with Detective Richards. I was out; Richards was brought in as lead detective, and the Chief assigned Officer McGraw to the team for continuity."

That surprised me. Richards hadn't mentioned anything about his promotion. "Did the Chief give a reason for taking you off the case?"

"About a hundred of them. He was hot after you called us on our procedures at Darrin's funeral."

I winced. "I'm sorry."

"You were right on. I was against it myself, but Mayor Clemons insisted. The jerk. He set the whole thing up and then his bright cop, McGraw, kept losing you."

"McGraw reported to Clemons?" I said.

"Of course. You've got to know, in a volatile setup like this, the Mayor is going to have some ears on the inside. McGraw was assigned to head the surveillance on you by Clemons himself. McGraw flubbed it, and I got the blame."

"Are you angry with me?"

"I gave that up about a year ago and no matter what you do, I promise, I'll never blame you again."

"You feel sorry for me because I got shot and Darrin's dead."

"I blame myself for Darrin's death. I thought I had it covered. There's no way a sniper should have been up in the hospital parking structure. The Mayor's right there. I'm totally to blame."

I didn't say anything. Maybe because I also suspected it was his fault. That had always troubled me. No one should have gotten by Steve's team. But it also bothered me that Steve was up in the parking structure when the shots were fired. Why didn't he see anything?

"Billie, there's something else. I may be imagining this, but I don't think so."

"What?"

"I think I might be a suspect in Darrin's murder."

"*What?*" I tried to act surprised.

"It's the way things are unfolding. Effectively I'm on paid leave. They've got me here filing records instead of out in the field. It's supposed to be a punishment, but it feels like I'm in the frame."

"You mean for Darrin's murder?"

"Not just Darrin's murder, but the attempts on your life too, including when *you* were shot in the warehouse. They're going through my phone records. I think they're searching for any calls I might have made to The Jet. And I was on the scene during both of the other attempts."

"But you were at my house when The Jet was shot."

He shook his head. "I only got to your house ten minutes before you. Before that I was following another dead end lead. The address my informant gave me was out in North Portland and didn't exist."

"North Portland? Anywhere near Cathedral Park?"

"About three miles, but I never got a call on the shooting. I could have been there in a few minutes, but for some reason communications got mucked up and no one called me. Could be they suspected me even then."

"So you don't have an alibi."

"No." He said. "I could easily have shot him and returned to your house."

"Did you know I was at the Pirate Festival when The Jet was shot?"

"Shit no. What were you doing there?"

"He wanted to warn me about something. He told me not to trust the police. He was about to tell me why, when he was shot to death."

"Oh my God, you must believe me. I didn't try to have you killed. I'm being set up. You *do* believe me, don't you?"

"That depends on how you answer my next question, and I want you think carefully before you answer it."

"Okay," he said, dead serious.

"Did you ever say or imply to anyone you thought I might be gay?"

He jerked his head back, his eyes opened wide and he laughed out loud.

"You? A lesbian? Okay I can understand why someone who doesn't know you might think so, but honest, never in my life. You hit on me so many times I couldn't have kept track with a scorecard. It was all I could do to act like I wasn't interested. One thing I didn't want to do was get demoted for having a relationship with my partner. Ethically it's just wrong. I'm old school and you represent a new breed of police officer so I don't think you ever got that, did you?"

I felt my face blush. Was it excitement or embarrassment?

"Did I answer your question correctly?" he said. "Now do you believe me when I say I didn't try to kill you or your brother?"

I hugged him. "Of course I do."

I had to say it. But in my heart a doubt lingered. I tried to brush it away, but . . .

Chapter 21

"I can't get Mrs. Fleming on the phone," Angel said. "I've tried all day, but it rings forever and then goes to message."

"Funny she would call and then not be available when we try to call her back," I said. "Is she still at the same hotel?"

"Yeah, *The Comfort Suites* on Airport Way. I called the desk, but they said they haven't seen her today."

"Have there been any other calls?"

"No. It's been really quiet this afternoon. I haven't even heard from your brothers."

"I talked to them after I met Richards at the shooting range," I said. "Dag said Chris has gone missing again. Dan's been filling in over at the East Precinct. He said Jason is out on patrol in East County too. He thinks the Chief is keeping them at arm's length so they can't do any snooping into Darrin's murder case."

I checked my watch. It was five-thirty and City Hall offices were surely locked up by now. I wanted to have another crack at the layout later in the evening to find out why The Jet snuck in and what he might have learned.

"You feel like going for a ride?" I asked Angel.

"Where to?"

"The Comfort Suites. I have this uneasy feeling Stella Fleming held something back from me the last time we talked and now I'm concerned about her safety."

We left the house by the back door and entered the garage

through the side. The sun was an hour and a half from setting, but the lighting inside the garage was dim and shadows filled the gaps. I pushed the automatic door-opener button and waited for it to lift. It didn't open. I pushed the button again and nothing happened. I flipped the light switch and the bulb failed too.

Angel bumped into me. "What's the matter?"

"I think the power's out. The door won't open and the light won't turn on."

"That's ridiculous," Angel said. "The house lights are on and there's not enough power out here to trip a fuse."

I walked to the rear bumper of my car and squinted to see if any wires were loosened at the garage door opener apparatus. As my eyes became used to the darkness, I spotted a stray white wire from the garage door leading up to the ceiling where it joined another white wire leading back to the overhead motor. The wire appeared caught at the edge of the guide rail which tracked the pulley system.

"Maybe this wire got snagged when the door closed or opened last," I said.

"Hmm," Angel said. "What about the overhead garage door light?"

"Probably just burned out."

"Well how are we going to get the damn door open?" Angel said.

"Dan showed me what to do when this happens." I walked toward the door opening, reached up and grabbed a small wooden handle dangling from a braided rope overhead and pulled. A metal plate unlatched from the garage door, separating the door from the pulley system.

"Now we can lift the door manually."

I wedged myself between the door and car bumper, grabbed the metal handle in the middle of the door, and tugged. The door opened a couple inches before I had to stop.

"I think I pulled a stitch. Can you help me?" Angel stood a few feet away at the edge of the garage door, staring.

"What is that?" she said.

"What is what?"

"If the power is off to the garage door, why is the little red light on?"

She pointed to a little plastic sensor box, which shot a red beam across the width of the door to stop the garage door from closing if a child or some object lay in its path. I bent over the sensor box and felt more wires I'd missed before in the dark. These wires were black. They led in another direction from the white ones.

Were the black wires also part of the garage mechanism? I squatted and ran my fingers back along the black wires between odd pieces of wood, lawn chairs and other junk leaning against the wall. After following the wire hand-over-hand for about seven feet, I stopped and gawked up at the other set of wires overhead. Why would there be two sets of wires?

Angel watched intently, and I ran my fingers along the cord for another foot or so when I felt it. It was smooth, metallic and tube shaped.

"Uh Oh!" I sputtered. "Let's get out of here."

"What is it?" Angel said.

"A big pipe bomb."

We scurried back around the front of my car and I bumped my hand and my keys against a headlight. The car's horn bleated in steady increments. It scared the hell out of us and we ran for the door. It wasn't until we got outside and away from the garage, that I realized I had accidently triggered the fob on my keychain which set off the remote car alarm.

My garage is detached and about fifteen feet from the side of my house and we were at the back corner of the house. So when I managed to tap the remote fob on my key chain to stop the bleating of the car horn, three things happened concurrently.

First, the horn went silent. Second, my garage left the ground in thousands of various sized debris. Third, the blast laid us out on the grass like helpless fish floundering out of water.

Some of the smaller pieces fell on us, but I lay in stunned amazement at seeing most of them shoot straight up in the air as high as 100 feet.

"Jeez," Angel said. "I can't hear anything, except a ringing in my ears."

"The bomb went off," I said to no one in particular. I sat up and rubbed my ears to stop the ringing. "Are you okay?"

"I'll live, but that's more than I can say for your car. Make the ringing stop."

There were flames coming from where the garage used to be. They quickly engulfed the shell of the building and shot up 50 feet over my car.

"I didn't like that car anyway." I lied. It was a 1990 Mazda Miata, a cool little red convertible with a cherry body and troublesome engine, and I loved it. "I'm going to get a better car."

I noticed a figure pacing around the driveway in front. It started toward us, and I instinctively reached for my purse to get my gun only to realize I'd left my bag on the hood of my car.

"Damn," I said, "my purse is burning up in there."

"I've got mine," Angel said. "Do you want me to call 9-1-1?"

"I need a gun."

"Why didn't you say so." She reached into her purse and pulled out a snub-nosed revolver. I grabbed it and raised it toward the dim figure approaching."

"Hey, hold on; it's me."

"How did you get here so fast?" My eyes slowly focused on Steve.

"Thank God you two are all right. I thought the worst when I heard the explosion."

"You were here when it blew up?" Angel said.

"Yeah, I thought I'd stop by and make sure Billie was doing okay. I was on the front porch ringing the doorbell when I heard the car alarm go off. Then all hell broke loose. The blast practically knocked me on my butt. What happened?"

"Pipe bomb," I said, deciding to lower my gun. "A big pipe bomb."

Angel and I staggered up off the ground and walked toward the front yard. When we got there, we saw Earl sitting in a blue BMW across the street. He stared at the garage in awe.

"Earl," Angel hollered. "I'm over here."

"He turned his head in our direction and got out of the BMW. "What happened?" he said. "Are you okay?"

She ran to him in tears, and he grabbed her tight and squeezed.

"I was so scared," she said. "A bomb in the garage exploded right after we got out. I thought I was a gonner."

"There, there," he said. "I'm here. You'll be okay." He held her in his arms and whispered something into her ear. She put her chin on his shoulder and winked at me. *See, this is how you do it*, she was telling me. I felt more alone in the moment than any time in my entire life. Angel had someone to hold her and tell her he was there for her, and I didn't. Steve circled the garage in the distance.

"What are you doing here?" I asked Earl, after their embrace.

"I came to see if my best girl wanted to go out to dinner. When I saw the fire, I was stunned. It never occurred to me anyone would be in there."

As if taking a cue from Earl, Steve finally stepped up to me and draped his arm around my shoulder. I should have been thrilled, but for some reason it made me feel creepy. I pulled his arm from me, and he took a step back.

"Everybody okay back here?" It was Officer McGraw. "I called the fire department."

"How did you get here so fast?" I asked.

"I was doing my rounds. The Mayor told us not to follow you anymore, but said we should patrol the neighborhood a couple times a day to make sure you were okay. I decided to swing by on my way home."

"Maybe if you'd come around a little earlier, you might have noticed someone putting a bomb in my garage."

"Now that you mention it, I did see someone around here earlier," he said. "It was that Chris guy. He was knocking at your door about lunch time. He waited and when nobody answered he sat on the porch for a few minutes and then got into his fancy car and drove away."

In the following minutes, three fire engines, an ambulance, and several patrol cars screamed up to my burning garage. A west wind blew the flames toward my house and firefighters raced to put them out before they made contact. The heat from the fire became so intense we had to go out to the street and watch helplessly.

When the bomb squad arrived, the neighborhood was evacuated up and down the block and most of the neighbors gave me dirty looks. This wasn't the first time I had interrupted their routines with one of my little situations. All I could do was stand helplessly answering questions from a bomb squad technician as my neighbors gawked from Northwest 23rd, which was now closed to rush hour traffic and causing one hell of a traffic jam in Northwest Portland.

TV news crews filmed as firefighters shot streams of water from across the street at angles as far away as they could get from another possible explosion. The result was they were able to keep water on my house and my next-door neighbor's houses, but the garage and my car were left to burn.

It was eight o'clock, about two and a half hours after the blast, before the last ember was extinguished. My brothers had arrived concerned and left frustrated at their inability to find my assassin.

My little Miata was so hot you could see steam rising from molten metal when the lights hit it. The firefighters saved my house, but the paint on its side blistered and peeled badly.

Sgt. George Arthurs pulled me to the side of what used to be the garage. The side the bomb had been located. He had a pleasant round face, balding grey hair and a patient if not fatherly demeanor. He had worked with my father on the force before my dad's death and remained close to our family.

"From what you've told me, it sounds like it was an improvised explosive device or IED," George said. "The kind militants used in Iraq to take out armored trucks. This was nasty one. Someone wired it to your garage door opener to explode when you crossed the red safety beam or used your garage door remote or wall switch.

"They must have crossed a wire somewhere and that's why your garage door failed to open. Maybe they broke the overhead lights so you wouldn't see their handiwork, but we have no way of knowing for sure. Everything's gone."

"I noticed a black wire near the door that didn't seem to belong," I said.

"Yeah, well lucky for you," he said. "If you hadn't seen it, you might have crossed the path of that beam and detonated the bomb when you tried to open the door manually."

"But it exploded when I tried to turn my car alarm off," I said.

He shook his head. "You're car remote wouldn't have affected anything."

"Why did the bomb explode then?"

"Probably somebody was parked nearby with another remote to the bomb. When they heard the car alarm honking and realized you were in the garage, they decided to go for it."

"They were watching me?" I shuddered and realized how close I'd come to death again.

"That'd be my guess. Did you see anyone before the blast?"

I watched Steve and Earl engaged in animated conversation with Angel on the porch. I hadn't seen anyone before the blast, but Steve was on my doorstep during the explosion, Earl and McGraw showed up seconds later, and McGraw said he'd seen Chris hanging around earlier in the day.

"No," I said, absently. "Not until after."

"That could be important too. Make sure you tell the investigating officer."

"Steve was the investigating officer until today. He filled in Detective Richards a few minutes ago."

"Well that simplifies things," Sgt. Arthurs said. "I hate to keep seeing you under these circumstances. First your poor brother was killed and now this. Be careful. Maybe you should take a little vacation until things settle down."

"I can't do that, George."

"Yeah, I know. But stay safe." He gave me a hug and sauntered off to sift through the debris.

"Any luck coming up with a suspect?" I asked, approaching Angel, Earl and Steve.

"Steve's come up with some new information about Mrs. Fleming," Angel said. "He said the police have her pegged for the murder of her husband."

"That's insane."

"I told him, but he thinks otherwise."

"It's not what I think, it's what the investigating detectives think," Steve said.

I knew in any murder the spouse was always the top suspect. However, Stella Fleming was in another state when he was killed. At least I hoped she was. I never thought to check. To me she was just a woman frantic to find her husband.

"What would be her motive?" I asked.

"She had an insurance policy which pays $500,000, double for accidental or violent death," Steve said.

"So they think she arranged his death to appear like an accident?"

"They did at first," Steve said. "But upon further investigation of the bloated body, the coroner found two small caliber slugs in him."

"I didn't see any bullet wounds."

"The swollen body hid the bullet holes, but the coroner found them on a second look. The detectives think he knew the person who shot him because he was killed at close range."

"So it had to be his wife? Maybe he had a girlfriend here."

"They're considering the possibility, but they haven't been able to find anyone in Portland who knew him. It makes it hard to come up with another suspect. And apparently his wife has been asking the insurance company for payment. Of course they didn't want to pay without finding a body."

"Seems logical to me," Earl said.

"Do you think you could put up with a houseguest tonight," I said to Angel. "I don't think I could sleep here after this."

"Probably a good idea," Steve said. "It's not safe to be alone."

I ignored the comment and kept my attention on Angel.

"I think it's a good idea too," she said. "You don't mind her staying tonight do you, Earl?"

Earl greeted me with a sour puss. "No, I think it's best under the circumstances."

"Oh, I forgot. You two wanted to go to dinner."

Angel smiled sheepishly. "Earl's been staying the night lately."

"Oh, I didn't know things had progressed that quickly."

We rode in Earl's sedan because Angel's little Volkswagen was totaled and my Miata resembled burnt toast. I sat in the back and suggested we go by Stella Fleming's hotel on the chance that she might be home this time of night. I wanted to get her side of the story and didn't want Steve tagging along for obvious reasons.

When we got to the hotel we stopped at the office and got her room number. The clerk tried calling her, but got no answer. The hotel was new and modern with a glass elevator that sported a view of the airport lights and a busy little strip of motels and fast food restaurants.

We rode the elevator to the fourth floor and stepped out into a hallway with commercial paisley brown carpet, beige walls, and a slight smell of cigarette smoke. When we approached Stella

Fleming's door, I noticed a *Do Not Disturb* door hanger and rapped on the door anyway.

We waited, but there was no answer so I rapped again, louder.

"I'll be right back, I have something in my car that will help," Earl said. He returned a few minutes later with thick copper tubing rolled in a loop and slipped up to the door.

"These aren't too hard to get open." He unwound the copper and began bending it while measuring it from the floor to the lever-style door knob. He shaped a hook at the door handle and bent it so it resembled a "V" with a hook at the top. I watched as he slid the tubing sideways under the door and turned it upright, snaking the hook up to the door lever. He brought the tubing back out and reshaped it, then slid it back under, snagged the inside door latch and tugged a few times. The door eased open and Earl smiled. "See what I mean?"

Where did you learn to do that?" Angel said.

"I'd like to take credit for the idea, but I saw a 17-year-old do it on a YouTube Video."

I shook my head at the ever resourceful Earl and stepped through the door. When we entered it was obvious someone been there before us. A few of her clothes and underwear lay on the floor. The rest were jumbled in a dresser drawer. The bed was made up, but the covers were loose and the mattress sat slightly off-kilter. A notebook mouse sat on the nightstand but there was no laptop in sight.

A slim black purse lay open next to her bed. I bent over it and didn't like what I found inside. It was a small caliber hand gun. I lifted it by the trigger guard with a motel pen. It was a revolver similar to Angel's and it was easy to see two bullet chambers were empty. I wondered if it was the murder weapon used to kill her husband.

"Looks like we were wrong about Mrs. Fleming," Angel said.

"It appears that way." I said.

I laid the gun on the bed and picked through the purse with the pen. Things were all mixed together like someone dug through it, but I couldn't see anything obvious that might be missing. There were car keys, makeup, a checkbook, more makeup, lip balm, a few pens and eyeglasses in a case. What I didn't find was the picture of Mr. Fleming she had shown me when we met last.

"Uh oh." Earl stood at the bathroom door. "Better come and see this."

I went over to the door and opened it wider. In a bathtub of crimson water, lay Mrs. Art Fleming. A blue pallor colored her chin and lips. Her head slumped over the back of the tub. A bloodied straight razor blade lay on the bathtub ledge.

We stepped closer and Earl reached over and lifted her arm. There was a deep cut across the inside of her wrist. Earl frowned. "Suicide?"

"Or meant to look that way," I said.

"Oh my, poor Mrs. Fleming," said Angel. "This hasn't been a very good day."

"It's been a terrible day for Stella." I bent over and touched the bloodied water. "It's cold and from the looks of her she's been dead for a long time."

"Maybe since this morning after she called you," Earl said.

"Yeah, that's what I was thinking," I said. "The *Do not Disturb* sign on the door would have been put there for the maid this morning."

"A private suicide," Earl said. "So no one would find her in time to rescue her."

Angel shook her head. "Or a private murder."

Chapter 22

I watched somberly through the fourth floor hallway windows as blue and red lights flashed along Airport Way and glided into the hotel parking lot below. I couldn't believe so many people were dying around me.

First Darrin, then The Jet, Art Fleming, and now Stella. My life continued to spin out of control, and I needed to stop the spinning before I got sucked into the vortex of death and depression.

As the proverbial noose tightened around the neck of a dead person who could no longer defend herself, I refused to believe the evidence onstage. The gun in Stella's purse obviously was a plant. A very short, unsigned suicide note, implicating her in her husband's death, sat on display on the bathroom vanity and the scrawling was illegible enough to be considered the scratches of an insane person, despondent enough to end her life.

We watched as the police sealed off the room. Angel went for coffee and brought a cardboard Starbucks box back for the investigators. Officer McGraw showed up and interviewed Earl, then me, and finally Angel. He seemed satisfied we were, for the most part, telling the truth.

McGraw grilled *me* the longest, wanting to know her identity. He winced when I told him about her hiring me to find her husband and about Art Fleming's body being discovered a few days ago.

"Crap. She's the lady who was going to be arrested for her

husband's death," he said. "I talked with the investigating detective at lunch today. We'll have the gun in her purse checked to see if it matches the slugs they found in her husband's body. Her conscience must have caught up with her."

"There's something wrong with this whole scenario," I said. "She had a picture of her husband in her purse when I met her. She held onto it like it was the most important thing in her life. It's not there now and . . ."

"You went through her purse? Christ, you may have contaminated vital evidence."

"It was before I knew she was dead. We found her in the bathtub a few minutes later."

"Did you handle the gun?"

"No. I mean I fished it out with a hotel pen. I didn't touch it. I know it appears bad for her, but I don't think Mrs. Fleming killed her husband. The suicide note looks bogus to me and someone went through her purse and took her husband's picture."

"Why would anyone take a picture?" McGraw asked.

"I don't know. Maybe her killer thought it might be too sentimental for her to be carrying if she murdered her husband."

"Doubtful. The coroner ought to be able to tell if she was restrained or if she suffered any trauma prior to her death, but all the evidence points to suicide."

"What do you mean, you want us to drop you off downtown?" Angel said. "I thought you were going to spend the night at my house."

"I've already ruined your night enough," I said. "You and Earl were going to go out to dinner and spend a nice evening together. I still have some unfinished business. Earl, can you drop me off at City Hall?"

"I guess we could do that," he said. "But what are you going to do there this time of night?"

"Hopefully meet a friend." I dialed Eileen's phone number and got her on the third ring. "Eileen? Are you busy?"

"Just curled up with a good book," she said. "What's up?"

"I'd like a little tour of your office and maybe a few of the commissioner's offices."

"Are you crazy? I can't get you past the guard this time of night."

"*You* can get past the guard, can't you?"

"Well, I can tell him I have some important work to do before morning, but the commissioners' offices only work by key card at night."

"I know. I remember seeing the slots for them when I paid a surprise visit to the Mayor."

"They're on a timer," she said.

"Can you get me in the building?"

"Not through the main lobby. Okay, if you meet me at the exit door on the Fifth Street side of the building I can get you up the back stairs from there. But we'll still be locked out of the commissioners' offices."

"Let me worry about that. Can you meet me there in fifteen minutes?"

She hesitated. "Okay. But I look dreadful."

Earl dropped me off down the street from City Hall and he showed concern. Bless his duplicitous little heart.

"What are you up to?" he said.

"I'm up to finding out how The Jet got out of City Hall without being seen by the cameras." I thought Earl went a little green around the gills. It was too dark to tell for sure.

"I don't think that's a good idea," he said. "They'll throw the book at you, if you get caught."

"If I get caught, I'll know who to blame." I bent over and glared at Earl through the open car window.

"Well I'm not going to say anything," he said. "But I still think it's a bad idea. You want we should hang around? Just in case?"

"No. I'll be fine. Eileen will be with me."

"Be careful," Angel said. "Call and let us know you got home safe. Otherwise I won't sleep a wink."

"I will. And Earl, if you really want to make sure I don't get caught, there's one thing you can do."

A few minutes later I was cooling my heels outside the City Hall doors on Fifth Street. I cooled them for twenty minutes before a door opened with a piercing whine, which was louder than any alarm that might have gone off. It probably wasn't that loud, but as it was nearing the midnight hour it certainly seemed so.

"Sorry," Eileen said. "One of the guards wanted to gab. Then he wanted to walk me up to my office, and I had to come down the back stairway."

I stepped in from the cold, cloudless night and witnessed Eileen in all her dreadfulness. Her hair was immaculate. She wore perfect makeup, a slimming pair of black dress slacks and matching sweater, and smelled of lavender. I suspected it was something more in the way of fashion which detained Eileen. I looked down at my own outfit. Blue jeans, a white blouse, and sneakers, and I smelled of smoke. Everyone dresses better than me.

"What's that for," Eileen asked, pointing at a roll of copper tubing hooked on my belt.

"You'll see," I said.

We climbed the stairs, and she used her ID card to gain entrance into the receptionist's office. We pushed the little gates open, and I made straight for Bob Blaney's office.

"If I open his door with my card key, they'll know I went in there at, cripes, eleven-fifty-five at night," she said, sneaking a peek at her watch. "I'll be fired. And the cameras already caught you coming in with me."

"No one will view the security tape unless they have a reason to, and we aren't going to give them a reason," I said. "What happens if someone opens the door from the inside?"

"It wouldn't register anything. It's the card that triggers the system. What are you doing?"

I pulled out the quarter-inch copper tubing Earl reluctantly parted with at the car.

"Watch," I said, manipulating the wire to make a giant coat hanger similar to one Earl had used to get us into Mrs. Fleming's hotel room. I noticed on my earlier visit that the doors were equipped with lever handles, not the rounded knobs.

I slid the copper device under the door and tried to catch the lever on the other side of the door. It felt like I was catching something, but I couldn't get it to grab. It wasn't as easy as Earl's demonstration earlier. I reshaped the wire as Eileen kept one eye on me and the other on hallway outside where I heard footsteps in the distance.

"Hurry up," she said. "Someone is coming."

A click, a downward turn of the door handle, and we were inside in the next instant. We waited in the dark, holding our breaths, until the footsteps faded.

"That's so cool," Eileen said. "Now what?"

"Now we search for clues."

I flicked on the office light. Blaney's desk was neat to a fault. No paperwork or other obstacle was on his desk other than a small thin computer screen. I didn't see any kids' pictures or award plaques. There was a small color photo of his wife, Gloria, on an oak lateral filing cabinet and three motivational pieces of art on the walls. *Soar Like an Eagle,* one of them suggested, and a fierce bird of prey hovered above the lettering.

There was a door which backed to the side hallway, but it wouldn't open. When I tugged at the knob, I noticed the antique nails driven through the door at an angle into the door frame.

"It's been nailed shut and for some time," I said. "So how did The Jet get out?"

"Maybe he snuck out the way he came in and somehow evaded the camera," Eileen suggested.

"I wonder." I pointed to a large folding screen, decorated with oriental branches and flowers.

"The Japanese screen came with the office before Blaney was hired," Eileen said. "I'm surprised he kept it."

It stood nearly six-feet tall. I grabbed it at the ends and folded it shut, setting it aside. The shade hid a decades old secret. A slight rectangular vertical seam in the faded wallpaper was evident now. Years ago, someone pasted the material on the wall as an accent and, for whatever reason, covered a door too. Later, someone slid a knife along the door's edges to make it operational again.

I turned the knob and pushed it open about eighteen inches before it stopped. I slid through and found myself behind another wall, created by an oversized bookcase. Commissioner Tuttle and City Auditor Bob Blaney enjoyed a clandestine passage between their offices.

"What do you know?" Eileen said, pawing at remnants of another wallpaper design on the back of Tuttle's door. "I never knew this was here."

"It was a secret between these two men," I said.

Tuttle's office was the antithesis of Blaney's, with a filing system consisting of stacks of files and paper scattered throughout his office. A gold-plated golf club hung on a wall amid plaques and awards. The room had a slight scent of alcohol and on a hunch I opened the right lower drawer in his desk and found a bottle of scotch.

To the side of Tuttle's office, another door led to the side hallway. This door opened when I turned the handle. My eyes trailed down the hallway to Blaney's side door, which now we knew was bolted shut.

"The only way The Jet could have left by the side stairway was from Tuttle's office," I said. "But the video showed him going into Blaney's office.

"So The Jet must have known about the secret door," Eileen said. "The question is, who told him? Blaney or Tuttle?"

"He could have stumbled on it just like we did. Maybe he heard a noise and it scared him so he jumped behind the screen and saw the door. Or maybe he was in here talking to both of them. I wish I knew if they were still here when he entered."

"I wish I knew too. It still gives me the creeps, him slithering about like a snake," Eileen said.

We closed the doors, and I had just arranged the screen in front of Blaney's secret door, when we were startled by male voices echoing from the hallway.

"Someone's coming," Eileen said. "Hide under the desk, and I'll go out and see what's happening."

She flipped off the office light on her way out. It seemed like I was forever crawling under office furniture. I pushed Blaney's desk chair out and scooted under his desk.

"Eileen? You all right?" a voice boomed from the reception area.

I risked a peek from behind the desk. A glazed window between Blaney's office and the reception area distorted the forms, but I guessed it was one of the building security guards. I hoped he was the one who was her friend.

"I was just finishing up this report," Eileen said. "It has to go into the mail first thing in the morning. Is something wrong?"

"We got a call from Blaney," the guard said. "He wants us to do a search of the building. He didn't say why, but I'd better get you out of here. It won't be good if he finds you in here tonight."

"But I haven't done anything," Eileen said.

"I know," the guard said. "But I'm not so sure he'd understand."

I squinted at the window as the two figures moved about the outer office and the lights flashed off.

"Should we go down the back hallway stairs?" I heard Eileen ask.

"No," the guard said. "There's less traffic out front. Besides, we don't want to appear to be doing anything wrong."

Time to get the hell out, I decided. As the voices trailed off, I felt my way to the screen and moved it away from Blaney's secret door. I repositioned the partition and slid behind the bookcase in Tuttle's office, when the copper wiring, attached to my belt, snagged its hook on the door frame. I thought I'd been grabbed and nearly yelped. I unhooked myself and made for the door to the back hallway Eileen had suggested to me in her question to the guard. I opened the hallway door to dim fluorescent lights and was about to step out when voices clamored up the back stairs.

"He wants us to check his office first, then every office up here," a husky voiced drawled.

I pulled the door shut, retreated to my sanctuary behind the bookcase again, and waited to see which office they would search first.

"This has got to be a huge waste of time," a guard said, as he entered Blaney's office.

I closed the door between the offices. My plan was to scoot back inside Blaney's office after it had been searched.

A clicking sound behind warned me another guard just opened Tuttle's door. Shit. They were searching both offices at the same time, leaving me in a precarious perch behind the bookcase.

"Not much to search in here," a voice said, from the other side of the bookcase.

A desk lamp flicked on and I heard the guard by Tuttle's bureau. Probably peeking under it, I thought, and I was glad for once I wasn't hiding under office furniture. A minute went by and I heard a desk drawer open and a gulping sound. The guard helping himself to Tuttle's Scotch?

My hip was trapped awkwardly in the small space behind the bookcase. I tilted my body to flatten against the wall when the copper wire on my belt loop again betrayed me by making scratching sounds against the wall. I held my breath. The door to the back hallway opened and closed. Had he left? A few seconds later I heard another noise. It sounded like a desk drawer closing.

Then I heard movement and my reeling senses told me he was about to find me behind the bookcase. I pinned the copper wiring tight against my leg and pivoted toward the door behind me. I pushed it open a crack and, thankfully, Blaney's office lights were off. The screen stood about eighteen inches from the door, enough to allow me to slide in.

A second later the doorknob twisted in my hand. I held it tight and held fast on the door. Another tug, then the tension on the knob was gone. The door to Blaney's office opened again but the lights stayed off.

I realized I was holding my breath. I listened to the guards' rustling sounds on each side of me, slowly let my breath out and tried not to suck oxygen loudly back into my lungs.

"There's no one here," a voice finally drawled. "Nothing seems out of place. Okay, we'll keep looking. How soon will you be here? . . . Yeah, I'll check the reading on your door lock to see if anyone accessed it."

The guard was talking to someone on the phone and I guessed it was Blaney because we were in his office. Worse, it sounded like he was on his way and with his reputation of being methodical he would make them search the entire City Hall again.

Blaney's door opened and the other guard chirped: "That the old man?"

"Yeah."

"What'd he say?"

"Keep searching. He's coming down."

"What's going on?"

"Said he has his office alarmed and someone or something set it off."

"Did you check behind that screen."

"What screen? Oh yeah."

"Did you know there's a door behind there?"

"Nah, it's just a wall."

The office light flicked back on. I could tell where this was going and gently twisted the doorknob.

"Yeah, there is. Come here. I'll show you."

A flashlight hit the screen as I wafted through the doorway. I closed the door tight and held the doorknob with a vice-grip.

"*See.*" The voices were muffled, but I understood them.

"There's a doorknob. Why did they leave the wallpaper over the door?"

"Maybe they don't use it."

"Sure they do. Someone used a razor blade to cut the wallpaper around the door."

The knob tried to twist in my hands. I clamped down harder on it.

"It's locked. I tried it from the other side."

"Maybe they don't use it anymore. I hear they've been fighting about something lately."

The voices trailed off and I heard the outer door in Blaney's office close. Drips of perspiration stung my eyes. I wiped them with my arm and leaned against the bookcase. I felt it give and turned to find it swaying. I reached around the corner and grasped the front and pulled it back to me. It obliged, pinning me against the wall and, before I could recover, it cascaded forward again. A deafening crash sliced through the silence.

"What the hell was that?" a voice hollered, from the reception area. "It came from Tuttle's office."

The bookcase blocked the exit door to the back hallway. I climbed over the top of the shelves and struggled mightily to pry the door open enough to slip through. The door gouged me on my still healing chest wound. I winced and scraped through.

In the hallway I heard a radio flash a command somewhere at the bottom of the back stairway. "Get up here. We have an intruder," a voice squawked.

"I'm on my way."

There was an elevator to my left. To my right I saw a door with a handicapped sign. I twisted the knob and entered a one-toilet bathroom. I locked the door, flipped on a light switch, and spied a small sash window about five feet from the floor. I stepped onto the sink and opened the window just enough for a slender female P.I. to slide through, or so I hoped.

"Did you see anybody coming down the stairs?"

I froze atop the sink. The voice belonged to Blaney.

"No," a guard said.

"What about the elevator?"

"It hasn't moved all night."

All right. We're going to scour this floor. Whoever broke in, is still here."

"Did you find anyone?" It was a woman. Gloria? Why was she here?

"Nah. But somebody knocked the bookcase over in Tuttle's office. They could still be in there."

"Open the door." It *was* Gloria.

Geez, I thought. I've really stumbled into a hornet's nest. I took the copper tubing from my belt. It was folded in sections. I unrolled it and fished it through the window. I bent the end to fashion a hook I could tie through a metal grip on the inside of the window and coiled it in a knot.

The bathroom door rattled behind me. "It's locked," Gloria said. "Who's got the key?"

"Probably the janitor."

"I'll bet she's in there."

"She?" Blaney said.

"Billie Bly," Gloria said. "I'll bet it's her."

I didn't want to wait to hear the end of *this* conversation. I arched my leg over the window ledge and pulled myself up to straddle it.

"Find the janitor and get a key," Blaney said. "Let's find out."

"I'm on it," the drawling voice said.

I ducked my head back, raised my other leg, and slid it through the window, rotating my body so my stomach rested on the ledge.

A sharp pain shot though me, reminiscent of The Jet's bullet. I wheezed and wanted to cry. Instead I scooted out slowly with a firm grasp on the ledge. I said a prayer and started a hand-over-hand movement down the copper rope. I slid faster than I planned and summoned every muscle in my arms and shoulders and hands, to resist the gravitational pull.

My hands grew white hot and I continued my slide, clutching at the tubing with my feet now. It helped slow my descent. When I finally stopped sliding, I hung precariously about 30 feet from the ground. A streetlight illuminated thorny barberry bushes directly below me. My copper lifeline would get me, maybe, eight feet closer to the ground. Add another seven feet from my hands to my feet and it would be a fifteen feet drop, I figured. Not much I could do about that.

I methodically moved one hand down after another. I repeated the hand under hand motion until I was within a foot of the end of the copper rope and stopped to survey my situation.

It was going to hurt like hell landing in the barberry bushes. I'd brushed up against them once at Dan's house. He used them to deter a would-be burglar from sliding through his bedroom windows. I thought if I could just swing a bit, maybe I could steer clear. My hands already ached. I planted my feet on the wall and pushed, swung awkwardly a few feet forward and returned to bounce off the wall.

I pushed away again and got a little more momentum. My swing improved and I figured two more practice motions would get me clear of the bushes. I wondered which would be worse, falling 15-feet onto hard ground, or having my drop cushioned by the spiky bushes. The choice was taken from me when the knot at the window unraveled.

I bounced off the barberry bushes and crashed onto clay earth beneath the grass. It knocked the wind out of me, and I lay there unable to breathe. I was about to black out when I heard a friendly voice.

"Billie? Are you okay?" It was Eileen. "My God, you could have been killed."

I don't remember much after that. I recall telling her to get the copper tubing, and the next thing I remembered was waking up the next morning naked in bed with Eileen.

Chapter 23

Now I'm not a prude. I've awakened in a strange bed after imbibing in too many drinks or otherwise making poor choices. The result wasn't without its share of shock. When the fear transcended from heart-stopping panic into guilt-ridden anxiety, I usually remembered how I got there and maybe who I was with, and I made a firm resolution to not let it happen again.

Nowhere in my resolutions did I ever foresee the necessity to include waking up in bed with another woman. When my eyes opened, I rolled over on my side and there she was. Her newly styled hair with the blond highlights not cvcn mussed. She rustled under the covers and rolled from side to back, her eyes closed and her mouth grinning at the ceiling.

I lifted my sheet and peered down at my body. It was riddled with scratches, although they seemed to be healing. The scar below my breast was red and angry, proof that I wasn't following doctor's orders. I wasn't totally naked. Eileen had left my bra and panties on.

I slid out from under the sheets and located my clothes on a chair. They smelled like smoke, but I felt fresh. Had I showered last night? After dressing, I popped into Eileen's master bathroom and ran her brush through my hair. For the first time in a long time my hair fell perfectly into place and even bounced playfully against my face. And my face was radiant with what I can only relate to as the after-sex glow. Great, I thought. What had I done?

And why couldn't I remember anything?

It was nearly eight by my watch. I didn't know why Eileen was still home, and I didn't want to ask her at the moment. Maybe she was afraid to go to work after the ruckus the night before.

I slunk out of her apartment and found myself about a mile from home. Since I had no car, money, or purse, and I didn't know the connecting buses, I began walking. It gave me time to think. Why couldn't I remember anything at Eileen's? My last memory was of falling from the window at City Hall, and Eileen bending over me. Slowly a few more tidbits came to me. One of Eileen dragging me to her car parked at the side of the street and wanting to take me to the hospital. I remembered telling her I was okay. She insisted we go to her home so she could nurse me and make sure I was all right.

After fruitless attempts to remember how I got into her bed, my thoughts turned to the door between the offices of Commissioner Tuttle and City Auditor Bob Blaney. Why did they keep it a secret? Did The Jet use it to sneak down the back hallway the day Chris and his friend saw him go in and not come out? I was wondering where in the heck Chris had gotten to, when I turned the last corner and saw him sitting on the wooden steps at my front porch.

Then I saw what was left of my garage. It had burnt nearly to the ground. What was left of it was charred black. My sweet two-door sports car was a pile of molten plastic and metal. The smell of smoke lingered in the air, sending me into an immediate flashback of the prior day's events.

"Hi Billie." Chris's call brought me back to the present. He didn't make a move to get up as I approached. His head drooped a bit and he seemed to struggle just to meet my gaze.

"What happened to your garage?"

I sat next to him on the stoop. "Spontaneous combustion." I didn't want to scare him off again. "Must have been all those oil rags and gasoline cans I kept in there."

"That's too bad. It was a nice garage."

"Yeah. It had a nice car in it too. By the way, where's your new ride?"

"Ah, I decided against it. Too expensive." He motioned toward an old red Chevy pickup, rusting at the wheel wells and freckled with dents. "That's going to be my car for a while. Since I'm not going to take your money, I figured I'd better watch mine. The money I got from the city won't last long."

I nodded. I should have been happy he planned to follow through on his promise not to take my money, but I had too much on my mind. "Where have you been?"

"Here and there," he said. "Staying with friends. Trying to stay under the radar. Someone tried to kill me again yesterday."

"Oh? Tell me about it."

"I was down at the City Hall. My lawyer met me there and the lawyers had me sign some papers. When we were done I walked across the street and got a hot dog at one of those vending carts. Got me some sauerkraut on it with all the fixings."

"So far no one's tried to kill you," I said.

"I'm getting to it," Chris said. "I was sitting on a bench, eating my dog and I see one of those commissioners. What was his name, Turtle? No Tuttle, that's it. Anyway I see him talking to your assistant's new boyfriend. I wondered what the two of them could have in common."

I remembered that McGraw said Chris was at my house at noon yesterday, implying he might be responsible for the bomb. I wondered which of them was lying.

"Could you hear what they were talking about?"

"A little. The Commissioner dude . . ."

"Tuttle."

"Yeah, Tuttle. He's telling the guy in the T-shirt with the naked lady on his arm . . ."

"Earl."

"Okay. Well Turtle was telling the naked lady guy that he

didn't hire him to speculate about things. He had a job to do and as far as he could tell, this guy hadn't done shit."

"What did Earl said?"

"Something about *these things take time*. Then something about if he moves too fast he'll make people suspicious. I couldn't hear everything. Besides they caught me listening. They totally turned and stared at me at the same time. I knew I was busted so I thought I'd better move on. None of my business what they were arguing about anyway."

"So, who tried to kill you?" I asked.

"The naked lady guy, uh Earl. I was about six blocks away and he followed me and tried to run over me in a tow truck. A big one. I stepped off the curb and had to jump back. His back wheel ran over the curb."

"Is it possible that he was just turning, and you weren't watching where you were going?"

"No way. If I hadn't heard the truck's muffler stack roaring, he'd a flattened me."

I thought about the likelihood of Earl trying to run Chris down because he might have heard something in their conversation. I also considered the possibility that Chris might know something more than he was telling about Darrin's murder and The Jet. And although Earl may have spotted him downtown, I didn't believe he would try to kill him.

But what did I know about Earl? Not much. Angel liked him and she was usually a good judge of character. I knew that he was a P.I. who preferred to be thought of as a tow truck driver. I remembered Eileen said he had worked for Tuttle before. What was Tuttle involved in this time? From the conversation Chris overheard, it could be anything. Tuttle was anxious something be brought to a conclusion and Earl didn't want to break his cover. As a tow truck driver, a P.I., or an assassin? I wondered.

"Well, what about it?" Chris had been talking to me.

"Huh? What about what?"

"Hiding me out at your house for a couple of days. Someone wants me dead I tell you. I need a safe place."

"Why not?" I got up from the step. "Now that my brothers are gone I'm sure I've got a room you can use."

He stood up and followed me to the front door. I fumbled for my keys and unlocked it. Nine o'clock and Angel wasn't at work yet. We hadn't been busy lately anyway. When people around you start getting killed, word travels quickly through the grapevine.

Chris barely stepped through the doorway ahead of me when two marked squad cars squealed around the corner and pulled up abruptly on the curb in front of my house.

"What the hell's going on?" Chris cried. "Oh no. Are they after me? I haven't done nothing."

I was still in the doorway as Sgt. McGraw jumped out of the first squad car.

"Shut up and get up the stairs," I huffed in a whisper. "Bedroom to the right. They haven't seen you. Lock the door."

I heard him scuffling up the stairs, probably three at a time, as I smiled at the rapidly approaching McGraw and two jogging officers.

"Where the hell have you been?" McGraw growled. "Don't you ever answer your phone?"

I knew they weren't coming for Chris. I figured I was about to be arrested for breaking into City Hall the night before. Somehow they had evidence of my visit. Probably they already checked the security camera. I supposed it was too much to hope that Eileen's security guard friend might have found the video and accidently erased it.

"I spent the night at a friend's house. I just got home," I said.

McGraw didn't read me my rights. Instead he seemed concerned.

"We've been trying to get hold of you since early this morning. We found out who killed your brother."

"That's great. Who is it?"

"We'd better go inside. We haven't arrested him yet and you might be in danger until we do."

"But . . ."

"Inside! Now!" McGraw pushed me back off the porch and through the front door. The other two cops brushed by us and started searching the house."

"What are you doing?" I asked as the three of them drew their guns.

"No one down here," one of the cops said. "Let's check upstairs."

"Wait," I said. "There's no one here. I just unlocked the front door."

"Have to be careful," McGraw said.

I sweated it out as the two cops frisked the upstairs. Finally one of them yelled from the top of the stairway.

"There's one room locked."

I glanced up to see both of them pointing their guns at the door and figured Chris was probably peeing his pants on the other side.

"That's a storeroom full of junk," I said. "I lost the key a couple years ago."

"We'll have to break it down," McGraw said.

"Like hell you will," I said. "I'm not going to have you busting up my house. I can't afford it. I'm out of work, my garage blew up, my car's gone and I'm not sure my insurance will cover any of it because it's related to one of my cases. Unless you have a warrant, you'd better leave that door alone."

McGraw, gun drawn, looked disappointed. "Well, I guess that's that."

"Good. Now you can tell me who killed my brother."

"You'd better sit down," he said, pointing to the settee in the waiting area.

"I don't need to sit. Just tell me the name of the asshole who killed my brother, and I'll go and get him myself."

"It's Steve." McGraw offered a wry smile.

“Steve who?” My mind was numb and it didn’t get through.

“Steve, your ex-partner.”

He caught me as I slumped and guided me onto the settee. A loud ringing in my ears made it hard for me to hear his words.

“Steve? You’re crazy,” I heard myself saying.

But even as the words left my lips I knew it wasn’t really that crazy. In fact, it made a lot of sense. Richards told me he thought I was a bitch. Of course he admitted it when I confronted him, but said it was in the past. Why then, did he remain so distant throughout the investigation?

“It may sound crazy,” McGraw said. “But we got a tip the gun used to kill your brother was in the trunk of his car. We checked it a couple hours ago and found a sniper’s rifle hidden where the spare tire would be under the trunk carpet. Ballistics already matched the rifle with a bullet taken from Officer Bly’s body. They’re pretty sure it’s going to match the bullet taken from the little guy’s body at the park too.”

“There’s got to be some mistake,” I said.

“Steve was in the general area of Cathedral Park when The Jet was killed. We think Steve silenced him so he wouldn’t finger him as the one who hired him.”

“But he couldn’t have killed Darrin. He was with me at the hospital . . .” The words barely exited my mouth when I realized my error.

“He left you to get his car in the parking structure where the shots originated. We had men inside the structure and they would have seen anyone out of the ordinary. But it would be a simple thing for him to pull a rifle from his trunk to finish what The Jet started. Only he missed and killed your brother. But he didn’t panic. All he had to do was put the rifle back in his trunk and speed down to the crime scene. No one would suspect a fellow cop.”

My head reeled and my gut felt like it had been slammed with a sledge hammer. I didn’t want to believe any of this, but it rang true. Steve put himself in a perfect position to do everything

McGraw claimed and more. Could he have done it?

I hung my head, remembering the day at the funeral home when I surprised him and Dan. Steve was upset with me at first. He went outside to cool off, and I saw him talking on his cell phone. On the way home The Jet and his buddies tried to gun me down. I had wondered how they found me. The Jet had to be tipped off and the only two people who knew I was at the mortuary were Steve and Dan. And Steve made those damn phone calls outside while Dan and I did the paperwork inside.

I gazed into McGraw's knowing eyes and he nodded.

"I know it's hard to believe," he said. "It's getting to where you can't trust anybody."

My face flushed and I felt the rage building inside. The Jet said the same thing just before he died.

"Where is he?" I said.

"Don't know. We showed up with a search warrant at his house at five a.m. this morning. His car was there, but he wasn't. Someone must have tipped him."

"He left his car behind with the murder weapon in it?" I said. "That's pretty dumb."

McGraw shrugged. "Maybe he got a ride with someone else before we showed up, or we spooked him and he snuck out before we hit the door."

"So you have no idea where he is?"

"Not yet. We'll find him."

"You thought he might be here?"

"Not really," McGraw said. "He knows this is the first place we'd check. Listen, I'm going to leave the two officers here to watch over you. They won't be here long. I expect we'll have him in custody in the next eight hours. Still, we want you to be safe."

"Do you? Or do you want to keep me from going after him?"

"Give us a whack at him first. You don't want to go to jail for a cop killer. Let us handle it legal-like. Okay?"

I nodded. "I'll give you eight hours. No promises after that.

And the brothers can stay outside and watch the front and back doors."

"Fair enough," he said, and motioned the boys in blue outside. "But if you hear from him, call me right away." He gave me his cop card and I nodded.

After they left I walked gingerly up the stairs. My body ached from the fall the night before and my head throbbed. At the top of the landing, I paused and peeked over my shoulder to the front door to make sure no one was watching through the lead-glass window. I groaned and walked to the locked bedroom door and rapped lightly with my knuckles.

"Chris? It's me. It's okay, they're gone. You can come out."

I waited for a minute, wondering if he had slipped out the bedroom window. Then I heard a faint rustling behind the door. A weak voice said, "Billie?"

"Yes. Open up." The latch clicked, the door creaked open and Chris's white face peered out."

"Hey it's okay. I wouldn't have let them get you. Besides they weren't after you anyway."

"They want your ex-partner," he said. His voice trembled and his lower lip quivered.

"How did you know? Could you hear us from up here?"

"No," he said, opening the door. "I found him."

Standing behind Chris with a gun jammed in the small of his back, stood the man whom McGraw said murdered my brother.

"Hi Billie," Steve said with a crooked smile. "Sorry to show up unannounced. I needed a place to lie low for a while."

And me without my gun.

Chapter 24

"What the hell's going on?" I said.

We were downstairs and Steve had lowered his gun now that the cops were outside. He stood at an angle to the window where he could watch the patrolmen.

"I dunno," he said. "I couldn't sleep much last night and then I heard a noise outside my house this morning. I went to the window and squad cars were lining up down the street. I turned on my scanner and the dumb asses were organizing my takedown on the radio. They must have thought I was asleep. Anyway, I heard them saying I was wanted in your brother's murder. After I threw up, I got the hell out of there."

"McGraw told me they found a sniper rifle in the trunk of your car," I said.

"Impossible. It's a frame up."

"All the cons in stir say they're innocent too," Chris said, apparently feeling braver since Steve holstered his gun.

I gave Chris a dirty look. "McGraw presented a pretty solid case."

I told Steve about the anonymous call, about the gun hidden in his car, his proximity to each shooting, and the police theory he was trying to silence The Jet before he could talk. Steve just sat and listened, occasionally nodding his head, as I presented the prosecution's case.

"It's not true. Not one word of it," he said. "I wouldn't harm a hair on your head, Billie. I couldn't because I . . ."

"Are you all right?" I saw a single tear in the corner of his eye.

"Yeah. I couldn't hurt you." He wiped the emotion off with the back of his hand. "Hell, I've been in love with you almost since the first day we partnered."

"What?"

"He's dishing you a load of crap," Chris said. "Don't believe him. He's in a jam and he's trying to butter you up."

Normally Steve would have gone for the jugular on a mouthy perp, but he just sat there like he was in shock.

"Shut up, Chris," I said. "How can you say you love me when you've gone out of your way to avoid me ever since I left the force? Even since Darrin's death, you've basically abandoned me when I needed you the most."

"I haven't abandoned you. I've been working on this case day and night trying to find Darrin's killer."

"A phone call once in a while would have been nice."

"What would I say? We're like oil and water. Every time we get together one of us blows up. I figured any relationship between us was doomed from the start."

"You big moron. The reason I always get so damn upset with you is because you won't give me the time of day. If you'd ever let me know you cared, I would probably have melted in your arms."

"Really?"

"Well, maybe. I don't know. We've never gotten that far."

He stood up and walked over to me and draped his arms loosely around my waist. "I *do* care for you."

"I care for you too," I said, enjoying his soft brown eyes.

"Yuck!" Chris said, and turned away.

Steve bent over me and touched my lips with his. We embraced and kissed softly for what seemed like an eternity. When we broke for air, I smiled and took in the moment before I spotted something shiny on a nearby table. I took his hands in mine, smiled, spun him around, reached the nickel-coated bracelets, and handcuffed his hands behind his back. It happened so fast it even surprised me.

"Yeah. Way to go, Billie." Chris turned back toward our brief scuffle. "I thought you were buying his sob story."

I took Steve's gun from his shoulder holster and stepped backwards.

"What the hell? What are you doing?" he said.

"Making a citizen's arrest."

"What about all the bullshit about how you loved me."

"I said I care for you." No sense in committing too much this early in a relationship. We just got to first base.

"If you turn me in before I can clear my name, I'm dead meat."

"You wait until you're in a real jam and say you need my help, and oh by the way, you're suddenly in love with me. And I'm supposed to believe you? I'm sorry, I don't think I can."

"But Billie. . ."

"Besides, it's safer for you to be in custody. You're liable to be killed out on the street by some revenge-minded cop."

"I didn't kill Darrin," he said. "I'm telling you it's all a mistake. And I won't be treated with kid gloves once they get me downtown."

"I'll have a talk with the arresting officer."

And that was that. I closed my heart, denied the ache inside me, and called McGraw on my cell.

I decided I needed clarity and a break from all the recent drama. Something about this whole business didn't feel right and there was too much stress floating around in my head. So after McGraw hauled Steve off as a startled Angel and Earl arrived, with a high-fiving Chris yelling in my ear, I had asked Angel to book me on a flight to Pocatello to visit the Fleming ancestral home.

The smallish recently remodeled Pocatello airport lay on the western outskirts of the city along the winding Snake River. We descended across a reservoir and touched down on an abbreviated landing strip. The sky was blue, but there was a chill in the late afternoon breeze as I walked to the rental car. It came with a GPS unit, and I spent ten minutes trying to enter the address of the Pocatello City Hall.

I pulled up fifteen minutes later alongside a dreary building painted in three horizontal stripes of brown tones. The building was cheerier inside, with lemon and lime flavored walls. I wandered down the hall to glass doors with a city emblem.

A tall, thin, middle-aged woman with a '70's bouffant black hairstyle and eyeglasses the size of pickle jar lids, sauntered across the medium-sized office with a stack of file folders in her arms. I must have startled her because the folders slipped through her fingers as she turned her head and her folders sprawled across the floor.

"Oh, I'm sorry," I said.

She huffed deeply from the floor: "What do you have to be sorry for, Dear?"

"I think I scared you."

"I drop stuff like this three or four times a day. I'm supposed to be the city clerk, but since the layoffs I'm about the only one here most of the day. Sarah comes in from two-to-five on Mondays and Fridays."

In an artful scoop, she gathered the folders from the brown linoleum floor and stacked them on one of the three desks in the office. Then she walked over to the front counter and winked at me.

"What can I do for you, Honey?"

I showed her my ID and told her I was investigating the deaths of Mr. and Mrs. Fleming.

"Oh my God," she said. "Mr. Fleming's dead? And his wife too?" She took two steps back and plopped on a desktop. "Was it a car accident?"

"They were both murdered."

She shook her head. The pickle jar glasses highlighted her olive irises as her eyes widened.

"*Murdered?* How awful. The poor man has had more than his share of bad luck."

"Can you tell me about it? The bad luck?"

"Well I shouldn't say anything about any employees, past or present," she said. "But poor Mr. Fleming got such a raw deal and now he's dead. Somebody's got to know he was a nice guy."

"What do you mean?"

"He worked here for years and one day he was accused of embezzling from the city. He would never do such a thing and they never found the money—oh they discovered a couple extra thousand in his savings he couldn't account for—but he didn't have the $500,000 they said was missing."

She leaned back on the desk and shook her head, as if in deep thought.

"What happened?" I asked.

"Well, the city auditor found some irregularities in his bookkeeping and notified the city council. The auditor's report showed funds were transferred to bank accounts under a phony name which he says he traced back to poor Mr. Fleming."

"What happened to the rest of the money?"

"Nobody knows. Still, the prosecutor had enough of a case to get him seven years in the Idaho State Pen. I heard he got off for good behavior a few years ago and was back in Pocatello. I haven't run into him though."

"Could I talk to his supervisor?"

"Ben Miller? He died suddenly a year after Mr. Fleming was sentenced. Heart attack."

"Mmm. Too bad. What about the city auditor? Is he around?"

"Robert Paul left for greener pastures a couple years ago. He left a forwarding address in New York City. Think I got it somewhere."

She walked over to a gray steel filing cabinet and opened the bottom drawer. “Here it is.” She wrote the name, address, and phone number down on a scrap paper and handed it to me. “Don’t tell him where you got it.” She winked again.

“Is there anyone else around here who knew Mr. Fleming and might be able to answer some questions?”

“Doubt it. He was one of those studious types, you know. Kept to himself a lot. Never saw him around town with anyone but his wife. You might talk to his mother. She lives over in Chubbuck.”

I got the number and called Mrs. Delilah Fleming. Five minutes later I pulled up to a 50’s ranch-style track home with brown grass and myriad weeds. Delilah Fleming answered the door in a green paisley housecoat. A cigarette hung precariously from her lip as she pushed the screen door open.

“You Missus Bly?” Her voice cracked and sad eyes peered at me through a wrinkled face.

“Miss Bly,” I said. “I’m not married.”

“That’s okay, Sweetie. You still got time.” She chuckled. “Come on in.”

Like the little bit of Pocatello I’d seen so far, the furniture was left over from the seventies. Her carpet was green shag and the wallpaper peeled some. If Art Fleming stole money from the city, she never saw any of it.

“I’m investigating your son’s death,” I said.

“I understand.” She stubbed out her cigarette in an overflowing ashtray. Tears welled up in her blue eyes, and she wiped her face with the sleeve of her housecoat. “Sorry. I knew something bad had happened to him, but when I finally got the news from the cops . . . well, it didn’t make it any easier.”

“Uh, I’m afraid I have more bad news, Delilah. Your daughter-in-law was found dead in her motel room last night. Foul play is suspected.”

Tears streamed down her face. “Stella, dead? Oh my. Is the world coming to an end? How did it happen?”

“The police are treating it as a suicide, but they are also

looking at it as a possible murder." Well, I was anyway.

"Who would possibly want to murder Stella?" She quieted for a moment, taking it all in.

"It must have something to do with the money stolen from the city. Art said he was innocent and I wanted to believe him. I mean, I did believe him, but there was always a little bit of doubt. After he got out of jail, he was obsessive about proving his innocence. But everyone involved in the case was gone. He was able to start his own insurance agency, but he didn't do too well. Stella told me he spent most of his time on the job trying to track down the city auditor back in New York somewhere."

"Did Art ever reach him?" I asked.

"He told Stella he left a couple of messages and suddenly the number was no good any longer."

"Sounds like Mr. Paul didn't want to be found."

"I guess. Art hired a private eye, but the guy didn't find anything, and Art couldn't afford to keep paying him."

"Why did your son go to Portland?"

"He had a convention to go to. He called me from the hotel the night he arrived and that's the last I ever heard from him."

She started sobbing again and I waited.

"Did he say anything about his plans when he called?" I asked.

"He said he had a dinner date with an old friend he had run into and that maybe his luck was about to change. I asked him what he meant, and he told it was a secret. He'd explain it to me when he got home. He sounded excited."

"Did he happen to mention this old friend's name?"

She sighed. "No. Just an old friend."

"Would you know many of his friends?"

"He didn't have many after he went to jail. There's a few old high school buddies, a few women he dated before he met Stella. I think I could remember some of them."

She took about half an hour writing names down--mostly after going through Art's high school yearbook, which she had kept all these years. There were only ten names, six men and four women. Most of them dated back to high school. None were familiar to me.

"What about the city auditor, Robert Paul? Was he a friend of Art's?"

"Not anymore. I mean they used to golf together for a while, but about a year before Art was arrested something came between them. I think Mr. Paul was having an affair with some married woman and Art thought that was wrong."

"Do you remember her name?"

"I don't think Art ever mentioned it. He seemed embarrassed about it. Stella might have known, but I just don't remember."

I thanked Delilah for her help and promised to let her know if I found out anything further about her son's and daughter-in-law's deaths. I took the list of names and added Robert Paul and even the supposedly deceased Ben Miller to it. I wanted to have Angel check to see if any of the names now lived in the Portland area. Something about Art Fleming's imprisonment seemed fishy to me, and I wasn't going to take anything at face value. Delilah Fleming promised to call me if she thought of any other of Art's friends.

I stopped at a little Philly cheese steak sandwich place in downtown Pocatello and contemplated who else I might be able to talk with and came up empty. *The Idaho State Journal* newspaper offices were across the street so I decided to research the infamous theft from the city of Pocatello.

A helpful receptionist walked me into a back room with a computer and showed me how to research their articles on-line. I spent an hour and came up with several computerized versions of the news events: *City Auditor Accuses Investment Officer of Embezzling $500,000; Fleming Indicted for Embezzlement, Claims Innocence; Auditor Says Money Gone; Fleming Turns Down Plea Agreement; Jury Convicts Fleming, Sentencing Tomorrow; Fleming Gets Seven Years.*

The stories were long and tediously accurate, but something seemed to be missing. I swirled around in my chair and saw a wall of bound newspapers with notations on them. I found one dated the month of the trial and pulled out the oversized bound volume. It didn't take long to find what was missing from the online stories.

The hard copy pages had more pictures. And on page one with a banner story of *City Auditor Office Accuses Investment Officer of Embezzlement,* was a picture of Ben Miller. I stared at the picture and shook my head. I hoped I might recognize Art Fleming's supervisor as a Portland official. The mug staring back at me, with a mole above his lip and weasel-like dark eyes, bore no resemblance to anyone I knew.

I searched through the stories hoping to find more pictures of the players in the city's scandal. The two main players were city auditor Robert Paul and Miller. I found one other photo of Miller, but none of Paul. I did a search of Miller's name in the newspaper files, thinking I might learn something about him that would be helpful and turned up nothing.

I had hoped to find a fresh lead on the Fleming murders and had nothing to show for it except upsetting a grieving mother and flushing three hundred dollars down the drain for airfare and a four-hour car rental.

I tried to enjoy the ten-minute drive out to the airport, slowing to admire a clump of mountains which surrounded the city and nearby valley. The scenery was ruined by a stiff breeze carrying the odor of rotten eggs. A few minutes later I found the awful smell's origin, a J. R. Simplot potato processing plant. It seemed to sum up my entire trip.

Chapter 25

I arrived home in time for dinner. I was grouchy and tired and not much in the mood for what greeted me. Dan met me at the door and took my briefcase. Loud voices boomed from the dining room, and I turned the corner to see a family dinner in progress. Seated at the table were Jason, Dag, Angel, Chris and Earl. Dan pulled out an empty chair for me and I slid in.

"You're just in time," he said, "Angel cooked spaghetti and meatballs."

Angel passed a plate of spaghetti to me and everyone wanted to know where I'd been and what I learned. I covered the trip with them right up to my discovery of the J.R. Simplot plant. Then I filled them in on my midnight visit to City Hall the previous night. Dan and Dag shook their heads at me and tried to cover their grins with their hands.

"That poor Eileen called for you," Angel said. "She's worried you might be upset with her and wanted me to have you call her as soon as you got back."

My face flushed as memories returned of waking up in bed practically naked next to her.

"I'll call her later," I said, without much conviction.

"Steve's going to be arraigned tomorrow afternoon," Dag said. "The prosecutor must feel pretty confident."

"Why so fast?" I said. "I figured they would sit on him for a couple of days and shore up their case."

"I heard Mayor Clemons is pushing it," Dag said. "He's under a lot of pressure from the public and the police union to find Darrin's killer."

"I have a hard time believing Steve could have become a serial killer just for revenge against me."

"Stranger things have happened," Jason said. "A woman up in Oregon City shot a guy in Dunkin Donuts because she thought he swiped one of her maple bars."

"If it was a jelly-filled donut, I could understand," I said.

"Yeah, but the donut was from his own bag. Her bag was on the other side of her on the counter," Jason said.

"Case of mistaken identity," Dag said.

"How many years did she get?" Angel asked. "Bet she got a baker's dozen."

The jokes got considerably worse as I attacked my meatballs and once I think I snorted a spaghetti noodle through my nose or at least if felt that way. After things settled down, I told everyone what Steve had said about being framed before I cuffed him, managing to leave out *the kiss*.

"Sounds like someone's got it in for him," Jason said. "They must have had him in their sights for a little while."

"You got any theories about who else might be after you?" Dan asked me.

"I've got plenty of theories. The problem is keeping the players straight while I investigate four murders."

"Four?" Dan said.

"Yeah. Darrin, The Jet, and Stella and Art Fleming. As much as I hate to say it, Steve is a good fit for the murder of Darrin and The Jet and at least one attempt on me. I keep wondering why Steve slowed down, allowing The Jet to pull alongside and shoot at me."

Dan tapped his fork nervously on his dinner plate. "I've known Steve for quite a few years and he's always been a straight arrow. I can't see him straying now."

"I know, but remember how he stepped outside for a few moments at the funeral home. I saw him make some calls on his cell. By the time we left, we had picked up The Jet as a tail. How did he know where I was?"

"I don't know, but . . ."

"And just before The Jet was iced at Cathedral Park, he told me his handler was a cop and I shouldn't trust anybody."

Jason whistled. "Man, that's heavy stuff. You sure about this?"

"Ask Chris. He was there."

All eyes turned to Chris, who was slumped in his chair, hiding behind two large meatballs heaped on a mound of uneaten spaghetti.

"I, uh, it's like she said. A cop was involved. I don't want to talk about it."

Chris appeared agitated and nervous as we talked, and he wasn't eating. I realized he was avoiding Earl's glance and slapped my hand to my forehead.

"I forgot. Earl, Chris thinks you tried to kill him."

Earl sucked a noodle into his mouth. "What are you talking about?"

"You tried to kill me." Chris's spine stiffened I could tell he was trying to be brave.

"He said he saw you talking with Commissioner Tuttle downtown near the hot dog stand." I nodded at Chris.

"He's wrong," Earl said flatly. "He must have me mixed up with someone else."

"I don't know. He gave me a pretty good description right down to your naked lady tattoo."

"The naked lady man," Chris stammered.

"I *was* down there yesterday, but I didn't see Commissioner Tuttle," Earl said.

"Chris said he heard Tuttle say he hired you to work on a case," I said. "I know you have a private investigator's license. Eileen told me. I also learned that you worked for Tuttle once before a few years back on an elections violation case."

"Okay, I talked with him," Earl said. "But I can't tell you about what. It's confidential."

"I can understand that. It must be difficult working under a man like Tuttle, who wants results now and is trying to undermine your cover. I mean if you were to be too overt the person you were investigating might become suspicious."

I stopped short of telling Earl he was investigating me.

"Listen, I don't know what that creep told you, but it's a bunch of bull," he said in a low voice. "I'm working a case, but it's not related to you. I promise."

I watched Chris. His eyes seemed to plead with me and he glanced back at Earl, who seemed unperturbed. I was about to say something when Angel spoke up.

"Earl Monroe Thompson! Are you courting me just to get inside information about Billie?"

"No, I swear," he said. "Don't jump to conclusions. I'm dating you because I like you."

"Eileen said you dated her to find out information about an investigation," I said.

Angel jumped up from the table muttering under her breath. She was crying, and I felt like a heel. She had asked the question I was dying to ask, but couldn't without her hating me. As it was, she'd probably hate me anyway.

Earl started to get up to follow her, but Dan grabbed his arm.

"Sit down," he said. "It won't do any good. She just needs to get it out of her system. Maybe tomorrow."

Earl sat down shaking his head. "You've got it all twisted up, and I can't tell you what I'm doing. I'm certain it has nothing to do with Billie."

"Then can you explain why after Chris saw you and Tuttle talking, not ten minutes later you tried to run him down in your tow truck?" I asked.

"Are you kidding?" Dag said. "When?"

"Yesterday around lunch time," Chris said. "I just stepped off the curb and this naked lady's man came around real fast and tried to run me over."

"Ridiculous," Earl said.

"It's true. I heard you coming and jumped back. Your exhaust roared when your truck jumped up on the curb and nearly killed me."

Earl started to say something and stopped short. "Where did this happen?"

"Fourth and Madison," I said.

"I—I got a call to pick up a car over in East Portland, and I had an appointment with a client in an hour. I was in a hurry to make the tow, drop it off and make my appointment. I remember hitting that curb. But I didn't see you there; my mind was miles away. I'm sorry, man."

"I saw you both look at me," Chris said. "You knew I was listening in. You were trying to kill me."

"Hey, I remember you now. I saw you coming out of the Mayor's office when I stopped off to meet Tuttle."

"I was signing papers with the Mayor and the lawyers," Chris said.

"I didn't see any lawyers. I saw you and Mayor Clemons come out into the lobby alone. He was patting you on the back and telling you something about doing a good service to the city or some crap like that."

"I was signing papers for my lawsuit."

"Billie, did you ever consider maybe Chris, here, has been acting as a mole for Mayor Clemons? Doesn't Clemons have a feather up his butt about you?"

"What?" Chris said. No. I . . ."

"I'll bet Clemons has him following you around to spy and report back," Earl said. "Is that what you've been doing, creep?"

"No. She's hiding me out because someone is trying to kill me. *You* are trying to kill me."

Chris got up and started to leave. He hesitated and returned for his untouched plate of spaghetti, a fork and napkin, and scurried up the stairs to his bedroom.

"Boy, you sure can empty a room," Jason said to Earl.

"I tell you, I'm on your side," Earl said. "But you'd better watch that guy. I'll bet he's stooging for the Mayor. In fact, I'll prove he is."

Earl stabbed a meatball, jammed it in his mouth and marched out the front door.

"Angel sure is a good cook," Dag said. "Did you notice how everyone wants to take their dinner to go?"

"Who else have we got as suspects?" Dan asked.

"Now I guess we have to add Chris to the list," I said. "There's the Mayor, who hates my guts, and he seems to have Gloria working for him to keep me in line. Commissioner Tuttle may be involved now because he's obviously hooked up with Earl somehow."

"You think Earl is a suspect?" Dag said.

"I have for a long time," I said. "I just don't trust a man who dates two women at the same time. In the beginning, I thought he was just a louse. Then Eileen tells me he's a P.I., and he seems to have this knack for inserting himself into my investigations. Hell, who knows what Angel's been telling him. Now it's this thing with Chris. I don't think Earl was trying to kill Chris, but Chris's observations certainly struck a sore spot with him."

"Jeeze, you're painting a conspiracy here," Dan said.

"And The Jet said his handler was a cop. Earl looks like a cop, don't you think? I mean if he changed out of that T-shirt."

"He looks ex-military and he has a lot of confidence in himself," Jason said, "so yeah, he could pass for a cop."

I forked the last wad of spaghetti into my mouth and talked around it. "The only other cop I can think of is Steve. Do you think any cops on the investigative team might be jaded?"

"I know most of them personally," Dan said, "I doubt it. I don't know McGraw well, but he has a lot of ambition so I can't see him mucked up in anything which could jeopardize his career. I'll ask around. See if I can pick up on anything suspicious."

"Wasn't Steve the first one on the scene when your garage blew up?" Dag said.

"I thought about that," I said. "Earl conveniently appeared too. And Officer McGraw showed up a few minutes later and said he'd seen Chris hanging about when he drove by earlier to check on my safety."

"They all had a chance to place the bomb," Dan said.

"The one thing that continues to eat at me," I said, "is when The Jet go into Blaney's office and how did he know to exit through the secret door in Tuttle's office?"

"You said he was looking for a clue as to who hired him," Dag said. "He also went into Mayor Clemons' office. Maybe he was looking for blackmail material and stumbled onto the door like you did. If he hadn't been paid, he probably wanted some leverage."

"I hadn't thought of that," I said. "Crap, it's too late to find out now. After sounding the general alarm at my break-in last night, they're probably waiting for me to try something stupid again."

The next day started out bad and never got better. Angel stayed the night because as she said "my ride went home" and although she said she didn't blame me, I seemed to be getting the cold shoulder. Chris and I got into an argument over what Earl suggested about him informing to the Mayor, and he stormed out of the house.

Angel settled into her work demeanor so I gave her the list of names of Art's friends Delilah Fleming had given me and asked her to see if she could find any of them living in Portland. To the list I added Robert Paul. It was a hunch which already hadn't panned out, but I gave her Paul's last known address and phone number in New York and asked her to run him to ground if he was living in Portland.

I asked her to track down Bob and Gloria Blaney's home address. It was about nine in the morning, and I was willing to bet Gloria was a night person and probably just waking up. I gave Angel my itinerary and told her to call me right away if she turned up any of the names in Portland.

At the last minute, I decided to add my green blazer to matching slacks and white blouse. I checked my makeup, removed my lip gloss and added a magenta shade of lipstick. My hair was fly-away so I added some hair spray. I hoped I might catch Gloria in her housecoat and maybe for once she would be the frumpy one.

I found a matching green purse but it was too small for my gun. I took off my blazer, strapped on a shoulder holster and gun and donned the jacket again. By the time my taxi pulled up to her Laurelhurst home 40 minutes had elapsed. I thought I saw her through a dining room window drinking coffee as we pulled up so I paid the cab driver and knocked at the door. I waited and knocked again and there still was no answer. I was sure I saw someone through the window. She must be home, I thought.

There was a doorbell so I pushed and held it tight. A not too pleasant melody chimed throughout the house. Three minutes later the door opened and there stood Gloria in a powder blue dress, hiked distastefully above her knees, perfectly coiffed black hair, lipstick three shades redder than mine, killer high heels and killer legs. I almost gagged at my luck.

"Are you the one making all the racket? I didn't hear you from the bathroom. I was just putting the finishing touches on my face. Oh, dear. You have a smudge on yours."

She whipped out a dainty kerchief from nowhere and wiped the edge of my lip. "There that's somewhat better; no, it isn't. You should check it yourself."

I opened my purse, still standing at the front door, and checked my face in my compact. The witch had smeared lipstick from my lips to my cheek. I grabbed the handkerchief from her and dabbed off as much as would come willingly.

"I wondered if we might talk for a few minutes?" I said. "I have a few questions I'd like to ask you."

"I'm afraid not, Dear. I have an appointment with the dentist in twenty minutes. Then, I'm meeting friends for brunch, I have some volunteer duties at the hospital, and several appointments during the day. You should really should have called ahead, you know."

"I was just wondering about your little affair with Mayor Clemons."

"Affair? Why we're just good friends. Actually I've known him for years. We went to school together at the University of Oregon. He, Bob and I spend a lot of time together since Bob started working for the city."

"Bob was appointed by the Mayor when the former city auditor abruptly resigned mid-term, wasn't he?"

"Listen, Honey, I simply don't have time. If you want to have a talk with me, the earliest I could fit you in would be this evening."

"When?"

"Bob and I are going to meet at Finnegan's along the Willamette River for a late dinner at eight-thirty. We could have drinks there at eight. Does that work for you?"

"I guess it will have to."

"You know where it is?"

"On Swan Island, in the Industrial district. I've been there."

"Oh, here's my cab. I'd offer you a ride but I'm going in the opposite direction."

Before I had a chance to ask her what direction she was heading, she tucked her purse under her arm, closed the door behind her and swept past me down the steps to the cab. I fumbled through my purse for my cell phone and realized it had burned up in the fire.

Damn, I've got to get a car, I thought, and walked three blocks to Glisan Street to catch the next bus downtown, cursing the tramp,

Gloria, all the way. I felt we were heading for a showdown, and I wanted to make sure I had plenty of ammunition before I tangled with her again.

Chapter 26

I'd gone about twenty blocks on the bus when I remembered Honest Hal and his car lot on Northeast 21st and Sandy Boulevard, and I hopped off of the bus at the next stop. Glisan Street intersects Sandy at Northeast 20th, so I only had to walk a block.

Hal deals in previously owned cars, and he has a liberal trade-in policy and easy credit. He was a former client of mine who got into hot water with the law when he bought a fleet of previously owned cars the previous owners were still looking for.

His story about having received ownership papers from a man who represented himself as a legitimate auto broker fell on deaf ears with the cops because of the forged documents. The broker disappeared, of course, and all the contact information Hal had on the man turned out to be bogus. It took me about a week to follow a cold trail leading to the missing broker.

Hal was so appreciative he offered me a lifetime purchase special: at cost. Today I was going to take him up on it. I walked onto the lot with red flags flowing overhead, balloons on car antennas and prices marked with soap on the windshields. Most of the cars were late nineties models, a few older and a few newer.

"As I live and breathe, it's Billie Bly," a voice echoed over the highway traffic on Sandy Boulevard. "I thought you were dead and buried."

I turned and saw the tall, slim car dealer walking toward me, dressed in chinos, a white linen shirt, and bolo tie with a turquoise stone, his feathery red hair flowing in the wind. He shook my hand with both of his and displayed a gap between his two front teeth.

"Good to see you," he said. His greeting turned into a bear hug, and he slapped me on the sides of my shoulders. "I thought sure you were dead for a while. Sent you flowers when you were in the hospital."

Honest Hal was just that. Honest and always sincere and compassionate. I never understood how he could be successful in the used car business.

"I came to shop for a car," I said.

"Got a trade in?"

"No."

"What happened to that cute little Miata?"

"It got blown up," I said.

"Ouch. You've had that for a long time."

"Seven years. I called her Betsy."

"I got just what you're looking for," Hal said, and walked me over to a Smart Car, a white two-seater, with New Jersey Police insignias on the doors.

"They bought five as a trial for local malls and decided it wasn't a good fit."

"It's really small," I said. "How fast does it go?"

"Seventy-miles-per-hour is top speed listed by the manufacturer, but these police specials will do eighty-five. How about it? It's cute, it's hip, and it's you."

"I don't think so," I said. "It would draw too much attention. Not a good idea if I'm tailing someone or on a stakeout."

"I can have it painted a dull color. Price is eighteen thousand, you can have it for fifteen."

"That's cost? Maybe I'd better look around some more."

"This car is hot right now. If I wanted to wait a while, I might get twenty-five grand, which is about what it cost new."

I walked down the line of cars and stopped at a cute red older sports car with a full sun roof. It was British and low to the ground, the red paint impeccable, new tires, and leather seats.

"I thought you wanted to blend in," Hal said.

"I can't help it. I have a thing for smaller, sporty, red cars."

"I just picked it up last week," Hal said. "It's a '73 MGB GT. Has a rebuilt engine, the works. Wife lost her husband to cancer and couldn't bear to see it sitting in the garage. He spent years restoring it. She said it's a pity people can't be given new life like cars."

"What did you say? People can't be brought back from the dead? I wonder."

"It's listed at eighty-five hundred. I paid four thousand below book for it because she just wanted to unload it. You can have it for six thousand."

I reminded him of our lifetime agreement and he let me have it for five thousand. I wrote a check on my credit union's line-of-credit account after test-driving the spiffy little red demon and promptly nicknamed her Myrtle. She had plenty of power and performed even better when I shifted gears smoothly.

I took Myrtle up to Washington Park and put her through her paces on the winding curves above the Rose Gardens. By the time I arrived downtown it was noon. I plugged a meter on Southwest Fourth and walked along the park block to the hot dog stand where Chris spotted Tuttle and Earl.

I ordered a dog with onions and relish and noticed Tuttle, sitting on a park bench, apparently deep in thought as I slid down next to him.

"Hello," I said.

"Hi," he said amiably, not looking up at me.

"You come here often?"

"Huh, yeah. Three or four times a week. I love their polish dogs."

"They are pretty good," I agreed.

He glanced up from his meal. "Oh it's you. It's been a while since I've seen you, except at the funeral."

"Yeah, I noticed I never got a visit in the hospital."

"Believe it or not, I meant to," he said. "But with campaigning and homeland security drills I lost track of the time."

'That's okay. I wasn't exactly your favorite person."

"The lawsuit, you mean. Nah, that was just business. I thought it was pretty funny when I heard what you did to that guy in the revolving door--until he sued the city."

"I didn't see it coming either," I said.

"You got a bad break. A couple of bad breaks, including your brother. How are you holding up?"

"I'm hanging on by a hair, Commissioner. The only thing keeping me going is the thought of finding Darrin's killer."

"But I thought they caught him. Isn't it Steve Thomas—your former partner? He's going to be arraigned this afternoon I understand."

"In two hours," I said.

"Are you going to attend?"

"Maybe. I've got a busy day lined up."

"Then let's not waste time," he said, taking another bite from his dog. "What's on your mind?"

"What do you think is on my mind?" I said.

"I have no idea. Something to do with your brother's death, I would guess. Sounds like you aren't convinced Thomas did it."

"I'm not sure about it. I want to think he didn't do it, but the case against him seems pretty convincing. What do you think?"

Tuttle took another bite and chewed for a while.

"Something's off kilter. There's a strange vibe in the air around City Hall these days. Weird things are happening. People seem not to be themselves. The Mayor is crankier day after day and more stubborn. We've had office break-ins, nobody's talking to anyone, and . . . well I'd better just leave it at that."

"Can you tell me about the break-ins?" I asked.

He looked over his shoulder and back at me.

"Last week someone broke into my office and rifled through

it," he said. "And a few nights ago someone broke into Bob Blaney's office and apparently escaped through the exit in my office."

"Was anything taken during the first break-in?"

"I can only speak for myself," he said. "Some drawers were open and papers moved around on my desk, but nothing was missing."

"Was that what you and Blaney argued about last week?"

"How--?"

"I've got sources."

"Whoever it was, first came through an interconnecting door between our offices. Then it happened again a few nights ago. The thing is, the door was kind of a secret. It was covered by wallpaper and blocked by a Japanese folding screen and my bookcase. No one knew about it except Bob and me. It used to be our private little joke. One of us would get silly or tired at the end of the day and visit each other."

"Why did you two argue?"

"It's a lot of things. I accused him of searching my office. He denied it."

"What did you think he was looking for?"

Tuttle became tight-lipped.

"You got pretty upset," I said. "You could be heard yelling at him in the outer offices."

He grimaced. "I felt violated and I was mad."

"Was that because he accused you of being involved with his wife?"

"No! I mean, he did accuse me, but it was completely untrue. Gloria asked me out to lunch a few times, and she flirted with me like she does with all men. But I'm happily married and it didn't go anywhere."

"Gloria seems to me to always have an agenda. What did you two talk about?"

"Not much. She seemed to be getting at something without

really getting at it. She asked me about some things that happened in the past."

"What type of things?"

"She wanted to know about an investigation I spearheaded a few years back. She seemed fascinated by it."

"Was that the one you hired Earl for?"

"How did you know about Earl?"

"You were seen talking to him out here the other day. The person who saw you overheard your conversation. You didn't answer my question."

"Yeah, I've used Earl before. He's so unassuming and it's a mistake to take him at face value. There's a lot more going on there than you would think."

"So is he working for you now?"

"We talk from time to time."

"So your little talk out here with Earl was just a casual conversation?"

"Not exactly. He's working on a little matter for me. He was briefing me. I can't talk about the matter so please don't ask me about it."

"Does it have anything to do with me or my brother's death?"

"I doubt it."

"You aren't a hundred percent sure?"

"Nothing's a sure thing. I just don't see a link."

I sat thinking, momentarily out of questions.

"What's your angle here?" he asked. "Why are you so interested in me?"

I thought he was involved in Darrin's death somehow, but I didn't have a motive for him and it kept me in limbo. I decided to try the direct approach.

"I saw a security video of a short thin man, named Monty, The Jet, breaking into your office last week. He went into the Mayor's office, then into Blaney's and then yours."

I watched as the gears turned and Tuttle nodded slowly. "The guard said that video had been recorded over when I asked him about it later. Then it wasn't Blaney who rifled my drawers."

"The Jet was the one who shot me, and he was involved in killing my brother."

"Sweet Jesus. You don't think I . . . why would he be in my office?"

"I think he was looking for the person who hired him."

Tuttle's face turned white. "I wouldn't do something like that. Why would I want you or your brother dead?"

"I don't know. Why would you?"

He ignored the question so I asked another.

"You and Bob still chat between the secret doors?"

"Not lately. There has been some friction between us and Bob's become reclusive. I think he's having problems with his wife."

"Because she tried to seduce you?"

"How did you know? I mean, I didn't respond to her overtures even though it was hard not to."

I shrugged. "She tried to seduce me too. In my case she was trying to get information and steer me away from the investigation for the Mayor."

"I didn't know she went both ways." He laughed. "Heck, I didn't know you did either."

"I don't." My faced flushed. "She'd do anything to help her husband's career. Or maybe it's the Mayor she's hoping to latch onto."

"I don't pay attention to any of the office gossip I hear. I will say, however, it's well known Mayor Clemons would like to run for Governor someday, and he's grooming young Blaney for a place in his administration if it ever happens."

"You think it will happen?"

"Stranger things have." He paused for a minute and added: "I hope he doesn't take the Blaneys with him. It would be a mistake."

Chapter 27

After my meeting with Tuttle, I went City Hall to see if I could find Blaney or Mayor Clemons. I wasn't looking forward to this because of the possibility of running into Eileen. Blaney was out to lunch and so was Clemons so I decided to meet my supposed gayness issue head on.

I rounded the hall from Clemons' office to the reception lobby and entered the door. Eileen sat near the back, her hair frizzled and she was dressed in a brown skirt and similar colored blouse. Her glasses perched on her nose reminded me of the first day I met her. The last few times we were together she was like a peacock spreading her wings, but now she had reverted to her formerly dowdy self.

I mustered help from two other clerks in the office to get her attention and when she finally strolled to the counter, she was merely pleasant toward me.

"Hello, Billie. What do you want today?"

"Could we talk privately somewhere? I need to explain something."

"I've been trying to get you on the phone for the past day and a half. Why didn't you call me back? I was worried about you. This morning your assistant told me to quit calling."

"I'll explain, but not here, okay?"

She turned to one of the clerks. "Susan, I'll be gone for a couple of minutes."

Susan nodded and Eileen ushered me out the door and into the hallway.

"Talk," she said.

"Well this isn't easy for me," I began.

"It wasn't easy for me, either, to realize you've just been using me. Pretending to like me and then disappearing like our friendship was a one-night stand. I was worried about you. You were injured and I took you in and dressed your wounds, staying up all night to make sure you were going to be okay. I finally fell asleep and you snuck out on me. Not even a note."

"I'm sorry. I was confused. Put yourself in my position. I woke up in bed with you and I was naked. And so were you."

"You fell asleep," she said. "I didn't want to try to get a nightgown on you, so I just removed your clothes and tucked you in. What? Do you think I'm going to jump your bones or something?"

Two elderly ladies walked by and my face flushed.

"Oh my God. You *did* think I was going to jump you."

"I didn't know what to think. Angel said you were seeing someone new and she was kidding me about our dates. She said you might have something romantic in mind."

"You and me? Cripes, Billie. I've started seeing a new man a couple of days before my date with Earl. He's younger but he's very attentive."

I breathed a huge sigh of relief. "Tell me all about him."

"I don't want to jinx it by talking about him and getting my hopes up. That's why I never mentioned it to you before. We've only been on two dates. I wanted to wait and see if anything serious develops."

"Then you'll tell me all about him?"

"Do you want me to?"

"Of course I do. We're still friends aren't we?"

"Are we?"

I hugged her hard. "I like you. You're fun to be with and it can be hard to find someone you like who likes you too. Of course we're friends."

She teared up. "I thought you and Earl were just using me."

"Did Earl do something to you?"

She dried her eyes with a hanky as a group of rowdy students strolled past. "He wanted me to get him into Bob Blaney's office so he could go through financial records for the city."

"Did he say why?"

"No. I told him after the burglary the night before that I couldn't possibly go in snooping. He kept pushing me to do it until I started crying and then he said he'd find another way."

Eileen's head bobbed over my shoulder. Mayor Clemons walked through the lobby toward us. Eileen dabbed at her face with her hanky.

"I've got to go. I can't afford to be seen with you." And she was gone.

Bob Blaney walked alongside Clemons and the two chatted amicably.

"I was hoping to run into you two," I said, as they came closer.

"What can we do for you?" Blaney asked.

"Answer a few questions about Steve's arrest."

In Clemons' outer office, his secretary had just hung up the phone. She wore a conservative business suit which coordinated well with her weary eyes and grey hair.

"I made the call you asked about earlier," she said. "I expect to hear back soon."

"Fine," Clemons said. "See we aren't disturbed, will you?"

She nodded and displayed an awkward grin, which for some reason bothered me.

Clemons' office was spacious and tidy. The Mayor sat behind his desk and motioned me to sit in a chair while Blaney leaned against a window sill.

"So why was Steve arrested?" I asked.

"You've heard the evidence," Clemons said. "He killed your

brother. I told you if you would back off we'd get his killer."

"Gloria told me," I said. I could tell by Blaney's surprised look this was the first he'd heard of it.

"She was doing me a favor," Clemons said. "I wanted to get word to you unofficially that we were on the job and just needed a little time to put the pieces together. I'm afraid we may have jumped the gun a little though. I pushed hard to get the police to put a solid case together because there has been a lot of pressure to find Darrin's killer. I got a call before lunch from the District Attorney and he isn't going to prosecute Thomas until we have more to go on."

"What else do you need?" Blaney asked. "You found the murder weapon in his car. He had motive and opportunity. It seems to me to be more than a circumstantial case."

"Maybe he needs to be guilty," I said.

"You think he's innocent?" Clemons asked.

"He might be," I said. "I don't trust tipsters calling the police with incriminating evidence. And I don't think Steve was stupid enough to be driving around town with the murder weapon in his car."

"Are they going to release him?" Blaney said.

Clemons swiveled his chair toward Blaney and then me, smiling.

"They already have and you'd better watch yourself, Billie. You're not safe while Thomas is at large. He knows we're still putting together a case, and he might just be bold enough to try and finish the job before we can nail him."

"I'll keep that in mind, Mayor." I switched my attention to Blaney. "I heard your office was burgled a couple of times. Did they take anything?"

Blaney's face went from passive to stern. "How would you know about that?"

"Word gets around. And I *am* an investigator. It happened once last week and again night before last. Was anything taken?"

"No, and if I ever get my hands on the person who broke in, I'll wring their neck." Blaney made a twisting motion with both hands.

"You don't have any suspects?" I asked.

"Ah no. Well yes. But I've got to keep it on the q.t.," he said.

"What would anybody want in your office?" I asked, pushing for an answer.

"Ah . . . we're accepting bids for resurfacing the downtown bridges," Clemons offered. "Competition is fierce and the deadline is next week. We think someone was hired to copy the bids in hopes of winning the project."

"Have you seen the bids?" I asked.

"Oh, no. The council won't see anything until after the bidding process is finished. Bob here is the only one permitted, and he's not talking, right Bob?"

Blaney threw a quizzical look at Clemons and then responded. "Yeah, we're trying to keep the process honest. There have been complaints from participants during the last couple of projects we awarded."

Their hesitant remarks made me wonder if this was a story they cooked up in case anyone asked why The Jet might have been snooping around.

I played along. "These bidders think the fix was in?"

"Something like that," Blaney said. "The council is sensitive to their concerns so they developed this process. It seems to be working, but with these break-ins I'm more than a little nervous. I'm the one who gets blamed if anything goes wrong."

Clemons looked at his watch.

"Are you late for something?" I asked. I was beginning to feel the way I did the last time I visited him. Nervous.

"Me? Oh no," he said. "Just checking the time."

"He's waiting for the cops to show up and arrest you," Blaney said smugly.

"Arrest me? For what?" The odd look the secretary gave me made sense now. She spotted us coming down the hall through her glass window and had made the call the Mayor instructed her to make: to the cops.

"We know it was you who broke into my office the other night," Blaney said. "You and Eileen. Did you think we wouldn't check the video? Damn night guard tried to stonewall us. He's been suspended."

"Well, I'm pretty sure you didn't capture me on video," I said hopefully.

"I'm afraid we did," Clemons said. "It was an outside camera, but it was a little before the break in so we know you were in the vicinity. If Eileen wants to keep her job, she'll talk."

Clemons' secretary knocked on the door. "Do you want to talk to the security guards before they confront Eileen?"

"They have their instructions," he said. "Tell them to follow through and report back to me." She nodded and closed the door. In the background I heard mumbling.

"What are you going to do with Eileen?" I said.

"She's going to be escorted out of the building, pending an investigation and then terminated if she won't talk," Clemons said.

"The bum's rush," Blaney said, enjoying the moment.

"Shush, Bob. I wanted this to be a surprise."

"Judging by her face, I'd say we surprised her," he said.

"I think what he means is that he wanted to stall me until the police showed up," I suggested.

Blaney stood between me and the door. "You aren't going anywhere."

"You are," I said. I moved quickly and tried to shove him aside. He anticipated this and planted himself firmly, wrapping his arms around me in a bear hug.

"Bob, this isn't necessary," Clemons said.

I stomped on the instep of his foot as hard as I could and he released me and hopped backward a step. He came at me again as I started for the door. I balled up a fist and planted it on his nose with a crack. I opened the door to the outer office and spun around.

"You must be pretty desperate to have me arrested."

Clemons cocked his head at a stunned Blaney, sitting on the floor holding his bloodied nose, and then at me with a slightly amused expression. "Have a nice trip. You won't get far."

I entered the hallway in time to see two beefy security guards pulling Eileen out the door of her office. "Eileen, I'm sorry," I stammered.

"Don't worry about me," she said. "I'll call my union rep when I get home. You'd better scat. They'll be after you too."

I walked out with her and the guards and tried to hide behind them as two uniforms approached. I knew one of them and realized he would recognize me.

"Hi Billie, What's new?" Patrolman Hernandez said.

"Same shit, different day," I said, ready now to go to jail. I guessed they were on their way up to Mayor Clemons' office to get me.

"Isn't that the truth," he said.

"Isn't she the one we're supposed to arrest?" the other cop said.

"If she is, we didn't see her. You got that rookie?" Hernandez winked at me. "Better get going. It's going to get crowded real quick. Lots of chatter on the radio."

"Thanks for the bulletin," I said and smiled at him. I guess he didn't want to be the cop to arrest Darrin Bly's sister.

I couldn't stay and talk with Eileen so I ran up the block toward my car in the rain. A squad car drove by and I turned toward the building. Another cop car was parked on the corner a half-block from my new ride, so I meandered the other way toward the waterfront.

I ducked into a building doorway, out of the drizzle and watched two more police cars, going in opposite directions, stop in the middle of the street and talk for a few seconds. Word was out I got away and these guys were searching for me.

I drifted inside Pioneer Place, a multi-story building of retail stores, and looked through the shop windows to the street. I didn't see any cops outside, but I felt I was being watched. I glanced casually over my shoulder, but didn't see any storm troopers. In fact, not many people were about as the rain showers intensified. I walked a ways and slipped into a boutique and hid behind a female mannequin draped in the latest fall colors.

I sat for a few minutes pondering what to do next and decided to make for the light rail on Southwest First Avenue. I wanted to get out of the downtown area where a squad car could turn up at any moment. I imagined a police dispatcher was organizing a grid search. A few minutes later I hit the street and again I felt the omnipresence of some sinister being.

It wasn't until I reached the Max line I spotted a figure dart behind the corner of a building. I dropped my eyes to the street and jogged across the slippery tracks to wait for the Max train.

When I turned and looked back over to the corner I was greeted by a flash of light where the figure had stepped out from under a store awning. Before I could react, the Max train brushed in front of me and at the same instant I heard a metallic ping of a bullet striking the trolley as it passed in front of me, followed by the muffled pop of a gun with a silencer.

I weighed my chance of getting away on the Max and thought it would be too easy for my assailant to catch up or to call police. If I'd been thinking clearly, I would have realized he wasn't going to call the cops. He wanted me dead.

The Max passing in front of me gave me good cover for a moment, and I turned and ran through some party tents still set up near the Willamette River. I ran a block up Waterfront Park and was greeted by more tents laid out over a four block area in preparation for the next weekend's Food Festival. I ran past four or five tents, kneeled behind one and grabbed my gun from my purse.

The shooter wasn't in sight, and he couldn't cross over to the park without my seeing him so I sat and waited. The rain shower stopped, but witnesses weren't about to take a chance and stroll through the park yet. Five minutes went by and I was thinking whoever had taken a shot at me must have jumped on the train. It had four cars so it might take him a while to realize I wasn't on it.

As I considered this, I sensed movement behind me. I twirled with my gun in hand and saw someone walking in the opposite direction about a hundred yards away. I blinked at the apparition in disbelief. The man walking away from me on the boardwalk along the river looked like Steve. Had *he* tried to shoot me? I started toward him using the food tents for cover.

He walked slowly, more like he was deep in thought than stalking me. I was 30 steps from him before I could get a good look at his face. It *was* Steve. He turned toward the seawall and looked over the edge for a moment. I was hidden behind part of a band's sound stage nearest the water.

He turned back and at the same time I heard a rustling noise from behind me. My view of whoever made the noise was cut off by a wall of stage partitions and tents. I'd have to walk around the maze to find the source of the noise and Steve was approaching. I crouched between two wooden boxes trying not to breathe while footsteps scuffed through the grass, coming closer and closer.

The footsteps stopped a few paces away. "Come on out, Billie," Steve's voice thundered. "I know you're back there. I saw you."

My gun greeted him first and the rest of me followed. I waved the gun motioning for him to move to my left out of the line of sight of a passerby.

"I got you now, Steve. You won't get another chance."

"Chance at what?"

"Killing me, of course." I motioned for him to turn away and patted him down. "Where's your gun?"

"I don't have one. I just got out of jail."

I backed away and he turned toward me again. "How did you manage that? I heard they had a solid case."

"I don't know," he said. "One minute they claimed to have me dead-to-rights and the next minute the D.A. drops the case because of insufficient evidence. It doesn't make any sense to me."

I shook my head. "Maybe they let you out so you could finish the job. And you almost did. Where'd you drop the gun?"

"I told you, I don't have a gun."

"Don't give me that. You took a shot at me over by the Max line ten minutes ago with a silencer."

"Bull. I've only been out of jail for half-an-hour, and I didn't have time to go home and get my gun. I've been wandering back and forth down here trying to make some sense of all this. Why did they arrest me? Who framed me? Why did they let me go?"

I had that familiar feeling of being watched again. But Steve's face showed defeat and frustration. I knew then what had to be done.

"Have you got a cell phone?"

He dug one out of his coat pocket. "Battery's getting low. I wasn't able to charge it in jail."

I glanced at it, hoping it would work long enough for my needs and put it in my pocket. The park was vacant, and we seemed to be completely alone.

"I'm sorry, Steve. One of us has to die. And the other has to disappear."

"What do you mean?" he asked.

I told him what I meant, and he went for my gun. We wrestled for control and it went off. We both fell behind the sound stage and the gun fired again.

If a casual observer happened to be watching they might have seen a long heavy bundle of canvass being hoisted over the seawall, possibly by a volunteer worker, or they might not have seen anything at all because of the structures in the park. A bicyclist speeding by on the sidewalk along the seawall could have heard the splash.

Chapter 28

My gun has no silencer and the two retorts echoed through the empty park as the drizzle continued. After the disposal of the body, I went to a metal plate I'd noticed near the sidewalk.

A newly constructed stage, festooned with white nylon banners advertising a local band, protected me from view in case someone watched. Under the plate was a dirty hole with electrical plugs apparently used to provide power for the music shows.

The hole was damp, but the rain had not turned it to mud and although I checked for bugs and black widows, I was sure they would crawl up to me when darkness was restored. The opening was just large enough to hold a child or a flexible woman. Flexible I wasn't, because of post-surgical shooting pains, but I climbed inside anyway and contorted my body. The sun made an appearance as I pulled the metal plate over me.

I left a two-inch gap facing the seawall so I could spy on anyone with an unnatural fondness for murder. I was sure the person who shot at me earlier must be lurking nearby, and I hoped I might get a first glimpse of my brother's killer. I didn't have long to wait. A man loped up to the seawall and gazed over the edge where Steve's bundle went over.

The now harsh sunlight spilled through the gap and blinded me a bit, but when the husky man in a polo shirt turned away from the river and dialed a number on his mobile phone, I have to admit I was surprised. Just when I thought I had a handle on this case, I was looking at a suspect I had recently eliminated. Earl spoke earnestly into the phone and peered back over his shoulder where the body plummeted.

I opened Steve's phone and sat in the dark, punching in Angel's phone number and typing in a text message: *"Don't believe anything you hear about my death, but don't tell anyone you've heard from me—especially Earl."* I also instructed Angel to call the city clerk I'd interviewed in Pocatello and ask a question.

It was three o'clock and it promised to be a long day. I took another peek and saw four people standing at the seawall now—Earl, two civilians and Officer McGraw. Within minutes more cops showed up and established a perimeter, pushing people away from the crime scene.

I could imagine what would happen next as I tried to realign my body into a more comfortable position.

Crime techs would go over the scene looking for blood or other clues—they would find none--and surmise all of the evidence was in the canvass bundle tossed into the Willamette River. Likely the Multnomah County River Patrol would be called in and divers would start looking for a body.

As I waited for nightfall I reviewed my two cases. One involved the attempts on my life, Darrin's murder, and the termination of The Jet. The other case started out with the disappearance of Art Fleming, an unknown from Pocatello, who eventually turned up dead in the Willamette River near the industrial area of the Port of Portland. This was followed by his wife's death within days of her arriving to identify her husband's body.

I tried to think of a connection between the two cases because my gut told me they had to be related. I also felt Earl had been involved somehow because he was working for Tuttle and Tuttle worked for the city. Art Fleming worked for the city in Pocatello. As hard as I tried, I couldn't find any connection between anyone working for the City of Portland and Art Fleming.

And yet, the only way I could make sense of any of this was if somebody who was out of the picture, wasn't. What was it Honest Hal had said about the widow who missed her husband? She said: *It was a pity people can't be given new life like cars.*

And that's what got me thinking—maybe they can.

An hour passed. Then another, and another. I fell asleep for maybe twenty minutes and was startled awake by voices directly over me. I hadn't been able to hear any conversations earlier, but now I heard Officer McGraw talking to someone.

"I'm sure it was Billie who got tossed into the River," he said. "How do I know? At least two people saw Thomas drop her body over the seawall. She was wrapped in a canvass tent."

I realized the conversation was one-way. McGraw was talking on the phone to someone.

"We'll find her. . . I know—I know. Don't rag on me. The divers showed up two hours ago and they're looking for her now. . . They have to deal with the outgoing tide and currents. She could be a mile down the river."

I hoped the bundle was a mile down the river. I didn't want anyone to know I was still alive yet. I had an important appointment to keep without being hassled by the police and their arrest warrants. As long as they thought I swam with the fish, they wouldn't be looking for me on land.

"I gotta go. It's going to be dark in an hour." McGraw signed off and apparently walked away. I realized I'd been holding my breath. He'd been close enough to spit on me if the angle was right and I had been afraid to move. I adjusted my legs to try and get some feeling in them and my head hit the steel plate.

The bump created a metallic echo, and I felt footsteps tromping toward me. I held my breath again.

"Did you hear that?" someone said. "Something's in there."

"Probably a rat," another voice said.

"Maybe we should check."

"You want a rat should jump out at you?"

"I got my gun. Just lift that lid up slowly and I'll blast the son-of-a-bitch."

"You want to fill out the report on why you discharged your firearm at a rat during a criminal investigation? Get over there and push those TV cameras back. This ain't any reality show."

Footsteps on the sod above me faded, and I breathed softly in case the other cop decided to sneak a peek at the rat. He didn't. I sat for another hour as dark cumulus clouds crowded in to usher darkness in early. It was seven-fifteen when I heard a voice shout to clear out until morning. Thirty minutes later I dared to sneak a better look in the night and pushed the steel plate up about a foot. Two dim figures hovered at the far edge of the police tape.

I climbed out of my hiding spot and gingerly crossed through the tents, holding my aching side and chest. I noticed a lone boat on the river chugging along and the two people at the wall watching intently. I guessed the divers were still at work.

Minutes later, still aching from sitting so long, I struggled to climb into my MGB, which had accumulated two parking tickets. I crossed the Morrison Bridge and took I-5 to the Swan Island exit. A few minutes later I pulled into Finnegan's' parking lot. It was eight-fifteen and I was supposed to meet Gloria at eight, but I took a minute to call Angel at home on Steve's barely charged cell phone.

"Thank God you are all right," she said. "The TV news said a woman had been thrown into the river downtown. We all thought it was you, but I told your brothers you said not to believe anything about your death."

"You can tell them I'm still alive. Did you contact the clerk in Idaho?"

"I did and she identified two pictures," Angel said, and told me who they were. "What's going on?"

"I'll tell you later. I have an appointment with Gloria now."

Finnegan's was once a desirable restaurant especially for Sunday brunch, but with the increase of trendy eateries in Portland in the last ten years, it has suffered. Now it's dated, the hotel style carpet is faded and the lighting is dim and gloomy. The only draw these days is the view of the Willamette River and a fair bar.

The bar is where I found Gloria, chain smoking outside on a patio and looking over her shoulder every few moments. I sat in a corner inside the bar and watched as she pulled a cell phone out of her purse and hit the speed dial. I couldn't hear what she was saying, but she was animated enough for me to see she was upset. I got up and stepped out onto the patio.

"Hello, Gloria. Sorry I'm late. Traffic was murder."

"Oh My God," she huffed into the phone. "I have to go. She's here . . . I don't know. Why don't you find out? I'll take care of things here."

"Am I interrupting?" I asked.

She turned off the phone. She took a final drag on her cigarette and stubbed it out on a patio table.

"No, Honey. I was afraid you weren't going to make it, and Bob cancelled on me too. Thought I was going to spend the evening drinking alone. Why don't we go for a walk on the sidewalk along the riverfront? I've been sitting all day, and I could use the exercise."

She had changed out of the blue dress and high heels I'd seen her in earlier and wore a black low-cut evening dress with more sensible heels. When we entered the lounge again, two business men leered at Gloria. She left a twenty-dollar bill on the bar, gathered her purse and smiled at the men on her way out.

After we strolled a fair distance from the restaurant, she slowed to look at the river. The sidewalk took us within about ten paces of it for a stretch.

"You know, some people think you were dumped into this river," she said flatly.

"Really?" I said. "What would give them that idea?"

"I wonder?" She paused for a minute. "Witnesses identified a man matching your ex-partner's description dumping what looked like a body over the seawall downtown. The news media filmed divers combing the river at Waterfront Park looking for the body of a young woman. The police think it's you."

"I'm tougher than most people realize."

"You certainly must be. After all the attempts---and failures—on your life."

She stopped and gazed over the black water. "Isn't the view here breathtaking? It would be more so if it wasn't so dark. Still, you can catch glimpses of the river as the moonlight reflects off it."

"Was it like this the night Art Fleming was killed?" I asked.

She stopped and turned to face me. "How would I know?" The moon hit her face and I could see she wasn't surprised. She looked placid and confident.

"Okay," she said at last. "So you figured it out. I knew you would eventually. I've been told you're a bit of a bulldog once you get the scent."

"You shouldn't have killed my brother."

"Oh, I didn't kill your brother. But I did kill Art." She pulled a small handgun from her stylish black Coach purse and pointed it at me. "Would you like to know how?"

"I think I know enough."

"Humor me," she said, waving me toward the beach with the gun.

I stepped off the sidewalk onto the sand.

"It was a night like this only a bit warmer," Gloria said. "The weather has turned decidedly cooler, don't you think? Art called me earlier in the day to tell me he had figured out how Bob framed him for a bit of embezzlement in Pocatello. You know about that, I assume."

I nodded.

"I thought so. He called me at home while Bob was working. He made his accusations and I played along with him. I told him I married Robert Paul after Ben died and knew nothing about it."

We were along the edge of the river now and I could hear the swift current. I needed to keep her talking until I could get some kind of advantage.

"Ben Miller was your husband in Pocatello."

"That's right," she said. "We'd moved to New York City because he had a job opportunity. He died of a heart attack almost before we got unpacked."

I shook my head. "I'm guessing after you left town you murdered your husband, maybe with Paul's help, and then dropped into Pocatello to announce he had a heart attack. The perfect way to commit a murder. New to the city, no identification, possibly no address because you were probably staying at a hotel until the supposed job came through. And Ben Miller was just another John Doe without an address and I'm guessing no fingerprints on file."

"A new start," she agreed. "You're right. I had to stop in Pocatello about a month later and announce his heart attack to keep anyone from looking for him."

"Why did you two change your names?"

"That was Bob's idea. He and I were having an affair back in Pocatello. We decided then it was time for a change and planned how to get rid of my husband.

"Robert changed his name to Bob Blaney and I became Gloria Blaney. He's really good at manipulating figures and it turns out he's a good forger as well. He established new identities, a complete resume and he enlisted references at the various places he was supposed to have worked—paying for a few references along the way. It was my job to schmooze Mayor Clemons to get Bob appointed. Tuttle's the only one who followed through on references outside the Mayor's office, but he didn't find anything. It was so easy."

"But Art Fleming found you."

Gloria shook her head, frowning. "It was a stupid photograph taken at a charity event. Somehow it appeared on the wire service—one of those goofy photos—three Portland city figures,

Mayor Clemons, Bob and me, coaxing our rubber ducks down the river in a Ducky Derby. It was picked up by a weekly newspaper in American Falls, Idaho. Fleming stumbled across the picture and recognized us."

That explained why I couldn't find it. I was looking in the wrong newspaper.

"He must have been pretty angry," I said.

"He screamed at me over the phone. He and Robert had been friends until Robert and I started our little affair. I calmed him down and agreed to meet him at Finnegan's to discuss it. When he arrived, I told him I wasn't hungry and suggested we take a walk to help me work up an appetite. We talked until we were just about where we are now. I wanted to look at the water. He skipped a couple of rocks. When he looked back at me I shot him with gun very similar to this one, which I then planted in Stella's purse to incriminate her. Art just fell over. I removed his wallet and identification and rolled him out into the water. It was so easy."

"Is that what's going to happen to me?"

"If it worked once, it should work again."

"But it didn't work. I figured it out. Someone will guess how my death happened too."

"I doubt it," she said, aiming the gun at me. "I don't think anyone else is as stubborn as you are."

"I can think of one person, because it looks like my help just arrived."

"Come on, Dear. Not the old 'look behind you' gag. I thought you'd come up with something more original."

"Billie? Is that you?"

Gloria turned toward Chris as he lumbered down the sidewalk waving at us. She turned and fired at him, and I went for my gun. I heard Chris swear and saw him dive to the sidewalk. Gloria wheeled back and fired at me and I shot back. I felt the bullet tear into my shoulder and fired again.

"You bitch," she said, "I knew you were trouble."

She slumped and as she fell to her knees the moonlight captured an ironic smile on her face before she rolled into the shallow water. I checked for a pulse but her heart had stopped. Chris hopped up like a scared rabbit and ran in the opposite direction.

"Chris, it's okay." I shouted. "She's dead."

He stopped. "Was it her or you who shot at me?"

"It was Gloria."

"Why'd she shoot at me?" he asked, hesitantly walking back.

I could see he was watching my gun so I put it in my purse. "She was going to kill me and you interrupted her."

"Really? Then I guess I saved your life."

"Maybe," I said. "How did you find me?"

"I heard on the news you had been killed, but I didn't believe it. I talked with Angel earlier today, and she told me you were meeting someone here tonight. So I thought I'd come down and see if you kept your appointment."

"You were worried about me. How sweet."

"Yeah, well I saw Earl on TV. He was down by where your body was supposed to have been dumped in the river. I figured if he killed you then he would come after me next. He showed up at your place an hour ago to see Angel. I was scared so I cleared out and drove around for a while. Then I remembered this appointment. If I couldn't find you, I thought I'd visit my sister in Reno for a while."

I looked down at Gloria's lifeless body, the waves lapping at her face. Her beauty seemed to fade now in the dim light.

"We'd better call the police, and I need to figure a way to explain why I killed the wife of Portland's city auditor."

"You're bleeding," Chris said.

I got a hankie from my purse and put pressure against my shoulder. It's just a flesh wound. I'll be all right."

"Did you hear something?" Chris chirped. There was movement in some brush a hundred feet above the sidewalk. Gun shots erupted and Chris and I danced like the cowboys in the old TV westerns.

"This way," I called, running behind an oversized tree stump. Chris dove behind me in the sand as I retrieved my gun and returned fire. "You stay here. I'm tired of being shot at. I'm going after him."

"It must be Earl," Chris said. "He must have followed me."

"Shit. How am I going to explain this to Angel? Especially if I have to shoot him."

I moved silently through the shadows and worked my way across the sidewalk, angling to try to get around behind the shooter. Two shots came at me and I flattened behind some brush. I hit the ground wrong and the pain in my shoulder was fierce.

I lay prone, ignoring the pain and fired three rounds at the approximate position the gunman had shown himself. There was a yelp and a groan. I must have hit him, I thought. I struggled laboriously to get up and waddled up the hill. By the time I reached the spot where the shots originated, the shooter was gone. I heard a distant roar of a car racing out of the parking lot above.

"Shit," I said to myself. "At least I got him. Maybe he'll bleed to death."

I stepped carefully down the hillside among the dirt, sand, and brush and gradually caught up to Chris, still lurking behind the tree stump.

"You're supposed to be protecting me," he complained. "But every time I'm out in public with you, someone shoots at me."

I coughed for a minute, the running and the bullet in my shoulder affecting me.

"Let's call the police and let them sort this out," I said, walking back toward Gloria.

But Gloria wasn't there. We looked around to make sure we were at the right spot, then to see if there was any trace of someone carrying the body off.

"Are you sure she was dead?" Chris said. "Maybe she got up

and left." He looked back up the sidewalk toward Finnegan's.

"If she did, she forgot her handbag."

I opened it and searched for anything helpful. I found a newspaper clipping and unfolded it. My penlight flashlight revealed a photo taken at the Ducky Derby Gloria had referred to earlier. I guessed she'd retrieved it from Stella's purse, because I also found Stella's picture of Art. Stella *had* been holding out on me

I scanned the river and started to doubt my medical acumen about what causes a death, when I noticed a figure drifting among the ripples in the moonlight 50 yards downstream. It was Gloria, floating toward the ship terminals. I swore and scanned the light across the ground and water around me.

"What are you looking for?" Chris asked.

"Her gun."

"I don't see it," he said."

"Neither do I. The tramp took it with her."

"What do we tell the cops now?" he said. "No body. No gun. How do you claim self-defense?"

"Well, I do have this gunshot wound. And a witness."

He looked at me puzzled-like. "What witness?"

"You're right," I said. "I'm in big trouble."

Chapter 29

My first thought was to run again. Make an anonymous call to the police about a woman floating down the river and take my chances. But I knew if I did, all forensic evidence would be lost and it might take a year to find Gloria's body--if ever. And I could still be charged with murder if the district attorney's office portrayed Chris as an unreliable witness.

I called Dan, reassured him I was okay, and asked who I could call at the Central Precinct and get a fair shake. I knew the Mayor would try to use his influence to railroad me, we being such good friends.

"I think Detective Schmautz is working tonight," he said. "He's honest and he goes by the book. He won't let anyone influence his investigation. I could call him, but it would carry more weight if you made the call. I'll try to get over there after my shift."

"Absolutely not," I said. "Stay away. I don't want you, Dag or Jason brought in on any of this. I'm sure Internal Affairs has better things to do."

I called Schmautz and explained what had happened. He listened to the whole story without interruption.

"You know you're supposed to be at the bottom of the river," he said.

I explained why I wasn't at the bottom of the river.

"Someone's in the river. We have witnesses," he said. At that point Steve's phone beeped twice and went dead. The battery was gone.

I walked over to the tree stump and sat and wondered why it was suddenly so quiet. Chris wasn't one for leaving large gaps in conversation. He liked to fill in the gaps. I surveyed the area for him. *Where in the hell did he go?* I dared hope he went for a drink or maybe to guide police down to the crime scene.

But in my heart I knew Chris was no hero. He wanted to be, but he always disappeared when trouble reared its head. He was a hero to me, but an accidental one. I knew his heart was in the right place, but at the moment it wasn't enough.

"Damn it, Chris. I need you." Strong words from someone who likes to believe she doesn't need help from anyone.

It was a long night. I was weary, hungry, and in pain. Not just from the gunshot wound, but from my irritated chest wounds. My pain pills had gone up with my purse in the garage explosion and the Ibuprofen I substituted wasn't making it. An ambulance arrived on the scene within twenty minutes, but I wouldn't let them treat me until I was sure Detective Schmautz heard my account of the shooting. An hour lapsed before an EMT radioed the hospital about my shoulder wound and gave me an IV designed to reduce the pain.

Lights blazed through every area of the crime scene and portable generators hummed in the background as technicians crawled on the outskirts of the crime scene toward the spot where Gloria and I shot each other. Downriver two police boats chugged methodically, their spotlights bounced back and forth on the water's surface.

Eventually a radio cracked: "We found her. We're heading back." A chorus of cheers drowned out the generators.

Dan appeared a few minutes later and pulled me aside. I was

too tired to admonish him for coming. In truth, I was glad to see my big brother. He hugged me and I cried a bit against his shoulder where no one could see.

"I'm told you think the city auditor's wife killed Darrin," Dan said.

"She may be responsible, but she's not the one who pulled the trigger."

"Who did?" Dan asked.

"I don't know. She died before I could find out."

"They said your principal witness ran off."

"He's probably headed for Reno. He's got a ninety-minute head start and he's driving his beat-up red Ford Ranger."

"I'll make a couple of calls to see if we can head him off," he said.

"Make sure they know they're looking for a material witness who can help find a cop killer. He's unarmed and scared. I don't want him shot."

"Got it," Dan said. "Now here's what's going to happen. You're going to the hospital tonight for your gunshot wound. You'll be under armed guard because you are under arrest for breaking into Bob Blaney's office, and you are *also* a suspect in a possible murder."

"Murder? But I told Schmautz what happened."

"He's just doing his job. He won't be able to verify your story until after ballistics can match the bullet in you to her gun."

"Which is somewhere at the bottom of the river," I said.

"Maybe. Maybe they'll find it tomorrow morning. If you're lucky, they'll keep you in the hospital overnight. If you can talk the doctor into hospitalizing you for a day or two it might keep you out of jail long enough that maybe we could make some sense of all of this."

"I don't want to stay in the hospital. I've got to find Darrin's killer."

Dan raised his hand for me to stop. "Bob Blaney was notified about his wife's death about an hour ago. He's up at the bar being interviewed by two detectives, and I heard he's trying very hard to implicate you in every crime that's happened in Portland during the last ten years. The Mayor is being updated every thirty minutes and he's reportedly agitated as hell."

"I'll bet he can see his governorship floating down the river with Gloria's body." It hurt to smile, but thinking about the Mayor's predicament made me feel much better.

It was about three a.m. in the morning when I finally fell asleep in my hospital bed after convincing the ER doctor I would recover faster in the hospital than I would in a jail cell. Angel, Earl, Eileen, Dan, Jason and Dag waited patiently while I was diagnosed and delivered to my room.

I thanked them for coming and Angel left me a new cell phone programmed with my database of phone numbers of clients, contacts and even a few suspects.

They left about two a.m. and still restless, I went over the facts of the case in my mind. There was only one way things made sense, I thought. I decided I shouldn't be the only one still awake so I called Mayor Clemons at his home. It rang for a long time and went to message phone. I waited for a few moments and tried again a second and a third time. I was about to try his cell phone when the line clicked.

"Hullo? What is it?"

"Marshall?"

"Yeah."

"It's Billie. Were you asleep?"

"I still am. What do you want? What time is it?"

"It's time for you to face the music."

"What are you talking about?"

"I'm talking about murder, Mayor. Do you know what you've gotten yourself into?"

"Me? Yeah. I'm going to make sure you're locked up so long you'll be drawing social security in jail."

"And I'm going to call my reporter friend tomorrow and tell her all about the affair you've been having with Gloria the past couple of years."

"Oh shit, don't do that!"

"Also, I'm going to tell about how she led you around by the nose, implicating you as an accessory in four murders and a slew of attempted murders."

"Oh my God. I swear I didn't have any idea what she was involved in. All we had was a little innocent hanky-panky. You can't make these accusations. It's slander."

"It would be liable if it's printed in the paper, but you should know the truth is the best defense against slander or liable. And I can prove it."

"Oh shit!" He was quiet for a minute and then he said: "What do you want?"

I told him what I wanted and hung up. Only one of us was going to get some sleep tonight, I thought, and rolled onto my good side.

Chapter 30

I had given Mayor Clemons a list of the people I wanted brought to the hospital to visit me the following morning. He reluctantly agreed and promised to have them rounded up by ten a.m. I called the hospital's administration office and they agreed to let us use a conference room on the floor below my room.

Angel, Earl and Jason arrived at nine and helped me get dressed and locate a wheelchair. Dan told me the state police intercepted Chris on I-5, 150 miles south of Portland, and he was already in the conference room under police guard. He was cited for driving ninety-five miles-per-hour.

I was pushed by Jason into the conference room in a wheelchair only to face cold stares from a group of people who wanted to be anywhere but with me. Jason parked me in the middle of an oversized elongated table finished in rich cherry wood. Chris sat sulking at the far end. Mayor Clemons positioned himself at the head of the table nearest the door. Bob Blaney, sporting a black armband, sat next to him. Commissioner Tuttle was seated across from me. Earl and Angel filled in chairs to my left and Dan stood as a uniformed police guard near the door. Detective Schmautz, in plain clothes, sat next to Tuttle, and McGraw, also in uniform, stood behind them.

"I understand you're the one in charge of this get together," said an impatient man wearing a black Armani suit with a faded pink dress shirt and silk tie, sitting next to Mayor Clemons.

"Are you from the D.A.'s office?" I asked.

"I *am* Rex Stone, the Assistant District Attorney, and I don't appreciate being dragged over here on the whim of a civilian. My time is too important for such chicanery."

"Would you call finding the man who murdered my brother a waste of time?"

"Well no, but—this is highly irregular. We have trained investigators working on this and a suspect. How do you think you can find the truth when we've had hundreds of officers combing the streets for your brother's murderer?"

"If you will sit down and shut up for a few minutes, I'll tell you."

Mayor Clemens put his hand Stone's shoulder to stop him from standing up. "Go ahead, Billie. We're all ears."

"I think we have two more guests," I said, motioning to the door. In walked Steve in his rumpled brown sport coat with a uniformed Dag bringing up the rear. Steve looked around the room at the cast of suspects.

"That man's wanted by the police," Detective Schmautz said.

"He's been in custody since yesterday afternoon, under the care and guard of my brother, Dag Bly," I said.

Schmautz started to say something, but stopped himself, rapping his knuckles nervously against the table top. "Go on," he said, as Steve and Dag sat next to Earl and Angel.

"We'll have to start with some history," I began. "A few months ago I got a visit from Stella Fleming from Pocatello, Idaho. Her husband had attended a convention here a few weeks prior and never came home. He never called his wife. He never checked out of his hotel room. He seemed to disappear from the face of the earth. The police couldn't find him and one of them referred Mrs. Fleming to me.

"I didn't have any better luck as hard as I tried. I visited the coroner, and I checked death records, missing persons, hospitals, followed his itinerary when he was at the convention, talked to his colleagues, checked for credit card usage—nothing.

"Until a friend of mine made an innocent remark to me the other day about it was too bad people couldn't be given new life like cars. And I began to think maybe they could. Maybe that's what Art Fleming stumbled upon. An old friend with a new identity. *A new life.*

"Fleming had been unlucky in the last years of his life. He was framed for embezzlement of city funds and sentenced to five years in the Idaho State Penitentiary. Then one day a few years after he was released, he spotted two old friends, Robert Paul and the former Gloria Miller, in a newspaper photo and realized both were living in Portland and had changed their names to Blaney. Fleming had ended his friendship with Paul because of Paul's affair with Gloria, who at the time was married to Ben Miller, Art's supervisor. Paul repaid him by setting him up as the patsy in his little embezzlement scam against the city of Pocatello.

"Fleming became suspicious Paul might be responsible for the city's missing $500,000 for which he was convicted. So he came to Portland on the pretense of attending an insurance convention and called Gloria at home. She agreed to meet with him at the same place she met with me last night."

Blaney jumped from his chair and slammed his fist on the table. "You better be careful what you say." Officer McGraw grabbed Blaney by the shoulders and pushed him back into his chair. "She'd better not defame my wife. I'll sue her."

"I'm sorry, Mr. Blaney, but your wife told me she killed Art Fleming, and she killed Mrs. Fleming too. Both of them made the mistake of trying to contact you through her. I think Stella Fleming found the clipping of Gloria, you and Mayor Clemons and meant to blackmail you. Gloria killed Stella in her hotel room and took the news clipping with the incriminating picture of you from the room. I found it in Gloria's purse along with a picture of Art Fleming Stella had shown me earlier."

"I don't get it," Jason said. "How did Mrs. Fleming get the

news clipping, and if she had it why didn't she tell you?"

"Maybe Art's mother found it and gave it to her or maybe she had it all along and didn't know what to make of it," I said. "After Art's death, she put two and two together, and I guess she decided to handle the Blaneys herself."

"It *does* sound like she was going to follow her husband's path and try blackmail," Dan said.

"I felt she was holding something back from me when we talked last," I said. "She and her husband made the fatal mistake of thinking Gloria harmless when, in fact, she would have done anything to protect herself and Bob."

Bob Blaney's shrewd eyes pierced me, but he said nothing.

Schmautz got up and paced behind the table. "How do you know all of this?"

"It's the only way things fit. Gloria's ex-husband, Ben Miller, goes to New York to take a new job. Gloria comes back to Idaho a month later and reports he died of a heart attack. Then she winds up in Portland as Mrs. Gloria Blaney."

"So?" Schmautz said. "What does that prove?"

"As I mentioned earlier, the person she was having an affair with in Pocatello and Bob Blaney are the same person. Robert Paul also went to New York and he left a forwarding phone number with Pocatello, but it went to a message machine, and the calls were never returned. I think it was a way he could check and make sure there were no little problems that might surface later. Art Fleming tried to find him—even hired a private investigator until his money ran out."

I told them how Gloria bragged about Robert Paul becoming Bob Blaney and creating a new identity and a solid job history. She simply kept her own given name and added Paul's false surname.

"Gloria as much as admitted she killed Miller so she could marry Paul, who we know as Bob Blaney. She and Miller weren't in New York long enough to meet anyone or establish residency. She killed him and left him as a John Doe for the authorities to file under unsolved cases. Then she stopped back in Pocatello to tell his colleagues he suffered a heart attack so no one would think to look for him, which freed her to marry her lover."

"That's absurd," Blaney said. "This woman murdered my wife in cold blood and now she's trying to get away with it."

I ignored his accusation. "Angel contacted a Pocatello city clerk—you remember Grace don't you Blaney? We sent pictures of you and Gloria to Mrs. Johnson and she identified them as Robert Paul and Gloria Miller. I'm sure we can get Grace to come here and make a positive ID."

Blaney sank into his chair, his chin on his chest.

"So are you saying Gloria shot your brother?" Assistant D.A. Stone asked. "Why would she want him dead? It doesn't make sense."

"She didn't want Darrin dead. The assassin was trying to kill me, remember? Gloria was afraid I might track Art's death to her, and she found somebody to stop me. At first I thought her husband might have done it. After all, they were both trying to stay out of jail so they could tag along with Mayor Clemons to the state capital when he became governor."

"That's never going to happen now," Clemons said. "Why did I ever listen to that bitch?"

"Is that a confession, your honor?" Schmautz asked.

"Hell, no!" he said. "I did some things she asked me to, but I thought she was trying to help."

"What kind of things did you do for her?" I asked.

"Little things at first. She suggested I put a man on you to make sure you were safe. That way I could also make sure you wouldn't interfere with the investigation."

"Who did you have following me?"

"Sgt. McGraw. I had him assigned to me so he could report on your activities--when he could find you. Each time he lost you someone got killed. I thought of replacing him, but Gloria was against it. She said it would be best to keep a tight lid on things."

"What else did she ask you to do?" I said.

"She suggested we should cut Steve Thomas loose. She said McGraw could keep an eye on him and he'd either incriminate himself or lead us to you. That was before you paid us a surprise visit and then escaped from my office."

I looked at McGraw, then Steve. "No one else was assigned to watch me other than McGraw?"

"No. We couldn't afford to bring anyone else in on it."

I turned and glared at Earl. "Why were you the first one to show up at the scene when everyone thought I'd been tossed over the seawall?"

Earl stammered. "How did you know I was there?"

"I saw you. I was hidden a few feet away. You showed up almost immediately, followed by a couple of civilians, then McGraw. But *you* were the very first one on the scene. Were you following me, Earl?"

"No. I mean not so much following you as tracking you. I got a call from Tuttle. He said you were rattling his cage. He thought it would be a good idea to see what you were up to and I agreed.

"When I got to City Hall there was a real buzz. People were gossiping about Eileen being escorted out of City Hall by security and how the cops were looking to arrest you. I talked to one of the security guards and he told me you'd gone in the direction of Waterfront Park. Cop cars were cruising all the main streets so I headed for the riverfront. Then I heard muffled gunshots a block away and ran toward them. I was walking along the edge of the park a bit later when I heard two more gunshots further down. I ran toward them but I wasn't sure where the shots originated.

"Eventually I ran into a bicyclist and asked if he'd heard anything. He said 'no man, but some dude just threw a huge sack of garbage over the wall.' I ran to the seawall and saw what looked like it could be a body wrapped in canvas. I made a Nine-one-one call and then a man and a woman stopped and said they saw a woman of your description earlier. They were at the other end of the park when the shooting occurred and they came back to see what was going on."

I thought about what Earl told me. I figured he still could have been the one who fired the shot at me by the Max train.

"Is this going anywhere," Stone said. "It's starting to feel like a fishing expedition to me. I need something I can take to a jury. I've given you some leeway, but it feels like you really don't know who you're looking for."

"I'm getting there, if you can be a bit more patient, Mr. Stone . . . after Mayor Clemons told me there was a warrant for my arrest, I headed for my car, but I was blocked by police cruisers. It felt to me like I was being followed and I was right. Someone took a shot at me with a silencer at the Max stop. A silencer doesn't mute everything, so Earl could have heard it.

"I zigzagged toward the park and found Steve walking around like a lost puppy. At first I thought it was he who shot at me. I believed then he killed Darrin and, for a moment, I was thinking of plugging him and getting my revenge. But one glance at his face told me he was as confused as me. And I had the familiar feeling I was being watched again.

"Anyway, I realized why Steve was cut loose. It was to get more evidence against him. And what better way than to have him at large when I was killed. It wouldn't do to have me killed while he was in jail. They'd lose their scapegoat. You see, they jumped the gun in charging Steve.

"When I was away questioning witnesses in Pocatello, Gloria and Bob must have heard about it and got nervous. McGraw probably reported me boarding the flight. When I came back and wanted to talk to Gloria first thing the next morning, she panicked. It was time to finally get rid of the troublesome P.I. She talked the Mayor into releasing Steve and planned to kill me herself last night."

"Only we threw her a curve when it looked like I had killed Billie and thrown her into the river," Steve said. "That was our plan. One of us had to die and one of us had to disappear. So we made it look like Billie was dead, and then I had to disappear."

"We had to protect Steve too," Dag said. "He called me from a pay phone, and I met him under the Burnside Bridge. I took him home and have been babysitting him ever since. You know, to give him an alibi in case anyone else got killed."

Chris seemed to brighten. "Hey, does that mean I can leave? I gotta an appointment somewhere soon."

"Not yet," I said. "Can you tell me why you ran off last night?"

He scratched his head. "Well, like I said last night. Every time I'm with you someone shoots at me. I didn't want to take another chance. I mean the cops were coming, you know?"

"You didn't feel safe with the police coming?" I said.

"Nah. You remember what that little guy said before someone popped him?"

"About his handler possibly being a policeman?"

"Yeah, that's it. He said he followed his handler to City Hall and went through those offices to find the guy's boss. So I don't trust anyone now. Not the cops. Not anyone sitting at this table for sure. I just want to go somewhere safe. Even prison is starting to look better at the moment."

"So there you have it," I said. "The assassin working with Gloria to kill me could have been Earl, Steve, Chris, Blaney, Mayor Clemons, or Tuttle. Earl is a P.I. and has been working on some confidential investigation for Commissioner Tuttle. Maybe they were afraid I was getting too close to something or maybe one of them was working with Gloria. She had half the men in Portland leering after her.

"The Mayor and Gloria have been having an affair, and she's been leading him around by the nose. Maybe she got him to commit murder for her."

"That's a lie!" Clemons said.

I shrugged. "Chris showed up suddenly at Finnegan's and saved my life. But he is easily manipulated. Maybe he had been working for Gloria and had second thoughts. Maybe that's why he didn't want to stick around after I chased off Gloria's partner. And if the assassin hadn't taken a shot at me last night, Steve wouldn't have needed his alibi. But he was with Dag, so at least I know it wasn't him."

"Thanks, Billie," Steve said. "But I could have sent someone after you."

Dag shook his head. "He didn't make any calls."

"And of course, Blaney embezzled over $500,000 from Pocatello," I said. "He's knee deep in cover-ups. I bet he even siphoned some money from the city of Portland. Mayor, you hired Blaney. Have you balanced your books lately?"

"I don't . . . ." Clemons face turned red.

The D.A. smiled and almost licked his chops. He wrote notes furiously on a small memo pad.

"My guess is Blaney has been up to his old tricks," I said. "Tuttle became suspicious and hired Earl to find proof."

"Since you've figured it out, I might as well confess," Tuttle said. "I *did* hire Earl to prove that Blaney was embezzling."

Blaney reacted by sulking.

"So which one of them is the other killer?" Angel asked. "I hope it isn't Earl."

"Blaney and Clemons are the only two people with a strong enough motive to cover things up, but I don't think either of them has the guts to even order someone killed. Blaney is a wiz at numbers, but he's an embezzler, not a murderer. He'd just disappear and show up somewhere with a new identity. He probably knew what Gloria was doing, maybe even helped plan it, but he wouldn't be able to do the deed himself. And the Mayor isn't murderous, although I think he might like to make an exception for me. He just isn't very smart."

Clemons face reddened more.

"This secret assassin was someone working for Gloria," I said. "She hired The Jet to kill me in the warehouse because she found out I was looking for Art Fleming, and she had killed Art to protect her husband and herself so they could become rich and successful and move to the state capitol. When she somehow learned The Jet had been going through her husband's office, she had him killed. She already seduced someone with this contingency in mind and got him to do the deed."

"That sounds like something she'd do," Blaney said. "Why couldn't she just have come to me? We could have paid Fleming off and been done with it. Now all these people are dying, and she—she's dead too."

He started sobbing and I noticed McGraw behind him smirking.

"I guess that just leaves you, McGraw," I said.

"Me?" he said.

"You killed my brother and you also killed The Jet. You fired the shot that killed Darrin from the adjacent hospital parking structure. It was a simple thing. You were on watch for potential assassins coming after me when I got out of the hospital. When you took the shot all you had to do was to drop your rifle in your trunk. No one was going to search a police vehicle for the murder weapon. I'll wager it was still in your trunk when you drove me home that day."

"You're hallucinating," he said.

"You followed me when I went to Cathedral Park. It was dumb luck we went to meet The Jet. You probably brought your sniper rifle into the park planning to finally finish *me* off. But The Jet was in the line of fire, so you took him out first and then tried to kill me. When it was time to frame a patsy you tossed the murder weapon in Steve's trunk and phoned a tip to Homicide."

"That's a lie," McGraw said. "The D.A. said it. You're fishing. Hoping someone will take the bait. My only job was to follow you. Period."

McGraw paced nervously on the side of the room near a window and stopped to look outside as if for and answer. I backed my wheelchair away from the table and pivoted so I could better face him.

"The Mayor said you kept losing me whenever anything bad happened. He said you lost me when The Jet was murdered. Did you lose me again when my garage blew up? How about yesterday at Waterfront Park or last night at Finnegan's?"

"I was supposed to be watching Steve."

"But you didn't, did you? I think you were following me after I left the Mayor's office, hoping I wouldn't get caught long enough so you could kill me and lay the blame on Steve. But you missed again and by the time you got to the waterfront, you couldn't believe your luck. You saw or heard Steve and I struggle and the gunshots and you saw Steve carry a canvass bundle and dump it in the river. You didn't want to be *the* witness so you dropped back and let Steve go, figuring you could collar him later. You called Gloria, then the police dispatcher, and interviewed enough witnesses to be able to piece a case together against Steve."

"You can't prove a thing. I never even met Gloria before."

"I *can* prove it. You see last night when you were calling to report in to Gloria she was peeved. She wanted to see a body. You told her you were all doing all that was humanly possible, but the body could have drifted a mile down the river."

"I don't know what you're talking about."

"You shouldn't have been talking on your phone where anyone can overhear you."

"I don't know what you think someone heard. I reported to my Captain a few times and the Mayor once. That's all."

"I happened to eavesdrop on another conversation Gloria was having with you in Finnegan's a little later. I didn't get all of it. Just that she was surprised as hell to see me and told you so. You must have asked what I was doing at Finnegan's when I was supposed to be at the bottom of the Willamette River, and she said she didn't know. Or maybe she didn't know who was wrapped in the canvass in the river--it was a bit of stage metal Steve and I rolled into a tent canvass. Gloria directed you to find out what was in the bundle and said she'd take care of me.

"And she tried, but didn't succeed because my good friend Chris popped up unexpectedly to save my life." Chris smiled sheepishly. "But you had to find out what I was doing at Finnegan's. You heard the shots and raced to the scene in time to catch us standing over Gloria, obviously dead and partially floating in the shallow water, and you decided to avenge her death. Or maybe you were just protecting yourself by then."

"Is this true?" Schmautz said.

"Hell no!" McGraw said.

"Can you prove any of this?" Schmautz asked.

"I thought I wounded him last night when he tried to ambush me again. Maybe it was a flesh wound he could hide." McGraw's hand went instinctively to his thigh, and I knew I was right.

"You could check his thigh for a bullet wound, but I have another way to prove what I'm saying if you'd give me a minute to make a quick call." I rummaged through my purse and pulled out a cell phone.

Schmautz nodded and I searched for the proper button on the phone and hit *redial*. I waited for an answer as it rang again and again. No one spoke. Meanwhile, a vibrating noise sounded from the vicinity of McGraw. I raised my eyebrows.

"Is that you vibrating, McGraw?"

Beads of sweat formed above his upper lip. "I'll get it later," he said.

"You might as well answer it now. My party isn't responding."

He nervously fished the phone out of his shirt pocket and looked at it. "This is some kind of trick," he said.

"It's a call from the grave, you mean?" I said.

McGraw stared as his caller ID and Gloria's phone number.

"This is Gloria's phone," I said. "McGraw's number appears on her call history about twenty times yesterday."

McGraw raised a formidable service gun at me. "I guess the

charade is over," he said. "You." He pointed to Angel. "I want you to go around and relieve these gentlemen of their guns."

Angel scrambled out of her chair and walked over to Dan, Jason, and Dag and retrieved their hand guns and dropped them at McGraw's feet. She did the same with Schmautz. "Check the rest," McGraw said.

Earl gave up a 25-caliber revolver. No one else appeared to have armaments, but I knew Angel probably had three guns on her person or purse.

McGraw puffed himself up, feeling in control now. "It's all your fault, you bitch. Gloria was right about you. She knew you would never quit. That's why she wanted you dead." He wiped a tear from his eye. "We were going to get married."

"What?" Blaney and Clemons said in unison.

"Yeah, she said she loved me. We kept it on the quiet side because she had plans. She was going to be the wife of Clemons when he became governor, and I was going to be his personal bodyguard. We'd have plenty of connections and money opportunities and afterwards she'd divorce Clemons and marry me."

"Did you really think that would ever happen?" I said, incredulously.

"You bet. We were in love."

"Gloria doesn't divorce men," I said. "She uses them and she kills them. She killed her first husband, Ben Miller, so she could hook up with Blaney. She probably would have killed Blaney, or got you to do it, so she could marry Clemons. Of course, if she really was in love with you, I guess she could arrange for Clemons to have an accident. It would have to be carefully done, because the death of an ex-governor would be closely scrutinized. And what do you think would have happened when she got bored with you?"

"It doesn't matter now because she's dead. You killed her and now you're going to pay. He aimed the gun at me and Jason slowly rose from the his chair, with a determined look in his eyes.

"Stay where you are, Jason. I don't need another dead brother hero. He isn't going to kill anymore."

"Well, maybe just one more time," McGraw said. His brown eyes dilated and a mischievous sneer betrayed his intent. "Gloria will be able to rest when you're dead. I'm going to send you to hell."

"Before you kill me, I want to thank you," I said.

He laughed. "For what?"

"For letting me avenge my brother's death my way."

From between the side of my leg and the wheelchair I brought out Darrin's old service revolver. I'd asked Angel to bring it when she visited earlier. McGraw had the advantage because I needed to raise my arm and aim, and he would be quick to respond.

"Avenge your brother's death? How do you plan to do that?"

I pushed off the floor with my feet and the wheelchair scooted back and swerved to the left. McGraw reacted and put a slug where I had been. I raised my gun and quick shot it from my side.

Two more shots rang out from McGraw but they disappeared into ceiling panels as he fell to his knees in pain. He was dead before he collapsed on the floor.

"That's how," I said.

Jason ran to him, kicked his gun out of reach and checked his pulse. "He's gone," he said.

"Did you have to shoot him?" Clemons said. "If you knew he was the murderer, we could have had the drop on him at any time. Why didn't you let us in on it? We could have brought him to trial."

"Let you in on it?" I screamed. "When you did everything possible to come down hard on me and my brothers and Steve? You son-of-a-bitch. You almost single-handedly caused the death of my brother, The Jet and Stella Fleming.

"I just wish you'd give me a reason to shoot you."

Clemons cocked his head and thrust it out like a rooster. "You can't talk to me like that. I'm the god-damned Mayor of Portland!"

"What are you going to do, fire me?"

"I wouldn't count on your being Mayor for too much longer," Stone said. "Not after I launch my investigation of you and Blaney as accomplices in three murders."

Chapter 31

Two days later I had risen from bed early and drove to the cemetery to visit my brother. I knelt at the foot of Darrin's grave and said a prayer of thanks for God's help in finding his killer.

I told Darrin of the transpired events and asked him to watch over me. I thanked him for giving his life for mine, cried, placed a single rose on his grave, and made a decision to quit my profession.

I had planned to announce my retirement to my family and friends, and we sat at my dining room table a few hours later to share the latest news. The District Attorney's office charged Blaney with four counts of second degree murder and Mayor Clemons with two counts of second-degree murder. McGraw, of course, was dead so the taxpayers avoided the cost of a third trial.

"It seems a bit anticlimactic," Dan said of the arrests. "I mean we've been slogging through each day trying to find Darrin's killer and now that it's over I still feel depressed."

"We're all going to miss him so terribly," Angel said. She was comforted by Earl who took her hand.

"I'm sorry I couldn't tell you why Tuttle hired me," Earl said. "I was sure it didn't have anything to do with your brother's death. If I had any idea what was involved, I would have broken client privilege and told you about Tuttle's suspicion of Blaney."

"It would have given me the link I needed," I said. "I was treating these as two separate cases all along. I only went to Idaho to check out the Fleming angle because I was stuck and hoped by working on that case I might shake something loose in my brain. I thought I was at a dead end in Pocatello. All the players in the accusations against Fleming had disappeared.

"Ben Miller supposedly died of a heart attack and Robert Paul seemingly vanished without a trace. I thought it odd that the two people involved in putting Fleming in jail couldn't be found. But I couldn't turn up anything to disprove Fleming's claims of being framed except what he told his mother, and even she had doubts about her son's innocence."

"Delilah sure was excited when you told her you found her son's killer," Angel said. "I could hear her hooting through the phone."

"She was relieved her son was innocent of the embezzlement charges," I said. "In a small town, everybody knows the latest gossip. Delilah was stuck with the shame generated by her son's arrest and carried it for several years. She said she was going to call the editor of the local newspaper and demand a story with the new facts exonerating her son."

"When did you finally connect the two cases?" Dag asked.

"I was sitting in a hole down at Riverfront Park with Sgt. McGraw talking on his cell phone above me. He made excuses to someone about the divers not finding my body. At first I thought he was reporting in to headquarters, but I heard an edge to his voice. He wasn't defensive, more resentful.

"Earlier, I had realized the necessity of Steve's release to be the fall guy when they killed me. It became obvious all the juice on this case came from the city or someone connected with the city. When McGraw spoke on the phone it wasn't the kind of tone he'd use with the Mayor. There was a certain familiarity with the person, like you'd expect with a wife or girlfriend instead of his Chief or the Mayor.

"The Jet tried to find who pulled the strings and followed the cop who hired him. Probably, it was McGraw reporting to the

Mayor in City Hall offices. It occurred to me in that dark dank rat-infested hole, that Art Fleming worked at City Hall in Pocatello, which also had its problems with corruption.

"I wondered if there was a connection between the two cities so I asked Angel to email pictures of Mayor Clemons, Blaney, and Gloria to Grace Johnson, the receptionist I met in Pocatello, and *viola*. She identified the photo of Bob Blaney as Robert Paul, the former Pocatello city auditor, and Gloria as Gloria Miller."

"If you knew they killed Darrin, why did you let Gloria get the drop on you?" Dan said.

"I didn't have any proof yet, so I decided to put myself in a vulnerable position and see if I could get her to admit it."

"You almost got yourself killed." Jason huffed. "You should have called me for backup."

"I didn't have time. The cops were looking for me and I was playing hunches. Anyway, I had two or three ways I could have gotten the drop on her. I was just giving her enough rope to hang herself."

"It's a good thing Chris showed up when he did or you might have been killed," Angel said.

"I think if there's one thing that I've learned about Billie Bly, it's she can take care of herself," Earl said.

I was about to answer him when a knock sounded at the front door. I got up to answer it and was met by Steve and Chris.

"We were in the neighborhood and thought we'd drop in," Chris said. I ushered them into the living room. Chris sat at attention and appeared very earnest.

"Billie, here's a copy of a dismissal of my lawsuit against you. You turned out to be a pretty swell gal even if you did slam my head in that revolving door."

"Thanks Chris. What are you going to do now? Go to Reno?"

"Nah. I think I'll hang around for a while. I'm going to go straight. I still got my money from the city and I'm gonna invest in one of those Pay Day cash loan places. I hear those interest rates rock. It's like stealing money, only it's legal."

So much for going straight, I thought. Chris excused himself and went into the kitchen where Angel huddled around fixings for lunch.

Steve managed a little smile as we sat for a while in awkward silence. "I just wanted to apologize for cutting you out of my life," he said. "I think—I've always thought you were the greatest. But I never felt it would be right for us to get together—you know—because I enforce the law and you tend to break it."

"What would people say?" I laughed.

"I'd like to give us a shot," he said.

"You aren't worried about your promotions?" I said. "Because I know your supervisors are going to say: 'Steve Thomas is dating that Billie Bly scumbag. Anyone with such poor judgment wouldn't make a good Captain,' or whatever promotion you're going for."

"I don't care. I'd rather settle down with you than worry about a promotion."

"Settle down? That sounds good. I've been thinking about maybe retiring from being a P.I. Maybe get married and downsize into a nice house with a guy and a white picket fence. You could be that guy."

"I can't believe you're saying you'd quit," he said. "I figured we'd spend the rest of our lives bumping heads–me working the straight and narrow and you working the seamy cases P.I.'s take to make ends meet."

"I don't know. I've been shot at too many times on this last case. I think I need some time to mourn the death of my brother, and I don't know what I would do if anyone else was hurt because of me. It's probably best for me to give up being a Private Investigator."

"You're going to quit?" Earl said as he entered the living room. "Hey Angel, Billie's going to quit. You're going to be unemployed. Maybe you can settle down with me now."

"Yeah, yeah, you bet." Angel set a plate of sandwiches on the dining table as the phone rang. "Let me get the phone first."

"Hey Dan," Earl said. "Did you hear? Your sister's going to quit being a P.I."

"Is that so? Dag, Billie's going to quit the job."

"I could see it coming," Jason said. "Hey Sis, can I have your desk. It would look great in my home office."

"You got any P.I. stuff I could have," Dag said. "I might want to quit being a cop someday and . . . ."

"Hey Billie, there's a lady on the phone who wants to hire you," Angel said. "She thinks her ex-husband is trying to kill her. You want I should refer her to the cops?"

"Maybe I better take this call," I said to Steve. "I wouldn't want the poor woman to die on my watch."

"But what about settling down?" Steve said.

Dan and Dag laughed into their sleeves and Angel just rolled her eyes and handed me a note. "She's at this address. I told her you'd be there in 15 minutes."

"That was a short retirement," Steve said.

"I'm sorry, but I just have to take this case." I started to walk out the door and stopped. "Would you like to go with me? Maybe I could use a cop's perspective."

Steve shrugged and rose from the couch. On our way out the door I heard Angel make another wisecrack.

"It must be love. They're going out on their first date."

ABOUT THE AUTHOR

Don Weston is the Author of the new Billie Bly, P.I., series about a hard-boiled P.I of the feminine persuasion.

Don lives in Portland, Oregon, widely known, as of late, as the location for TV shows *Portlandia*, *Grimm* and *Leverage*. He is a member of Willamette Writers and Oregon Writer's Colony. He is the Volunteer Coordinator for the annual Willamette Writers Conference with over 1000 attendees, and works on the OWC conference committee staging author workshops.

He writes thriller mysteries "but somehow humor manages to sneak into my writing voice," Don says. He also writes a blog on writing and getting published called *I Love A Mystery*.

Coming Soon:

The Facebook Murders
Featuring Billie Bly

Billie Bly takes on her toughest case yet when she matches wits with a serial killer using Facebook to stalk his victims.

It starts when a client has her house burgled while on vacation to Maui because she posted her itinerary on Facebook and anyone could see she wasn't home.

Billie explores the online world of Facebook and realizes that most people don't fully utilize their privacy controls. She tries to track down some Facebook burglars to retrieve a groundbreaking computer design that uses a hologram as a computer screen and the Internet Cloud as a hard drive and stumbles upon a possible serial killer.

What Billie doesn't know is the killer has already infiltrated her Facebook page and she is about to become one of his victims. He believes they have been linked by fate and the only way for him to survive is to kill her before she catches him.

And worse, the police and her detective boyfriend don't give her suspicions much merit. Stubbornly, she investigates on her own with the help her her office assistant and a female sheriff's deputy who has been demoted to a library beat.

In the end, the serial killer has the upper hand. So why do we feel sorry for him and how will Billie survive?

Be sure to read this thrilling sequel in the Billie Bly series, tentatively entitled "The Facebook Murders," coming in 2014.

33609409R00162

Made in the USA
Charleston, SC
19 September 2014